A Little Christmas Faith

A Little Christmas Party

A Little Christmas Faith

Kathryn Freeman

Published 2018 by Choc Lit Limited
Penrose House, Crawley Drive, Camberley, Surrey GU15 2AB, UK
www.choc-lit.com

ISBN: 978-1-78189-411-8

Printed and bound in Great Britain by Clays Ltd, Elcograf S.p.A.

*To my boys, my husband, and my
mum. I love you all to bits.
To all those who love Christmas – may
this year be your best Christmas ever.*

Acknowledgements

They say never work with children or animals; Faith and Adam might agree with that, as it is quite possible a child and two dogs stole the show from them.

Chloe is a typical teenage girl. Though I have teenagers, they are of the male variety so a special thank you to my gorgeous niece, Tiegan who gave me some 'teenage speak' so I could make Chloe's character as real as possible. And thank you to the equally gorgeous Maddi and Gracie – for being my nieces, too.

Nip and Tuck are little scallywags, and their characters are based on two other canine scallywags I know: Ted and Oscar. A big thank you to them, for being such an inspiration, and to their owners (Jane, Tony, Emma and Tom) for allowing me cuddles with them now and again (the dogs, that is).

There is a host of other people I'd like to take this opportunity to thank:

My fabulous editor, who picked up my terrible gaffes, smoothed out the rough parts and made sure the final draft was far better than the first.

The Choc Lit Tasting Panel, who supported *A Little Christmas Faith* for publication, especially: Maureen W, Rachel A, Cheryl S, Anne E, Elaina J, Susan D, Melissa C, Gillian C, Heather P, Stacey R, Florina O, Margaret M, Sally SD, Gaele H, Linda T, Isobel J, Gill L, Els E, Hannah M and Liz R.

Book Bloggers. I'm so lucky to interact with so many wonderful book bloggers on social media. Their enthusiasm for reading and their kind support of writers is humbling. Thank you for taking the time to help this author.

Authors – including my fellow Choc Lit authors. I can't conceive of another profession where so much help, advice and encouragement is freely, readily, and happily given.

Family and friends (including Mum and Dad 2, Charlotte, Sonia, Neve, Gill, Laura, Michele, Sheyline and Tara). Thank you for still asking about my next book. It is coming!

My publisher, Choc Lit. Without them, this book wouldn't exist, because it was their idea for me to write my first Christmas book (*A Second Christmas Wish*), and their encouragement that led me to write this one.

You, my dear reader. Thank you so much for buying and reading *A Little Christmas Faith*. I hope you enjoy Faith and Adam's story. And I wish you a very Happy Christmas.

Chapter One

Only a fool would open a hotel ten days before Christmas.

Faith swept her hand lovingly across the gleaming oak reception desk; she guessed that made her a fool. A smile spread slowly across her face. At least she was a happy one.

The old wooden door creaked open and a smart looking couple in their late sixties strode in, the man dragging a ridiculously large wheeled suitcase behind him.

Faith hid a smile. 'Good afternoon, Mr and Mrs Watkins. Welcome to The Old Mill. The Lake District's newest, and if you forgive my bias, finest, boutique hotel.'

The lady chuckled, the curls of her silver hair bobbing. 'Why thank you. It's a delight to be here.' She elbowed her companion in the ribs. 'Isn't it Eric?'

The gentleman huffed. 'Would be if I hadn't had to heave this ruddy suitcase out of the car and across gravel that puts Brighton beach to shame. Who the blazes would put gravel in a hotel car park?'

Faith's lips twitched. 'A hotelier short of money, perhaps?'

The lady let out a *humph* sound. 'Ignore him. He's miffed because I couldn't decide which clothes to pack, so I put them all in.'

'We only live three miles away,' the man muttered, but his eyes were twinkling.

'We're staying in our daughter's new hotel for a few nights,' her mother countered. 'I wasn't sure what I needed.'

Faith laughed and went to hug her parents. 'Whatever you wear, I couldn't have a more perfect couple as my first guests.'

'Let's see if you're still saying that when she's complaining

1

about the vegetables being overcooked.' Her father picked up the case again as Faith began to lead the way to the room she'd allocated them on the ground floor.

'The vegetables will be perfect,' she answered. 'Mario and Antonio are fabulous chefs.' Faith was confident the restaurant was in safe hands, thanks to the Italian brothers. It was the rest of the hotel she was now agonisingly unsure about.

Behind her, Faith heard her father drop the handle of the case, leaving it to clatter to the floor. 'Good God.'

She swung round, following the direction of his eyes. 'What's wrong?'

Beside him, her mother's mouth gaped open. 'Oh my. It's very … festive.'

Faith studied the huge Normandy fir she'd begged the local garden centre to help her erect. At over ten feet tall, it did rather dominate the hallway. But wasn't that the purpose of a Christmas tree, to dazzle?

'Did you leave any decorations in the shop?' her father asked, his eyes skipping from the heavily festooned tree to the giant gold bells she'd hung over the fire place. Then across to the fairy lights she'd twisted round the old beams and the ivy garlands draped over the mantelpiece. Finally his eyes rested on the reindeer family in the corner, lit up like Oxford Street.

She bit her lip. 'Too much?'

'Not at all,' her mother cut in, giving her father a stern look. 'Christmas isn't subtle. It's cheerful, bold, over the top.'

'You can say that again.' Her father shook his head. 'When it comes to taking it all down, I'm busy.'

'Dad.' Faith bumped his arm. 'Don't talk of taking everything down already. It took me all day yesterday putting it up.' Worry niggled, squirming inside her like a bed of worms. 'I bought the decorations in the sales last year when I was planning to open the hotel at the end of October. I figured it would be a useful hook to get those early bookings. You know, position it as "The Christmas Hotel". Stay with us and experience all of the joy of Christmas with none of the effort.'

Her mother beamed. 'Like we're planning to do.'

'Exactly. Only then we had the building delays and I didn't dare take any bookings until I knew when we'd be ready. Now I'm opening with a week and a bit to go and so far my only guests are my parents ... although I'm delighted they're here,' she added hastily when her father coughed. 'A young couple with two young kids who arrive on the twenty-third. And a guy travelling alone who's booked the suite for two weeks. Arriving tomorrow.'

'Oh heavens.' Her mother clutched at Faith's hand excitedly. 'Your first paying guest.'

'Better hope he likes Christmas.'

On seeing her father's wry smile, Faith rolled her eyes. 'Okay, okay, maybe I went over the top, but there didn't seem much point having decorations and leaving them in a box. And anyway ...' She surveyed her handiwork. Perhaps it wasn't sophisticated. Perhaps there should have been some sort of theme, matching colours. But still. 'I like it.'

Stepping round the tree, she led them down the corridor, stopping at the end door. There she slid the key into the door of room number one – no modern card system for her.

Her mother let out a wistful sounding sigh as she walked in. 'Oh darling, it's beautiful.' There were tears in her eyes as she turned towards her. 'I'm so proud of you.'

'Really?' Faith wanted to believe her. She did believe her, most of the time. Yet those insecurities – what would her guests think? Would they like the rooms? – kept nipping at her. 'You don't think the grey walls are too austere? Is the purple too much?' She'd agonised for weeks over the colour scheme and the décor, in the end going with her instinct rather than her head. Modern and unfussy, she'd decided, rather than traditional to match the building. She liked the idea of the contrast and hoped it would accentuate the period detail of the seventeenth-century building.

Now she worried it looked ridiculous. Like she'd tried to pretend the old building was a shiny, new, modern one. With walls the colour of a prison cell.

Her mother patted Faith's cheek, her eyes glistening. 'The walls aren't grey my dear, they're dove. And I think the whole look is perfect.'

Faith smiled gratefully, her gaze drifting over to her father who'd just managed to manoeuvre the huge suitcase into the room.

'Anyone care what I think?' he asked, after poking his head inside the en suite.

'Don't tell me. You're disappointed you haven't got a Christmas tree in here.'

His usually gruff face relaxed and he chuckled. 'Christmas decorations aside, I think my daughter has made one hell of a hotel.'

Delight mixed with relief and Faith wrapped an arm around each of them. 'You know I couldn't have done it without you, don't you? Without all the Watkins family.' While she owned the majority of the hotel, it was her family – parents, sisters Hope and Charity and brother Jason – whose investments had turned her dream into a reality. The daft part was, she hadn't even been looking for a hotel yet. Not when she still had lots to learn about the business – and a deposit to save up for.

But then she'd seen The Old Mill advertised for sale. One viewing, and she'd fallen in love.

'We only provided money, darling.' Her mother sat down on the bed, smiling up at her as she sunk into it. 'It's you who's done all the hard work. Besides, we're expecting to become very rich on our investment.'

Faith laughed, though the kernel of unease in her chest refused to budge. Almost two years in the planning, a month since she'd started to advertise the hotel properly and only two bookings so far. She knew it was early days, knew the delay had cost her dearly in terms of Christmas guests. Knew too that the summer was the busiest time for the Lakes. Still, it was one thing opening your dream hotel. Another keeping it open long enough to make a living from it.

As her mother went to coo over the bathroom – grey slate tiles, walk-in shower, sleek white bathtub with curved sides – Faith pushed her worries aside. The restaurant had a handful of bookings tonight, she had a guest arriving tomorrow.

Baby steps.

Adam felt a prickle of guilt as he listened to his voicemail. A message from Emma. Again. It was the third year in a row she'd invited him to hers for Christmas. And the third year in a row he'd avoided her.

No, he told himself as he hauled his suitcase out of the cupboard in the spare room, careful to miss the neatly folded stack of bedding piled next to it – he wasn't avoiding her. He was going away.

It was just unfortunate he always chose to go away for two weeks over Christmas. Or at least he had, for the last three years. An image of Emma's face the last time she'd seen him flashed through his mind. The misery in her eyes, the coolness of her tone when she'd spoken to him.

He forced the image away and determinedly began to go through his wardrobe, methodically picking out what he needed. Work-out vests, gym shorts, two pairs of jeans.

A knock on the door stopped him in his tracks. Damon was early. Had to be, because Adam was never late. Adam expected punctuality, so he in turn was punctual.

Leaving the packing annoyingly half done, Adam went to answer the door. His friend stood huddled in the small porch, clearly trying to protect himself from the grim, wet December weather.

'Get your lazy arse out of here and into the car.'

Adam glanced down at his watch. 'You're five minutes early.'

'So, sue me. You always tear me off a strip when I'm late. Now you're giving me stick for being early. What's wrong? Have I interrupted something important? Mary Berry not finished showing you how to make lemon drizzle cake?' Damon's mouth formed what could only be described as a smirk. Clearly one of them was finding him funny. 'I know, it wasn't Mary, it was Nigella, wasn't it? She was licking the chocolate off a big wooden spoon, her tongue curling round the—'

'Can it.'

Leaving Damon standing in the draughty porch, Adam went inside to fetch his jacket. Served the bastard right for taking the piss out of him. So, he enjoyed cooking. Found it therapeutic, some of the time. He couldn't see what was so damn hilarious about it.

When Adam came back out again, Damon had retreated to the shelter of his car. 'I've guessed it,' Damon announced once Adam had squeezed himself inside. Clearly sports cars weren't intended for men of his size. 'I've interrupted your packing, haven't I? Because you're the one guy I know who packs the night before, rather than the hour before.'

'I'm the one guy you know who's organised,' Adam agreed. 'And I'd have finished packing if you'd been on time instead of early.' Fidgeting in his seat, he pressed the button that was supposed to push the seat back. Seemed it was already at the maximum. 'Why the hell do you drive a car meant for midgets?'

Damon flicked him a disgusted look. 'My car, which you're very welcome to be in, by the way, was designed for human beings of normal proportions. I doubt apes were part of the designers' brief.'

Adam let that one slide. With his beard, height and added

6

muscle since he'd begun working out borderline obsessively, he was probably closer to an ape than most people who drove a sports car.

'So, where are you sloping off to this year?' Damon asked as he sped up to overtake a lorry.

Adam shut his eyes. Over the eight years of their friendship, he'd learnt it was easier to spend the journey in blissful ignorance when getting a lift from Damon. 'I'm not sloping off anywhere. I'm having a well-deserved Christmas break in a hotel in the Lake District.'

Damon shook his head. 'Man oh man, the lengths you'll go to, to avoid Emma.'

'I'm not avoiding anyone,' Adam returned stiffly, though the guilt settled back in his stomach again, making him a little queasy. Or maybe that was Damon's driving. 'I wanted a change of scenery, that's all. The hotel was suggested to me by a client and I thought I'd give it a try.'

'Oh?'

'Jason Watkins. We designed his new shop. The hotel is his sister's.' Adam and Damon weren't just friends, they were business partners: architects with equal shares in their own practice. They worked surprisingly well together, despite everyone warning them against it. *You'll murder each other by the end of the week*, other friends said, knowing how different they were. Not just physically but in their outlook. Damon was talkative, easy-going, the life and soul of any party. Adam was more introverted, content to watch, his quieter personality turned taciturn over the last few years.

'What's so special about the place?'

Now that was something Adam couldn't answer. Truth was, Jason had mentioned it just at the right time, when Adam had been wondering where he was going to disappear to this year. He winced, mentally rephrasing that. When he'd been wondering where he was going to spend his well-earned Christmas break, this year. 'The sister only opened the hotel recently.' And he'd had the distinct impression, both from the way Jason had spoken, and the easy way the lady on the telephone had slotted in his two-week stay, that he was one of the first guests.

Damon winced. 'Oh boy, I hope she's ironed out all the problems before you arrive.'

'Why do you say that?'

'Come on, you're a perfectionist. You like everything just so. Your pencils lined up on your desk in the right order. Your cans neatly stacked in your cupboard with the labels facing forward. You're meticulous. If the duvet on the bed isn't turned down at precisely the right angle at night, you'll have a dicky fit.'

Adam raised an eyebrow. 'I didn't realise you were that interested in my bed.'

'Trust me, I'm not. Though there are others who are, from all accounts.'

'And whose accounts would those be, exactly?' Adam asked with a shiver of unease. He was a private man. He didn't go talking about his life to anyone. At least not willingly.

'Anita.'

Anita was their office manager, PA, receptionist – basically the woman ran the place. Without her they'd be sunk. So putting up with her uncanny ability to draw information from a person, seemingly without their knowledge, was a small price to pay. 'She should be working for MI5,' Adam muttered.

'Seems she can get anyone to talk. Even you,' Damon said cheerfully. 'And then she spills it all to me, so I know exactly what's going on in your bedroom, even though you don't tell me directly.'

As what was going on in his bedroom was actually a big fat nothing, Adam grunted but remained silent. Women might have shown an interest in him, but his own interest simply wasn't there any more.

'You know you should take some of those willing women up on their offer,' Damon said quietly as he turned into the pub car park where they'd arranged to meet a few more friends for a drink. It was a Friday night ritual. Didn't matter if you were single, like Adam, or married, like Damon. Friday night was boys' night. 'Might make you less grouchy.'

'I'd forget the psychobabble and stick to designing buildings if I were you,' Adam countered. 'At least it's something you're mildly good at.'

Gratefully Adam climbed out of the car. He knew Anita and Damon were trying to help but he was fed up with well-meaning people sticking their noses into his life, giving him advice, pushing him into things he didn't want to do.

Thank God he'd booked some time away.

Chapter Two

Nine days before Christmas

Faith took a gulp of her tea and tried to hide her disappointment. It wasn't her sister's fault she'd been offered work that would take her from now until the first week in January to complete.

But boy had she been relying on Hope to be with her during these next few weeks. Not just for another pair of hands, though she desperately needed those until her deputy manager started in January. What she also needed was Hope's emotional support. For the first time since she'd fallen in love with The Old Mill, Faith was scared she didn't have what it took to run her own hotel.

'Are you ever going to forgive me?' Hope smiled uncertainly at her from across the table. They were in the hotel restaurant, waiting for their parents to arrive so they could eat breakfast together. With a bit of luck, the fact that they weren't here already, waiting for the restaurant to open, was a sign they'd slept well.

'I suspect I will.' As a flicker of hurt flashed across her sister's face, Faith shoved aside her disappointment and squeezed Hope's hand. 'Of course, I'll forgive you. It's just I was banking on you being around to calm my nerves.'

Hope looked at her incredulously. 'You, nervous? You're the most confident person I know. Besides, you're not a novice at this game. You've studied hotel management. Worked in the trade. Didn't you practically run that last place you worked in because the manager was always off sick?'

'I know, I know. It's just …' Faith sighed, feeling a tug of emotion. 'This isn't only a job. It's my dream, and I don't want to screw it up.'

'Oh sweetie.' Hope shifted her chair closer and gave her a hug. 'You won't screw it up. Maybe I can ask for an extension on the article, help you out for a few days.'

'No, don't you dare.' Faith gave her a reassuring smile. 'I'll be fine.'

There were a few beats of silence, during which Hope started to twist her hands in her lap. 'Umm, there is one more thing.'

Faith couldn't imagine it was worse than leaving her high and dry without help for the next few weeks. 'Spit it out.'

'Would you mind putting Chloe to some use?'

At the mention of her niece, Faith groaned silently. She loved her, she really did, but a hormonal teenager was likely to be more trouble than she was worth.

'She's changed over the last few months,' Hope added, and alarmingly, now her voice was beginning to tremble. 'Tom and I don't know what to do with her any more.'

'What do you mean, changed?'

'She's started answering us back, being all sullen. I know mood swings are part of being a teenager and she was certainly never an angel, but there's been another shift recently. She doesn't seem happy any more.' Tears crept into Hope's eyes. 'She's put on weight and where she used to dye her hair lovely colours, the day she broke up from school she dyed it this awful tomato-red.'

Faith gave her a sympathetic smile. 'At least it's the right colour for Christmas.'

'That's what Tom said.' Hope dabbed at her eyes with a paper napkin. 'And now school is finished she just sleeps, watches television and gawps at the phone that's permanently glued to her hands. Most of the time she looks miserable. We thought if she could work with you, it might help. You know, channel her energy in a more positive direction. She can get the bus here and back so it wouldn't mean you having to do anything.'

Except make sure her unruly fifteen-year-old niece didn't blow the fledgling hotel's reputation. But Hope looked stressed and Faith wasn't exactly overwhelmed with guests. Maybe she could use the time to bond again with the niece she'd seen only fleetingly over the last two years. 'No problem. She can help me out on reception,' she found herself saying.

Relief filtered across Hope's face. 'Thanks baby sis. I owe you twice now.'

'Perhaps not. I could really do with the extra pair of hands, so this might work out well.'

Hope stared at her, a glint of amusement replacing the tears. 'Are you trying to convince yourself?'

Faith recalled the last time she'd seen her niece. 'Yes?'

'You always were the optimist in the family. Seriously though, I've told Chloe to be on her best behaviour. Oh, and …' she trailed off, looking awkward.

'You'd like me to pay her?' Faith guessed.

Hope grimaced. 'Sorry, I know that's taking a liberty, but Chloe will be more reliable if she sees this as a job rather than a favour to her aunt. Only give her the money if she pulls her weight, though.'

'Hey.' Faith gave her sister's hand a reassuring pat. 'Stop looking so guilty. Of course if Chloe's working, she should be paid. It will all work out, don't worry. When can she start?'

'When you do want her?'

'I've got a guest arriving this afternoon. I could do with showing Chloe the ropes before he arrives, if she's up for it.'

'I'll make sure she is.' Finally, Hope's face relaxed into a smile. 'Your first guest, eh? I wonder if he knows how special he is.' She waggled her eyebrows. 'They say you always remember your first.'

Faith rolled her eyes. 'Very funny.'

'At least your adverts are starting to work.'

'Not for this one. Jason recommended me, apparently. Seems Mr Hunter designed his new shop.'

'Wow, who'd have thought our brother would actually be useful for something for a change? I don't suppose Mr Hunter is tall, dark, handsome and single is he?' A gleam entered Hope's eyes. 'I'd really give Jason a high five if he was helping your business and your love life.'

Faith batted Hope away. 'Enough. The whole Patrick disaster proves I can't do this job and have a love life. All I want from Mr Hunter is a positive review on TripAdvisor.'

Chloe was going to drive her mad. From her position at the top of the stairs looking down across the hallway, Faith could see her niece on the reception desk, where she'd left her half an hour ago.

She was sitting on the stool, chewing gum and scrolling through her phone.

Damn it. Faith had been careful not to bat an eyelid when Chloe had turned up with her bright red hair. She'd held her tongue when she'd noticed the garish green nail varnish. Presumably another festive touch. But the gum she couldn't turn a blind eye to.

She started to walk down the stairs just as the front door opened. And a big hairy giant walked in.

Hairy perhaps wasn't the right word. His dark hair was cut short and his beard was more designer stubble; trimmed and neat. Giant was definitely right though. He had to be six-four at least, with shoulders he must have had a hard time squeezing through the old wooden door.

Her eyes scanned back towards Chloe, who was still blithely staring at her phone. How could she not have noticed him?

As Faith scooted down the stairs she heard the man clear his throat.

Still Chloe had her head down, totally ignoring him.

'Excuse me?' The man tried again to attract her attention, his voice deep but surprisingly soft for someone of his size.

Heart in her mouth, Faith dashed across the hall. In her anxiety to rescue the visitor, she ran too close to the tree, sending several baubles flying. *God damn it!*

Oh and joy of joys, one of them rolled to a halt right by the man's left boot. His extremely large looking boot, though to be fair it was very much in proportion to the rest of him.

He bent to pick it up, dangling the glittery silver bauble from his big hands.

Panting and embarrassed, she took it from him. 'Sorry. Thank you.'

A pair of direct grey eyes stared at her from a face that wasn't strictly handsome, yet still managed to drag all the remaining breath from her lungs. His nose was a shade too large, his chin a smidgen too square, his cheeks perhaps too angular, but by God he had something. A lot more than something. Rugged, she thought, trying to inhale some oxygen into her starving lungs. Rugged and very, very ... male.

Embarrassment turned into a fluster and she felt her cheeks burn with the effect of both. 'Aside from hurling Christmas decorations at you, is there anything else I can help you with?'

There was no reaction to her small joke. Just a steady gaze. 'I'm checking in. Adam Hunter.'

'Ah yes, we're expecting you.'

His eyes flicked over to Chloe, who'd finally put down her phone. 'So I see.'

Chloe stared up at him and shrugged. 'Didn't hear you come in.'

Faith cringed as she watched the interaction. It was like watching a glass rolling to the edge of a table, yet not being able to reach out and stop it from falling.

Mr Hunter's eyes narrowed in on the earphones dangling

from Chloe's ears. 'How could you hear me,' he replied, agreeably.

Faith studied his body language – and there was certainly a lot of body to convey that language – trying to determine whether he really was as calm as he sounded. The huge hands holding his case were relaxed, the expression on his face neutral. Yet if she were him, she'd be annoyed to the point of walking out.

'I'm sorry my niece didn't hear you,' she interrupted hastily, attempting a placatory smile. 'Chloe is helping me out over the Christmas break. It's hard to prise fifteen-year-olds away from their phones.' She held out her hand. 'I'm Faith Watkins, hotel owner. I'm delighted to welcome you to The Old Mill.'

Adam was starting to wonder about the wisdom of his decision to stay in The Old Mill Hotel. It had looked promising from the outside. He might spend his days designing new buildings but he had a soft spot for old ones; for the history, the tales they could tell if they could speak. The teenager on the reception desk, hair the colour of a post-box, he wasn't so enamoured with. He wasn't bothered about being ignored in favour of a phone – he was pretty damn good at ignoring others too, when he wanted to. He was more concerned at what it said for the rest of the hotel, if the best receptionist Ms Watkins could come up with was her rather sullen niece.

His eyes skirted past Faith Watkins and into the hall beyond her, the one smothered in so many Christmas decorations he could almost hear it groaning under the weight. Or maybe the groaning was coming from him. He'd come away to try and forget all about blasted Christmas. Not be thrust headlong into it. Sure he'd anticipated a tree and a few baubles – there was never any escape from the season – but he hadn't expected to be spending his fortnight in Santa's flaming grotto.

Thoughts of turning round and walking out jumped through his head but what would he do then? Drive four and a half hours back home? Accept Emma's invitation?

A cold shudder ran through him. Not an option.

He glanced back at Ms Watkins, only to find she was still holding out her hand, worry now marring her exceptionally pretty face. And yes, he had noticed. Just as he'd also noticed her sparky hazel eyes, her soft brown curly hair. She clearly thought he was about to blow a fuse and walk out.

He might like order, and The Old Mill looked to be more on the chaos end of the spectrum, but Adam wasn't prone to too many "dicky fits", despite what Damon thought. So he put aside his aversion to the over-the-top decorations and grasped Faith's hand, giving it a brief shake. He was a big bastard, he knew that, but it felt like holding a child's hand. Until she squeezed back, surprising him with her strength.

'If we could just ask you to complete a registration form.' Faith slipped behind the reception desk, shooting her niece a few looks Adam was pretty certain he could interpret. *Put the bloody phone away. Get rid of the gum.*

As Faith bent to retrieve the form, Chloe snatched it from her hands. 'You told me that was my job.' Chloe thumped the form onto the reception desk. 'You need to fill this out.'

Adam surprised himself by wanting to smile. He wasn't sure if it was at Chloe's angst, or her aunt's horrified expression.

'I also told you your job was answering the phone and greeting anyone who walked through the door,' Faith replied in an admirably mild tone.

The teenager raised her eyebrows. 'Okay, don't get lairy.'

They both turned to him then, Faith's brown eyes swimming in apology, Chloe's with indifference.

'Pen?' he asked.

As Faith opened one of the drawers, Chloe pulled a chewed biro out of her pocket and handed it to him.

Gingerly he took it from her. 'Hungry, were you?'

Chloe stared at him blankly, but her aunt's face, when she turned and saw the pen he'd been handed, was much more expressive. 'Chloe,' she muttered. 'We're supposed to be presenting a professional image.'

The teenager shrugged again. 'It works, dunnit?'

Lips twitching, Adam began to fill in the form. He was halfway through his name when he felt a soft warm hand cover his. For a brief moment his heart bounced. Then the hand disappeared and he found the pen he'd been holding replaced with a new black one, bearing the hotel name.

Faith smiled. 'I can't have my first guest filling in his registration form using a chewed biro.'

Though he'd suspected as much, Adam raised his eyebrows. 'First guest?'

Faith flushed. 'I wasn't going to admit that, but yes. Well technically you're my third, but the first two were my parents. They checked in yesterday.'

'Did they survive the night?'

He was treated to a smile of genuine amusement – different to the professional one she'd given him up until now. And damn if he didn't get a small buzz knowing he'd caused it. 'They did, thank you. They even slept in this morning and missed breakfast. Maybe you'll be able to do the same.'

Adam hadn't been able to sleep beyond 5 a.m. for the last three years. He gave Faith a small smile. 'Nothing would make me miss breakfast.'

Hastily he completed the form, which was immediately snatched away by Chloe. 'Says here you live in Windsor? Isn't that posh?'

Faith stiffened at her niece's question and Adam had a strong feeling the aunt was getting ready to slap a hand over her niece's mouth to shut her up. 'The Queen seems to like it,' he murmured.

17

Seemingly satisfied with the answer, Chloe dangled a heavy brass key in front of him. As he reached for it he was aware of Faith giving her niece a pointed look.

Chloe huffed out a deep sigh. 'I'm supposed to ask if I can help with anything else?'

He toyed with the idea of asking a barrage of questions just for the hell of it; the opening times of the restaurant, where the nearest cinema was, whether she could press his trousers. Then he figured making Jason's sister watch her niece's customer service technique any longer was probably verging on cruelty. 'That's all for now, thanks. Just point me in the direction of my room.'

Faith gave him a relieved looking smile. 'I'll show you.'

Picking up his case, he followed Faith Watkins' short, trim figure as she strode through the hallway – otherwise known as Santa's grotto.

'What brings you to The Old Mill, Mr Hunter?' She turned slightly to look at him. 'Visiting friends or family in the area for Christmas?'

Adam kept his expression neutral. 'No, nothing like that.' He stared up at the excessively decorated tree. 'I've actually come to escape Christmas.' The moment the words were out he wondered why on earth he'd told her the truth; to everyone else he'd said he wanted a break. A change of scenery.

Faith halted, causing him to bump into her. It was only a light touch but he felt a prickle of awareness as her curves brushed his arm. A feeling he hadn't had in a long time.

As her gaze shot up to meet his, he was struck again by how pretty she was. 'Oh dear.' Her eyes – actually closer to green than to brown, yet neither colour fully described them – flicked between him and the decoration-strewn hallway.

'I'm sure your other guests will appreciate them,' he found himself saying.

'I hope so.' She sighed. 'Still, if you see an elderly gentleman with a slight paunch, feel free to share your thoughts with him. You'll find a kindred spirit.'

'Your dad?' he hazarded, though it wasn't a difficult deduction considering her parents were the only other guests.

'Yes. He isn't a fan of my festive attempts either.'

The disappointment in her voice tugged at something deep inside him and for once Adam wished he didn't hate this time of year. Wasn't tortured by memories. He felt a crazy desire to apologise, though it was hardly his fault he didn't like Christmas. So instead he decided to change the subject. 'Your website said you have a gym here?'

Instantly her face brightened. 'Yes. Let's drop the case off in your room and I can show you that and the restaurant. It's not a big hotel so you won't get lost.'

'Jason said you'd just opened it.' Silently he gave himself a shake. What the hell was he doing? He didn't ask questions, didn't elicit conversation. Didn't speak until spoken to.

Oblivious to his shock, Faith smiled and began to give him a run-down of how she'd found the hotel for sale when she hadn't really been looking, but realised she had to have it. 'I've worked in the hotel industry since I left university and always wanted to have my own one day. Coming across The Old Mill by accident seemed like an omen. Someone up there telling me to change my plans. Now was my time. Mind you, it hasn't been plain sailing since then.'

He started to zone out as she talked about all the changes she'd made since buying it, though as he followed her down the corridor he enjoyed hearing the soft lilt in her voice. Appreciated the passion that burned from her eyes each time he caught her gaze.

She came to a stop by a giant oak door. 'This is you.'

Chapter Three

Faith's pulse sped up a few notches as she opened the heavy wooden door to the Cullin Stone suite.

Standing back to let Adam Hunter in, she offered up a silent prayer. Please God, let him like his room. It hadn't exactly been a smooth start, what with Chloe and her unique brand of hospitality, and him standing amidst her heavily decorated hall and telling her he'd come to escape Christmas.

His confession, or rather the expression on his face as he told her, was still etched on her memory. He'd looked lost, haunted. The words seemingly ripped out of him against his wishes. She'd had to bite her cheek to stop asking him a flood of questions, because she knew a private man when she saw one. And she suspected this one was probably already regretting telling her as much as he had.

'Is the room okay for you?' She stepped inside, trying to see the suite through his eyes. The big wooden bed had been plenty large enough when she'd checked it earlier, but now it looked too small for the man who towered over her. Just as the deep purple sofa in the far corner looked too feminine, the cushions too much. Adam Hunter looked like a man who favoured worn brown leather.

'It's fine. Thank you.'

Though the words weren't terribly reassuring – fine? – his eyes were warm.

'Would you like me to show you how anything works? You know, the television, the shower? There's a small kitchenette with a microwave and a fridge. The hotel has wifi, the code is on the card on the desk. There's a spare blanket in the top of the wardrobe. That's where you'll find an iron and ironing board, too. In the wardrobe, I mean, not on top.' Good God, someone stop her rambling. How many guests had she shown to their rooms over the years? So why was she making such a hash of this one? Because he was the first in her own hotel?

Or because she was aware of him in other, less professional, ways?

He shrugged off his coat, throwing it onto the bed, and her eyes ran far too eagerly over the physique he'd revealed.

When she realised his bulk was down to pure, solid muscle, she felt her blood heat.

'I can take it from here.'

His quietly spoken words jolted her from her lustful thoughts. 'Okay then.' For a second she stood, flummoxed and flustered, her natural ease with strangers having deserted her.

'The gym?'

'Yes, of course.' She clutched at the door handle, signalling for him to go first. Damn, she needed to sort herself out. Taking a deep breath she followed him out, trying to ignore the huge expanse of his back. The taut buttocks beneath the dark jeans. When she opened her mouth to speak, her voice caught in her throat and came out with a husky edge to it. 'Turn right. Past the restaurant.'

The gym was at the back of the hotel. The original owners had used it as another bedroom but Faith was positioning The Old Mill as a high-end, boutique hotel. It meant she could charge more. It also meant she had to provide more.

'Cullin Stone suite.' He glanced sideways at her. 'Where does that come from?'

Her embarrassing meltdown eased as she was able to focus back on the hotel. 'Ah yes. Cullin stones are a type of millstone. Made from a dark blue or grey lava, they come from Germany. I believe they were also known as Blue Stones, or Cologne stones ...' She trailed off. 'But you probably don't want to know any more than that.'

He gave her dry smile. 'Consider my millstone education now complete.'

Faith started to wonder who had embarrassed themselves most over the last fifteen minutes, herself or Chloe. And had it seriously only been fifteen minutes?

'Here you go.'

She pushed open the door with a flourish, her satisfied gaze sweeping over the two treadmills, exercise bike and step machine. The floor was a dark hard wood and in the corner, there was a rack of gleaming chrome dumb-bells. Fitting it out had blown the budget she'd set aside, but Faith had figured she'd use it herself so would be saving on gym fees in the long run.

A mirror ran the width of the room. Faith caught Adam's eyes in it – and her heart sank.

'Is it not what you wanted?'

He looked over at the dumb-bells, and then down at himself. 'I was hoping for weights.'

'Well, it *is* Christmas,' she said with false cheer. 'Maybe you can give yourself a break from them.'

His face turned from disappointment to something that looked like horror. 'I can't.'

'Can't?' It seemed an odd word in the circumstances. Unless. 'Oh, are you a body builder? Do you have a competition coming up?'

If he hadn't looked horrified before, he did now. 'Bloody hell, no.' He seemed to become aware of how blunt his response had been because he grimaced. 'Sorry. I just ...' His huge chest rose as he sucked in a breath. 'Exercising and weights are what keeps me sane.'

The words were said lightly, yet there was a darkness to his expression, a sadness in his eyes that suggested there was a degree of truth behind what he'd said.

'Oh.' All her disappointment channelled itself into that single word. She felt so deflated. Two years of anticipation, of planning, and she was finally showing her first guest round. Only he didn't like Christmas, and he needed a gym designed more for Mr Universe rather than for the average person.

She'd like to bet his feet hung over the edge of the bed tonight, too.

Tears pricked at her eyes and for a horrified moment Faith thought she might cry.

Adam stared at the treadmills, the rack of dumb-bells. This wasn't a gym, it was a bedroom with a few machines in it.

Damn it, why hadn't he checked when he'd made the booking that the hotel's version of gym, and his version, were the same?

A deep, frustrated sigh burst out of him before he had a chance to stop it. He hadn't been exaggerating when he'd said lifting weights kept him sane. He craved the burn, the adrenaline. Exercise so intense he didn't have time to think about anything else. The hours he spent doing it had lessened a little over the years, but it was still the only therapy that had ever really worked for him.

'I'm sure we can find you a gym nearby,' Faith said quietly. She gave him a smile that might have worked had it not been for the tell-tale glisten in her eyes. Or the droop of her shoulders. She looked like she'd just had the stuffing knocked out of her.

And he'd been the bastard to do it. With a heavy heart he studied the room again, trying to see it from her point of view. The neatly stacked white towels, the expensive wood floor that matched the dark wood of the dumb-bell rack. The thoughtful drinks fridge filled with bottled water. 'It's an excellent exercise room,' he stated firmly. 'I'm sure your other guests will appreciate it.'

Her lips twisted in an ironic smile. 'Are these the same guests who'll love the Christmas decorations?'

He winced. Turns out he wasn't just her first guest. He was her guest from hell. 'It's a great place you have here,' he continued doggedly, determined to give her something to smile about. He liked her real smile; the one that made her eyes dance.

'Just not what you were after.'

'I didn't say that. I'm sure everything else will be just what I'm looking for.'

Finally she turned to look at him. 'Does that include the carol singers I've booked for tomorrow?' His face fell. 'And the Father Christmas I've hired to wake all the guests up with a *ho, ho, ho* every morning?' He was just about to pick his jaw up from the floor when he caught the laughter in her expression. And shocked the hell out of them both by laughing back. It was an odd sounding noise, rusty from underuse, but it didn't seem to bother her because the smile was back on her face.

'I'm not your ideal first guest, am I?' he said after he'd caught his breath.

'Oh, I don't know. If you don't trash the room, and don't write a scathing review about the stroppy teenager who greeted you, or the poor exercise equipment, I'll feel it's a win.'

Adam found himself sharing a smile with her again as they walked back down the corridor. It was the first time in years he'd noticed the colour of a woman's eyes, the curves of her body. The cute snub end to her nose.

The first time in three years since he'd really laughed.

Within no time at all, he was back outside his room.

Faith's pretty hazel eyes glanced towards the door before drifting back up at him. 'I'll slide a note under your door with the address of the closest gym.' Her lips curved. 'A real one, with weights.'

'Thanks.'

There was an awkward pause. Suddenly he wanted to

ask her something, anything to keep her talking, which was frankly weird because he hated conversation. He was saved from having to think of that something – and wondering why he wanted to think of something – when two balls of white and brown fluff came barrelling towards him.

Faith let out a strangled cry. 'Nip. Tuck. What are you two doing here? Did I not shut the door properly?' She crouched down, patting the yapping dogs, kissing their ridiculous squished faces.

Not for the first time since he'd met her – and it had been less than an hour ago – Adam found he was trying not to smile.

Faith shot him an apologetic look. 'That scathing review we mentioned. Can you leave out the unruly dogs, too?' She gave them both a stern look. 'Nip, Tuck. Sit.'

The small dogs continued to yap and wag their tails, gazing up at her with utter adoration. And remaining resolutely on their feet. Faith let out an exasperated sigh and hauled them both into her arms. 'I got them from the animal shelter when I finally moved into this place. I figured I'd have twelve months to turn them into obedient hotel dogs.' She giggled while one of them – and who on earth could tell the difference? – licked her cheek. 'Turns out they're gorgeous but utterly impossible to train.' Her eyes drifted up to his. 'Do you have any animals?'

'Is now a good time to tell you I'm allergic to animal fur?' he deadpanned.

She gasped, then narrowed her eyes. 'Please tell me that's a joke.'

'It's a joke.' He reached out to scratch behind one of the dogs' ears. 'But no, I don't have any animals.'

'Well let me know if you have a burning desire to see what walking a dog would be like.'

He stared down at the pint-sized dogs in her arms – they had to be some sort of cross-breed. Whatever they were, he'd look bloody daft taking them for a walk. 'What are they, exactly?'

She laughed. 'Oh, they're Cavachons.'

'Cava ... what?'

'Cavachons,' she repeated slowly. 'A cross between a Cavalier King Charles Spaniel and a Bichon Frise. I'm guessing the owners gave them up because they refuse to do anything you ask them to. Except look cute. They're very good at that.'

'Well, they're ...' He racked his brain for a suitable description. 'Different.'

Faith smiled, though he wasn't sure whether it was at him or the dog currently smothering her in slobber. 'I'd better get them out of here before they wreck the place. I hope you have a great stay with us, Mr Hunter.'

'Adam.' He caught her eye, wondering what it was about her that made him want to put aside the formalities. 'I think you should call your first guest by their first name.'

She laughed softly. 'Well then, Adam, let me know if there's anything you need.' Her mouth curved wider. 'Or you could always try your luck and ask Chloe.'

Adam was smiling as he walked back into his room.

Chapter Four

Eight days before Christmas

Faith surveyed the restaurant with quiet satisfaction. Despite it being Sunday evening, there was a definite hum, and it wasn't just from her parents who were sitting at a table by the window. She'd opened the restaurant several months ago, figuring even though the hotel wasn't ready, The Old Mill could start to build a reputation as a place to go for a good meal. And thanks to the Italian brothers, it seemed to be working. Locals had started to eat in the cosy room with the wood-burning stove and big oak beams. With a bit of luck they would recommend the place to others, and word would get around.

Like a heat-seeking – perhaps that should be hot-male seeking – missile, her eyes zeroed in on the tall figure sitting alone in the alcove, reading a newspaper. There was something about the sight that tugged at her heart. He looked lonely. It wasn't just that he was sitting alone – she was used to the sight of guests staying in hotels on their own. Adam Hunter's loneliness emanated from his eloquent grey eyes; from a face that, she suspected, rarely smiled.

Why was a man as powerfully attractive, as vital as him, sitting alone in a hotel on a Sunday evening in the run-up to Christmas?

As if aware of her thoughts, he chose that moment to look up.

Faith jumped. Damn, he'd caught her staring. More correctly, he'd caught her ogling, though hopefully from this distance he wouldn't be able to detect the difference.

He gave her a cautious smile and her heart fluttered in response, drawing a sharp breath from her. When was the last time she'd felt this tingle of awareness, of excitement, just looking at a man? It had to have been Patrick, though try as she might she couldn't recall the feeling; she could only recall the sadness at the way their relationship had petered out. The following two years had been a hard slog, with no time for the lighter side of life: flirtation, romance. All totally worth it, she thought with quiet satisfaction as she glanced around the room. Her restaurant, in her hotel. But surely it wouldn't do any harm to enjoy a few moments in the company of this man who made her remember she wasn't just a hotel owner. She was also a woman.

Pulse hammering, she began to stride towards him, her route taking her past her parents.

'Darling.' Her mother reached out to grab her arm. 'Where are you off to in such a hurry?'

Faith turned so her back was facing Adam, just in case he could lip read. 'I'm going to say hello to my guest,' she whispered. 'He's the one in the alcove.'

Shamelessly her mother craned her neck to stare at the man in question. 'Oh heavens. He's, well ...' Picking up the menu, she started to fan herself. 'I can see why you're rushing past your old fogey parents.'

'I dispute both old and fogey.' Her father dipped his head, taking a much more surreptitious look. 'Big fella.'

Faith smothered a laugh. 'Thanks for the keen observation, Dad.'

'Go on.' Her mother flapped her hand in the general direction of Adam. 'Don't keep your guest waiting.' Then she leaned closer. 'Maybe you can introduce us later. You know, we're guests, he's a guest.'

'And why would you want an introduction?' her father asked mildly.

A wicked smile crept over her mother's face. 'He may like the more mature lady.'

'I'm just going to check he's happy with his room,' Faith

told them both firmly. 'Not to chat him up for myself or my mum.'

'Then you're missing a trick, dear.' Her mother winked. 'You won't get too many guests looking like that. Enjoy him while he's here.'

Faith rolled her eyes as she turned away, stifling a laugh when she heard her father mutter, 'What's he got that I haven't?'

The closer Faith got to Adam's table, the more her confidence began to ebb away. What did she say to him? *Hello, mind if I join you?* Did that sound as if she was coming on to him?

At that cringeworthy thought her steps faltered, but she could hardly stop now. Not when it was so obvious she'd been walking towards him. *You're just checking your guest is happy*, she reminded herself. He didn't – and wouldn't – know she was crushing on him. Drawing back her shoulders, she slipped on a professional smile as she neared his table.

'Mr Hunter. Adam,' she added, remembering his request. 'It's nice to see you in our restaurant. Is everything to your satisfaction?'

He eased back a little, his large frame dwarfing the chair he sat on. 'You mean aside from the rude receptionist, the tiny gym and the wild dogs?'

Though his expression was utterly serious, his striking eyes – such a contrast to his dark hair and short, dark beard – betrayed his amusement.

'I'd hoped we'd moved beyond those small hiccups,' she murmured, unable to drag her gaze away from his.

'The hotel manager is very attentive,' he agreed, a small smile now playing around his mouth. 'Though I suspect it's because I'm her only guest.'

'I believe she was just talking to two other guests,' Faith replied, playing along. Enjoying both the dialogue and the sexual undercurrent she could feel pinging between them.

His eyes crinkled. 'Ah yes, how are your parents?'

Faith gave up and laughed. 'Good, thank you. They're sitting over by the window. My mum asked to be introduced but I'm going to save you from that torture. Once she has an audience she'll talk for hours.'

'So I'm your escape route?'

She was having trouble hearing his surprisingly soft voice above the thump of her heart. 'Actually, I was thinking more of a diversion.'

Too forward, she scolded herself. What had happened to her professionalism? He'd come to get away from something. The last thing he needed was her pushing her company on him.

He angled his head, studying her, his expression thankfully more curious than annoyed. As if he was trying to work out what she really wanted from him. Or perhaps whether he wanted to provide it.

Finally he indicated the empty seat opposite him. 'I'm happy to be a diversion.'

Adam watched as Faith slipped into the chair. What had she meant by a diversion? If she was hoping for a pleasant chat to while away the evening, she'd come to the wrong place.

He didn't do small talk. Especially when he could sense his every move being watched by the sprightly looking grey-haired couple sitting by the window.

Faith nodded towards his empty plate. 'Did you enjoy it, whatever it was?'

'Steak and ale pie and yes, it was very good.'

Her lips twitched. 'And there was me thinking you were more of a couscous salad type.'

He knew when he was being wound up. 'Only on the days I do Pilates. Can I get you a drink?'

'Please don't feel as if you have to.' Suddenly the woman he'd assumed was assured and confident looked hesitant. Awkward. 'I understand if you'd rather not have company.'

'I'm glad to have company.' He wasn't sure who was the more shocked at his statement, her or him. He hated talking to people he didn't know – hell, he had enough trouble with those he did. Yet for some reason he wanted to talk to Faith Watkins.

She smiled, her eyes darting away from his and over to his glass of water. 'In which case I'd love a drink. As long as it's stronger than what you have there.'

'I was just about to order a coffee.' Because he was watching her – couldn't seem to take his eyes off her – he saw her dart of surprise. 'Is that allowed?'

A hint of red bloomed in her cheeks. 'Sorry, I guess you just looked more like a whisky drinker to me.'

'I am.' He glanced down at his watch. 'But it's a bit early for me yet. Is that an occupational hazard, second guessing your guests?'

She looked even more uncomfortable now and he wished his question hadn't sounded so curt. 'It is something I find myself doing. Nothing nasty, just wondering what they do for a living. Whether they're married. That sort of thing.'

For the first time in her company, he started to feel a sliver of unease. 'And what have you pegged me as?'

'At first glance I had you down as married.'

'Because?' he interrupted, keeping his expression carefully blank.

'Ah, because.' Her gaze dropped briefly to the table before coming back to meet his full on. 'Because women are clever, so the attractive men are usually taken.' Surprise rubbed happily against pleasure and some of his unease slipped away. When he stared into the depths of her eyes, a long-forgotten bolt of desire added to the mix. 'But you're travelling alone and don't wear a ring,' she continued, glancing at his left hand. 'Plus you're dining here rather than in your room while Skyping, so I'm going to say single.'

'Correct.'

She punched the air. 'Score one.'

'Am I allowed a go?' He didn't stop to think why a man who kept himself to himself was now so keen to ask questions of a stranger. To find out whether she was married.

'Be my guest.' Her eyes laughed back at him as she signalled over to the waitress for two coffees.

Adam suddenly really hoped his hunch was right. 'You've probably been hit on by every male guest over twelve you've been in contact with.' She didn't blush at his statement and he found he liked that. Liked her confidence. 'But buying your own place takes drive and a massive amount of time so my guess would be you're single, though not without offers.'

'One point each.'

As the warmth from her smile seeped directly from her eyes and into his, Adam felt another surge of desire. Bloody hell, he was not only flirting. He was enjoying flirting.

Their coffees arrived and Faith thanked the young waitress – who was apparently called Becky – before picking up the milk and waving it under his nose. 'I bet you take yours black. No sugar.'

Okay, so maybe he *was* predictable. He nodded over to her cup. 'White, no sugar.' She laughed, adding milk to her drink followed by two lumps of sugar. 'You're only adding sugar to beat me.'

She took a sip, lips still curving against the rim of the cup. 'I don't have to cheat to beat you. Now then, profession.' She narrowed her eyes, pretending to scrutinise him. 'First guess would be a lumberjack.'

He reared back in his seat, stunned. 'What?'

She waved a hand towards him. 'Come on, the big build, the beard. I bet your suitcase is stuffed full of checked shirts, too.'

'You think I spend my days chopping wood?' He wasn't quite sure what to make of that.

'No, no. I said first guess, but that's before I shook hands with you and noticed your palms aren't rough.' Self-consciously he stared down at his hands. *Was she saying he had girly hands?* 'My next guess would have been builder, but again that would be going with stereotype based solely on your big frame. Your hands don't work for that either, plus you told me working out keeps you sane, which suggests you spend your day sitting down.'

'It's not the reason I work out,' he murmured, regretting it immediately when her face lit up with curiosity.

'Interesting.'

'You're right that I sit down at a desk though,' he added quickly, anxious to divert her from the questions he could see brewing. 'Are you going to give me a final guess?'

Thankfully her competitive streak seemed stronger than her inquisitive streak. 'You don't look like an accountant, or a lawyer.' She cocked her head to one side, her eyes roaming carefully over his face. Embarrassment prickled at the back of his neck, along with a heavy sense of awareness. He found he was wondering if she liked what she saw. 'I'm going to stick with the building theme as you look like an outdoor man. Architect.'

For a moment he gaped at her. Then, as her lips started to twitch, he narrowed his eyes. 'You knew already, didn't you?' Finally the penny dropped. 'Jason told you.'

Laughing, she held up her hands. 'Okay, yes, I admit, he happened to mention how he knew you. But I would have guessed it anyway. Perhaps gone for civil engineer, but they're pretty much the same thing, aren't they?'

He bristled. 'There's a world of difference. Architects are creative, visionary. We focus on the aesthetics of a building. The look and feel, how it will work. Engineers are more practical. They take our vision and make it happen, if they're any good. The bad ones trample all over it.'

'So you're the vision, they're the reality.'

'Spot on.' No wonder he was enjoying talking to her. She was smart. 'My turn. You're a hotel owner.'

She laughed again, a sound he was coming to crave. There was nothing artificial about it. She let herself go, her curls bouncing as she shook her head at him. 'You're not getting off the hook that easily. You need to tell me why you think I wanted to own a hotel.'

His turn to study her, and he made the most of it. Long lashes framed her direct eyes, and a sprinkle of freckles graced her cheeks and cute button nose. Her lips looked soft and very inviting. None of which helped him with the answer to her question, but all of it made him want to get to know her more. To get closer to her. Something he was very out of practice at.

He gave himself a mental shake and dragged his eyes away before she became uncomfortable with his staring. 'You like people. Enjoy talking to them, even tall, bearded lumberjack lookalikes, so you had to work somewhere that involved meeting lots of new people. You're smart, so you needed a job that challenged your thinking.' He sifted through his thoughts until he thought he had the right direction. 'Your brother looks significantly older than you—'

'Jason's thirty-six. And to save your blushes, I'll tell you I'm twenty-seven.'

He'd guessed as much. 'You said your niece is fifteen, so I reckon that means you have another sibling quite a bit older than yourself.'

'Hope is forty.'

His lips twitched. 'Don't tell me there's another sister called Charity.'

Faith gave him a wry smile. 'She's thirty. Married with a four-month-old boy. And before you ask no, none of us are in any way saintly. And no, my parents aren't especially religious. Just ever so slightly nuts.'

'Duly noted.' He took a swig of his forgotten coffee, trying to get his head back into where he was in the conversation. Trying not to think about how much he wanted to kiss her. Or how terrified the thought made him. Hell, he didn't even know if the sexual side of him could still function. He cleared his throat. 'That makes you the baby of the family, which obviously means you have a need to prove you're a grown woman. Hence the desire to own your own business. Be your own boss, with nobody telling you what to do any more.'

'Though they still do,' she added. 'Every bloody day. But well done, I'll give you nine out of ten.'

'Only nine?'

'It isn't just that I like people, I find them fascinating. I like to observe them, which you should know because that's how we started this game.'

He put his hands up. 'You've got me there.'

'Also, I know this sounds a bit corny, but as a child, owning a hotel was all I ever dreamt about.'

He gazed back at her, seeing past the embarrassment and straight into the passion, the enthusiasm that burned in the depths of her eyes. 'It doesn't sound corny,' he told her quietly. 'It sounds amazing.' He wasn't sure he'd ever felt that way about architecture. He enjoyed it, sure, but he doubted his eyes lit up like Faith's when she talked about her hotel. 'Shall we call it a draw?'

'Oh no. We were both right about our marital status. Both nearly right about our careers. Only I was right about the coffee.'

'Which you added two sugars to, just to spite me.'

She smirked. 'Guess you'll never know.' Her eyes caught his, turning from highly amused to quietly serious. 'So, Adam Hunter, am I allowed to ask why you want to escape Christmas?'

And just like that, the happiness, the peace he'd begun to experience, disappeared in a flash. His muscles tensed and he was left feeling empty, hollow. 'It dredges up memories I'd rather not re-live.' He knew he sounded evasive, curt even, but he couldn't help it. The person Faith had been talking to just now wasn't the person he was any longer. Abruptly he stood. 'Thank you for the coffee, and for the conversation.' He nodded over to where her parents were still sitting. 'I'll leave you to talk to your other guests.'

Ignoring the flash of hurt he saw register on her face, Adam strode off towards his room. He was a solitary animal these days. He'd best remember that.

Chapter Five

The following morning Faith was sitting in the restaurant again, though this time having breakfast with her parents. Not coffee with a man who'd entertained her, made her laugh, complimented her. Then stalked away without a backward glance. She was still trying to work out what had caused his sudden departure; her question, or his lack of interest.

Yet for the half an hour or so before that, he'd seemed very interested.

'Earth calling Faith.'

She snapped her attention back to her mother. 'Sorry, what did you say?'

'I said have you seen anything of your mysterious guest this morning?'

'No.' And it wasn't for want of looking. He'd sparked something in her last night and though she knew crushing on a guest wasn't professional, she couldn't stop her eyes searching for him. Couldn't stop thinking how exciting, how thrilling, it would be to spend the run up to Christmas having a brief, sizzling affair. And she could tell, just by looking into the quiet depths of his eyes, that Adam Hunter could make a woman sizzle. The reserved ones were always the most deadly.

Her mother let out a frustrated hiss and Faith shook herself out of her fantasy. 'Sorry. What time did you say you were planning on leaving today?'

'We're not.' Now that caught Faith's attention. 'That's what I was saying while your head was caught up somewhere else.' Her mother gave her a knowing look. 'Perhaps I should say with someone else.'

'Mum,' Faith said warningly. 'Don't make things out to be bigger than they are. I told you last night, Adam was fun to talk to. End of. Besides, he's a guest. I can't go sleeping with my guests.'

'Rubbish, there's no rule stopping you. Admit it, you're intrigued by him, darling. And who can blame you.' Her father coughed, but like an out of control locomotive, her mother kept going. 'Maybe your old mum will find out more about him for you, now we're staying for a few more days.'

Faith took in a deep breath, praying for calm. 'You don't need to stay, you know. It was lovely to have you here for the opening but I can manage.' To her alarm, she felt a ball of emotion wedge in her throat. She loved her parents to death, but Adam had been spot on in his surprisingly perceptive comment about why she'd bought her own hotel. This was something she needed to do without her parents. Already she had them as investors. She needed to be clear that was where their involvement ended.

Her mother reached across the table and squeezed her hand. 'We know you can manage. We're not staying to interfere, or to keep an eye on you. We'd like to stay a few more days because we're enjoying it so much. We thought it would be lovely to spend the next week in our daughter's hotel rather than the four walls we usually inhabit.'

'Plus it'll save me killing myself getting those decorations down from the loft,' her father commented with a wink.

'We'll disappear if you get a rush of bookings,' her mother added. 'And we'll pay for the privilege.'

Her father gave her mother a mock glare. 'Minus family discount.'

Faith's eyes bounced between the pair of them, and she started to laugh. 'Okay, okay. I give up. Enjoy yourselves. Just—'

'Keep out of the way.' Her mother grinned. 'You won't notice we're here.'

Family, Faith thought as she left them to go and check on her niece. They were the most important things in her life. Even when they drove her crazy.

Speaking of crazy, Chloe was leaning on the reception desk, speaking into the phone.

'Yeah, we're open.'

Faith grimaced. She was going to have to find Chloe something else to do before she scared off all the potential customers.

'Dunno.'

'Chloe,' Faith hissed, coming up beside her.

'What?' Her niece glared at her, oblivious to the customer still listening on the other end.

Faith snatched the phone out of her hands. 'Hello, I'm Faith Watkins,' she said smoothly, turning her back on her niece. 'I'm the owner of The Old Mill. How can I help you?'

A few minutes later, following a very welcome query about a possible New Year's Eve party – thank God she'd taken the phone from Chloe – Faith ended the call and turned to her niece. 'Why are you being like this?'

Chloe jumped off the stool and shoved her hands on her hips. 'Like what?'

'Rude? Not caring whether you upset my guests, ruin my business?'

Chloe smacked her hand on the reception desk. 'What the flip have I done wrong now? You asked me to answer the phone. I answered it. You're as bad as Mum and Dad. Nothing I ever do is right.'

As they squared up to each other, Faith heard the clearing of a throat. She didn't have to look up to know who it was. The depth of the sound, the way her heart bounced against her ribs, gave it away.

Adam Hunter stood in front of the desk, towering over

both her and Chloe, his light grey eyes flickering between the two of them.

'Adam.' She wanted the ground to swallow her up. To rewind the last minute – or however long he'd been there – and do it all again. Without Chloe.

'Is there a problem?'

'Not unless you count the fact that my aunt is a dick,' Chloe muttered.

As Faith died another thousand deaths, Adam glanced at Chloe. 'I believe that's anatomically impossible,' he said mildly.

'Not in her case.' Chloe snatched up her canvas bag. 'Whatever. This place sucks. I'm out of here.'

Instinctively Faith moved to follow her, but Adam's large hand wrapped around her upper arm, stopping her in her tracks. 'Leave her. She'll calm down.'

Leave her? She tried to wriggle free. 'I can't. She's my niece. She's upset and I don't know where she's going.'

Adam's hold stayed firm. 'She's fifteen, not five. She won't come to any harm. Besides, she wants you to run after her. Don't play her game.'

'Since when did you become an expert on teenagers?'

He let go of her arm and gave her a small smile. 'I was one once.'

Gazing up at his lofty height, powerful shoulders, rugged face, it was hard to believe. 'I was one, too, but I can't remember ever behaving like that.'

'I can.'

She waited for him to elaborate, but of course he didn't. She was starting to realise Adam wasn't the chatty sort. Then again, for a while last night he'd seemed to really open up. 'You dyed your hair red, did you?'

Another smile, slightly wider this time. 'I grew it long instead, though for the same reason.'

Jeez, getting information out of him made getting blood from a stone look like child's play. 'And that reason was?'

'I wanted my parents to take notice of me.'

'Did it work?'

He grunted softly. 'Not in the way I'd hoped. I suspect the same is happening with Chloe.'

Faith sighed, thinking about her troubled niece. 'I don't understand. Chloe's parents love her to pieces. This is really cutting them up. We were hoping a change of scenery, a bit of responsibility, would help bring back the Chloe we used to know. Now I'm not so sure.'

'With respect, Chloe's issues are your sister's problem, not yours.'

Adam watched as astonishment spread across Faith's face.

'Chloe's my niece. She's family, so her problems are our problems.'

He felt a stab of frustration, though for the life of him he didn't know why, because none of this was his business. 'If you let her turn away potential guests, it's quickly going to become *your* problem.'

'I am aware of that, thank you.' She gave him a sharp look. 'You've already hinted you aren't close to your parents. I wonder, do you have any other family, Adam?'

For a split-second he felt a tightening of his chest. A difficulty in taking a breath. *Don't go there*, he willed himself. 'Not really, no.'

'Then perhaps that's why you don't understand.' Annoyance, or perhaps it was anger, flashed across her face. 'If you had family you were close to, you'd know you'd do anything for them. Anything.'

He heaved out a sigh, wondering how a man who liked to keep himself to himself had managed to wade knee-deep into someone else's business. 'Look, I didn't mean to upset you. I just sense how important this hotel is to you.'

It took a few moments, but slowly the tightness left her face. 'It is, and you're right. I need to have a chat with Chloe about how she interacts with guests.' She let out a deep breath and straightened her shoulders, giving him a smooth smile. 'All of this is really unprofessional of me, sorry. Was there anything I can help you with?'

He felt dismissed, which was stupid because he was her guest, not her friend. 'What's the best station for a train to Manchester?'

'They go direct from Oxenholme. It takes about an hour and quarter.'

Though he waited for it, hoped for it, there was no follow-up question asking why he was going to Manchester. He'd clearly pissed her off, big time. Feeling out of sorts, he nodded his thanks and headed for his car, glad to be getting out of the hotel for a while. As he scrunched across the gravel, Adam took a look over his shoulder at The Old Mill. Undulating roof tiles, whitewashed walls that were no longer linear. It wasn't slick, or smooth like a modern building, but friendly, inviting. It stood out not just in looks but in character.

A highly attractive hotel, with bags of personality, he mused. Much like the owner.

Adam stood in the doorway of the pub Damon had suggested meeting in, and frowned. Bloody hell, the guy couldn't have chosen a noisier, more crowded place to have what was supposed to be a quiet drink together. After buying himself a pint from the bar – one advantage of being tall, he was always served quickly – he forced his way through the raucous mass to the last free table. Next to the gents'. Nice.

Taking the seat furthest from the toilets – served Damon right for being late – Adam shrugged off his sodden coat (it was another beautiful day in the North of England) and took a swig of his beer. It said something for how sad he was that he'd agreed to spend an afternoon of his holiday having lunch with a guy he saw far too much of when he was at home. Damon was seeing a client in Manchester, and when he'd texted asking if Adam fancied meeting for lunch, Adam had thought, why not? Even for a loner like him, there were only so many damp, solitary walks he could manage.

Damon looked harassed when he finally appeared, after threading his way through the packed pub.

'Haven't these people got work to go to?' his friend muttered as he shook off his coat, spraying water liberally within a two-foot radius.

'I suspect *these people* are having lunch.' Adam thrust the bar menu at Damon. 'About time we did the same.'

Damon grunted, his sandy hair flat against his forehead. 'I've time for a quick pint and a bowl of chips with you before I have to scurry back to convince the most pernickety client on the planet – thanks for dumping him on me, by the way – that his blasted glass ceiling needs at least one support strut or the whole damn thing will crash down round his ears. These guys,' he continued, waving behind him, not giving Adam a chance to refute the "dumped" allegation, 'these guys are having a proper Christmas office party lunch. The type where you eat, drink and exchange rude jokes with your co-workers all afternoon before falling asleep in a cab on the way home. Something you, me and the delightful Anita never do because you always slink off on "holiday".' Damon signalled inverted commas with his fingers.

For the first time since he'd sat down, Adam took a proper look at the people around him. Many wore suits, a few sported silly paper hats. Laughter. There was a lot of laughter. Gaudy tinsel ran across the top of the bar, paper chains – for God's sake, who still made paper chains? – were hung from the ceiling. 'I can go,' he muttered. 'Leave you eating your chips by yourself.'

Damon huffed. 'Jeez. I see a few days away hasn't mellowed you.'

'Blame the season.' Adam stared moodily into his pint. 'I'll be back to my usual happy self in January.'

'Emma called the office.'

At Damon's blunt statement, the pint he'd been drinking shook in Adam's hands, slopping beer onto the table. 'What did she want?'

'What do you think she wanted? To talk to you. Invite you for Christmas.'

Panic shot through him. 'What did you tell her?'

'The truth. That you were on holiday.' Damon fixed Adam with a steely glare. 'You're being a right prick to her.'

Adam didn't know what to say to that. For once Damon was right. 'I know,' he muttered quietly.

'Then why do it? I understood why you wanted to avoid her that first year. Even the second, but if you ask me it would do you a world of good to see her now.'

'I'm not asking you.'

Irritation flared in Damon's usually calm, even-tempered eyes. 'Fine. Go on treating people who care about you like shit. See where it gets you in the long run.'

Adam hung his head. Jesus, what was he doing, being such a git to the one man who'd kept him sane these last few years? 'Sorry.' He gave Damon an apologetic smile. 'And thanks for dealing with Emma. Though you're wrong in thinking she's inviting me because she cares.'

'And you'd know that how, exactly? You decline her invitations with a text. You haven't returned a single one of her calls.'

Cold tendrils of dread, of fear, wound their way through him, tightening round his chest in a way he'd become all too familiar with. 'I don't need to speak to Emma to know what she must be thinking.'

Damon's expression turned more sympathetic. 'You know I've got your back mate, always. Just ...' He exhaled, twisting his pint glass round on the table. 'Just consider why she hasn't given up on you. Why she's still trying to make contact.'

Feeling too choked to speak, Adam nodded. He'd spent far too long considering it. Far too long remembering the last words they'd spoken to each other. *I think you need to leave*, she'd told him in clipped tones. As if he'd been a stranger turning up to her house. No, worse: an uninvited, unwanted caller.

Her reason for wanting to see him had to come from unresolved anger, blame, pity or duty. None of them sat well with him.

'So, how's the hotel?'

Adam clutched gratefully at the change in topic. 'Good.' He had a sudden vision of Faith, standing outside his door with her arms full of fluffy dogs. 'Surprisingly good.'

His friend did a double-take. 'Bloody hell, Adam. Beneath that beard, I can actually see your lips moving. You're almost *smiling*.'

'Piss off.'

Damon continued to study him, a contemplative look entering his eyes that made Adam distinctly twitchy. 'You've met someone, haven't you?'

'Hell, no.' Yet even to his ears his denial sounded too forceful, too defensive.

A grin broke out across Damon's face. 'A guest?' His eyes narrowed. 'Jason's in his mid-thirties, so his sister is likely to be around that age, give or take a few years.'

'Faith's twenty-seven.' Stupid time to remember that. Stupid.

Damon spluttered with laughter. 'Well, well. Who'd have thought it? It's been a long while coming, but a woman has finally caught Adam Hunter's eye. What's she like then, this twenty-seven year old hotel owner?'

He felt trapped, caught between wanting to talk about Faith and the feelings he'd been experiencing, feelings he thought he'd never experience again, and not wanting to say anything. Not wanting to tempt fate, to start raising his hopes, when actually her interest in him was only as a guest.

'She's very nice,' he said briefly, cringing at the use of the limp term to describe such an energetic, attractive, bubbly personality. 'Can we order the food now? I'm starving.'

Damon acquiesced, though as they ordered, and the conversation moved on, the glint in his eyes told Adam he wouldn't be hearing the end of this.

Chapter Six

Six days before Christmas

Working in her office the following morning, Faith was both surprised and relieved to hear Chloe plonk her bag down on the reception desk. She knew from Hope that her niece had gone straight home yesterday, only to slam her bedroom door behind her and not venture out for the rest of the day.

Closing the document she'd been working on, Faith walked out to see her. 'It's good to see you back.'

Chloe looked nonplussed. 'Am I not supposed to be?'

Faith smiled, giving Chloe's shoulders a gentle squeeze. 'You're exactly where you're supposed to be. What would you like to do today?'

In a gesture Faith was becoming familiar with, Chloe shrugged. 'Whatever.'

'We have a man due in shortly who's interested in holding a New Year's Eve party here, so I'm going to need you on reception for a little while.'

'Is it the guy who phoned yesterday?'

'Yes.'

Chloe gave her a hostile look. 'Didn't scare him off then, did I.'

'No, you didn't.' Beneath the bolshie glare, the "couldn't care less" attitude, Faith was sure she saw a hint of relief. 'Chloe, is everything alright? You don't seem happy.'

Chloe blinked, blue eyes vivid against her pale face and bright red hair. 'I'm fine.'

Because it was obvious Chloe was far from fine, Faith touched a hand to her cheek. 'I think there's something troubling you and I'd like to find out what it is, so I can help.' With a sigh, she let her hand fall. 'But I'm not going to press it. You know I'm here if you need me.'

Chloe didn't reply, just fiddled with the straps of her bag, avoiding Faith's eyes. She ached to see her niece so clearly unhappy, yet not prepared to talk about it.

'I thought we should make up some information packs for the rooms,' Faith said into the silence. 'I've already been asked where the nearest station is, and the nearest gym. Guests will find it useful to have information like that to hand. Staff, too, because not all of them will be locals. The new deputy manager joining next month comes from Bournemouth.' When Chloe again remained silent, Faith pressed ahead. 'Would you like to put a pack together?'

Chloe picked at her green nail varnish. At least it matched the green tights she was wearing today. She'd teamed them with a loose-fitting checked shirt and a short black skirt that might have fitted her a few months ago, but was now in danger of ripping at the seams. 'Is that to stop me answering the phone and talking to guests?'

Faith briefly debated how to reply. 'It's true we need to have a chat about how you go about that, yes, but I also thought you'd enjoy doing something different for a change. Besides, I'll still need you to help me out when I'm not around. So, what do you think?'

'I guess.' The phone in her hand buzzed and Chloe glanced down. Suddenly her face became even paler and her bottom lip started to tremble.

'What is it?' Faith asked gently.

'Nothing. Just a bunch of bitches.' She pushed the phone into her bag and once again Faith's heart went out to her.

'Girls from your school?'

'Yeah.'

When nothing else was forthcoming, Faith tried a different tack. 'What about those friends of yours, Alice and Tamsin, wasn't it?'

'Not my friends any more,' Chloe mumbled.

'Why not?'

Chloe huffed loudly. 'Leave it, Aunt Faith.'

She was loathe to, not now she was making progress, but tears welled in Chloe's eyes and Faith knew the last thing her not-quite-a-child yet not-quite-an-adult niece would want was to cry in front of her. 'Okay, let's change the subject.'

Chloe wiped at a stray tear. 'I saw that guy on the way here.' When Faith frowned, Chloe rolled her eyes. 'You know, the one who's staying in the suite. Big guy, beard, ripped.'

'You mean Mr Hunter.'

'Pretty sure you called him Adam.'

'Yes, Adam.' Faith couldn't believe it; her cheeks were growing hot. Damn, when was the last time she'd blushed – and over a man?

Chloe gawked. 'Oh-em-gee. You've got the hots for him, haven't you?'

It was on the tip of her tongue to deny it, but Faith took one look at Chloe's ear-to-ear grin and she started to laugh. If it took embarrassing herself over a man to bring a smile to Chloe's face, she was happy to oblige. 'He is rather attractive, yes,' she murmured, casting a quick eye around her to check nobody could hear her.

'For an oldie. He's out there running if you want to cop a look at his legs.'

As if on cue, the front door creaked open and a windswept, flushed and slightly sweaty Adam Hunter strode in. Faith couldn't stop her eyes from flickering down to the legs Chloe had mentioned. Long and powerful with a dusting of dark hair over well-defined muscle. She forced her eyes upwards, over his flat stomach and up to his broad chest where the heavy muscles of his pecs strained against the snug, long-sleeved running top.

Desire whooshed through her, making her blood feel thick and overheated. Her mind was a confused muddle of hormones; a teenager once again, in the throes of experiencing her first hot crush. She knew she was gawping, knew that Chloe was giving her a none too subtle grin, but Faith couldn't seem to snap herself out of it. 'Good morning,' she finally managed.

Adam wiped his forehead with his sleeve. 'Morning, Faith.' He nodded over to her niece. 'Chloe.'

Think of something to say. 'Been for a run?'

Beside her Chloe snorted. 'Duh. What gave it away?'

'The shorts?'

Her niece giggled. 'Thought you'd notice those.'

Faith willed herself not to blush as Adam glanced curiously between them. 'Everything okay?'

'Fine, thank you.' She nodded for good measure, hoping to God she didn't look like one of those nodding dogs that people put in cars. 'Isn't it a bit cold for shorts?'

He glanced down at his legs, which gave Faith another excuse to do the same. 'I warm up pretty quick when I run.'

'Guess that means you were right,' Chloe whispered, giggling, as Adam started to walk towards his room. 'He is pretty hot.'

Faith felt her cheeks burn again. Stupid to start crushing like this on a guest. Stupid. 'Umm, Mr Hunter.' He halted, that rugged face looking perplexed and, if she'd read him correctly, disappointed. 'Adam,' she corrected, suddenly aware he might still think she was annoyed with him from yesterday. He'd been trying to support her, she'd realised belatedly, not criticise her. 'I've asked Chloe to put together an information pack for the rooms. Could you spare her a few minutes this morning to go through what you think should go in it?'

He glanced down at his sweaty running kit. 'Am I allowed to change first?'

'Well yes, obviously—'

'Chill, Aunt.' Chloe rolled her eyes for the second time that morning. 'He's joking.'

And yes, now her fluster level had started to abate, she could see amusement lighting up those striking grey eyes.

'Give me fifteen minutes and I'm all yours.'

Thankfully Chloe waited until he was safely out of earshot before bursting into giggles. 'See, he's just told you he's yours.'

Faith let out a long, shaky breath. 'Sadly, even if that wasn't just a figure of speech, I fear I'm too rusty to take him up on it.'

'Rusty?'

'I haven't been out with a guy for … coming up to two years. Not since Patrick. I've been so focused on buying and doing up this place. Besides, my experience with Patrick taught me it's hard to juggle a full-on career and a relationship. Easier just to forget men for a while.' She gave her niece a long, questioning look. 'How about you, Chloe? Any boys caught your eye?'

Chloe's face turned the colour of her hair. 'No.' Immediately she turned away, making a great show of straightening up a pile of notepads that was already perfectly straight.

Faith took the hint and dropped the subject, though at least now she had an idea of what was troubling Chloe. It had something to do with a boy, and friends who were no longer friends.

Adam glanced at the clock out of habit. It had taken him exactly fifteen minutes to shower and change, just as it did every morning, whether he was going to work or not. He found it hard to turn off, hard to relax. Here he was in a hotel three hundred miles away from home, with nothing he had to get out of bed for, and he'd still woken up at 5 a.m. Oh he'd tried to go back to sleep, but his mind wouldn't let him. It was in those early hours, when it was still dark outside, that his thoughts often turned dark, too.

Especially at this time of year.

Sometimes he could fend them off, force himself to think

of other things. This morning though, even picturing Faith, and all the things he'd like to do to her, hadn't done the trick. In fact it had only made things worse, his mind bringing up images of another woman, her face glowing with laughter as she'd watched him put up their Christmas decorations. Directing him where to hang the silly yellow cab driven by Santa that they'd bought in New York. Where to put the mad saxophone-playing reindeer she'd bought in the sales.

Then her face the last time he'd seen her. Angry, her anguished eyes spitting fire at him. Her cold, bitter tongue wishing him dead.

Unable to bear the memories any longer he'd jumped out of bed, shoved on his kit and gone out for a long run as the sun had slowly come up.

The exercise had helped, as it always did. Now as he made his way to the reception desk, and to Chloe, he thought he could handle anything. Even a teenage girl.

But as he neared the desk he came to an abrupt halt at the sight of Chloe bent over her phone. Tears pouring down her cheeks.

Bollocks.

Crying teenagers were way outside his field of experience. Instinct told him to turn away, to give her some space. Hell, who was he kidding, he wanted out for his own selfish reasons. He had no clue what to do, what to say. Enough people had tried to comfort him over the years for him to know nothing ever worked, anyway.

Before he had a chance to decide whether to stay or bolt, she looked up.

'Is now a bad time?' *Of course it's a bad time. She's bloody crying.*

Chloe rubbed a hand vigorously over her face. Fifty years ago, a man faced with this situation would probably have had a handkerchief to give her. Adam had nothing except his wallet and room key.

'I, umm.' Her eyes darted in every direction but his.

'You don't have to explain,' he interrupted, belatedly realising he sounded too abrupt. Too much like he didn't give a sod. 'Not unless you want to.'

'No.' She tucked her phone into her skirt pocket.

'Where's your aunt?'

'Showing someone round.'

There was an awkward silence during which Adam racked his clueless brain for something to say. He was the adult here. It was up to him to make Chloe feel less uncomfortable. 'Shall we talk about this information pack your aunt was harping on about?'

Chloe swallowed, giving her cheeks a final wipe with the back of her hand. 'Guess so.'

To avoid crowding her, Adam chose to keep the reception desk between them, though now he was towering over her.

'You can sit round here. If you want.'

Chloe pointed to the second padded stool next to hers. Not wanting to offend, Adam walked round and wedged himself onto it. He caught Chloe staring at him and gave her a wry smile. 'I think they're intended for people smaller than me.'

As Chloe started to smile, he heard a buzzing noise coming from her pocket. Her eyes flew to where her phone was peeping out of the top and she started to pull it out.

'Why not leave it for a while?' he suggested gently.

She swallowed and tucked it back in.

'You know you don't have to look at it at all. Not if it's upsetting you.'

Her eyes welled again and she blinked rapidly. 'It's not. They're not.'

Ignoring the stray tears rolling down her cheek, he focused instead on her use of the term "they". 'Good. But say it was, say some halfwits thought it was clever to write nasty things about someone.' He was aware of her watching him, though every time he caught her eye, hers shifted away.

'If that happened, it would really piss the dimwits off if they saw that person had shut down their account.' He flicked her a glance. 'Hard to be nasty to someone when they're not listening to you.'

She held his gaze for a moment before looking down at the notepad in her hand. He wasn't sure whether he'd made any sense or whether he'd got the whole thing backwards and actually it wasn't a bunch of messages that were upsetting her. Still, at least the tears had dried up.

'Shall I tell you some of the stuff I'd find useful in a guest folder?' She nodded, and he began to talk.

Adam was aware of Faith before he saw her. Whether it was her subtle scent, or his pheromones mingling with hers he didn't know. But when he raised his head from where he'd been checking through the list he and Chloe had come up with, he was hit by a bolt of lust.

It seemed after years of inactivity, years when he'd not wanted to look at another woman, his libido had finally woken up and decided to play.

Standing next to Faith was a slender guy with slicked back hair, wearing a tight-fitting suit and exuding self-importance.

'Chloe, Mr Bannister would like his wife to take a look at our facilities before he makes up his mind about the New Year booking.' Though Faith was smiling, Adam had a sense that she wasn't feeling as relaxed as she was trying to look. 'Can you make a note in the calendar that she'll be round tomorrow at midday?'

Chloe slipped off the stool and opened the computer. 'What's her name?'

Tight-fitting suit raised his eyebrows. 'If you'd been listening, you'd have heard. It's Bannister.'

Chloe glared at him in the way of all teenagers when they think an adult is looking down on them. 'I meant her first name.'

'*Mrs* Bannister,' the suit replied cuttingly, before turning to Faith. 'I'll be honest with you Faith, having a teenager on the reception desk, especially one with hair that colour, doesn't fill me with confidence.'

Adam considered himself an even-tempered man, slow to anger, but Bannister's attitude had his temper bubbling to the surface. Faith might be hamstrung by the need to be polite to a potential customer, but he wasn't. With deliberate slowness he eased off the stool and walked round to the front of the reception desk, glad of his bulk, of his height. It meant he could look down on stuck-up squirts. 'I didn't realise hair colour and age were a prerequisite for efficiency.' Though he kept his tone mild, he hoped Bannister would read the irritation behind it.

The guy took a step back, and Adam felt a spurt of satisfaction. 'Who are you?'

'A guest.' He gave Bannister a cool smile. 'And I'm happy to vouch for the efficiency of both the hotel and the receptionist.'

From the corner of his vision, Adam saw Chloe's lips twitch.

With the wind taken out of his sails, Bannister nodded. 'Good to know.'

Faith turned her focus towards Adam and as her eyes blazed with gratitude, he felt another foot taller. But just as he watched her shoulders begin to relax, he heard the sound of scampering feet. They all turned towards the direction of the noise, which was coming from the hall. Like two fluffy tornadoes, Nip and Tuck came hurtling towards them, knocking baubles flying off the tree as they skirted perilously close to it.

'Oh my God,' he heard Faith whisper under her breath. And in the blink of an eye, her shoulders were back to rigid again.

Chapter Seven

The bottom fell out of Faith's stomach as she watched the dogs barrelling through the hall. For pity's sake, was nothing going to go right today? Mr Guy Bannister had been a total jerk, turning his nose up at everything she'd shown him, yet still keeping her dangling on a thread. If she didn't need the business so badly, she'd have told him to take a running jump, though he might have found it difficult in that eye-wateringly tight suit.

How on earth was she going to explain the appearance of two wild dogs in the foyer of the hotel Mr Pernickety was considering for his posh New Year's Eve party?

'Nip, Tuck, sit.'

Adam's firm voice brought the dogs skidding to a halt. Though they didn't park their bums on the floor, they did stand still, faces staring questioningly up at him.

Faith watched with mounting incredulity as Adam strode casually over to them and picked them up, one cute, fluffy bundle resting under each of his heavily muscled arms.

'Sorry. Must have left my room door open by accident.' Adam glanced at Guy Bannister with an admirably straight face. 'I didn't want to leave them in a kennel over Christmas. I'm sure you can see why.'

Nip and Tuck gazed up at him, heads cocked to one side, tails wagging, their expressions a glorious mixture of confusion and hero worship.

The sight was almost too much for her. Adam's bulging biceps wrapped round her silly, crazy dogs. Laughter bubbled inside, threatening to escape, and Faith knew she was only seconds away from totally losing it.

In desperation, she bit into her cheek.

Guy Bannister gave her a stiff smile and, thank you God,

walked towards the door. The moment she heard it clunk shut, laughter erupted from her. Bending over she gave in to it, laughing so hard her sides started to ache. Adam caught her eye and grinned, the dogs staring goofily up at him. Behind her, Chloe was almost in hysterics.

While Faith tried to stop laughing long enough to speak, her parents came dashing into the foyer.

'Oh my goodness.' Clearly out of breath, her mother's eyes darted towards Adam. 'That's where those little rascals ended up.'

Nip and Tuck were still gazing adoringly up at Adam, tongues hanging out of the sides of their mouths. 'You're nuts, you know that?' he told them before bending and letting them jump down.

'I'm so sorry darling.' Her mother gave her an apologetic smile. 'We popped in to check up on them as you'd asked, but your father didn't shut the door properly and they shot out.'

'Knew it would be my fault,' her father muttered.

Faith gave them both a reassuring hug. 'It's fine, no harm done. And not the first time it's happened, either.' She glanced up at Adam. 'Thankfully I have a guest who wants to spend Christmas with them.'

A slow smile crept across Adam's face and as their eyes met, her heart sped up.

'We'll take them back. Give them a quick run outside.'

Faith barely registered her mother's words, or her parents walking away with the dogs. She was totally unable to drag her eyes away from Adam's. 'I don't know where to start.' Her voice sounded quiet, husky. 'Thank you, for defending the hotel, sticking up for Chloe. Risking permanent damage to your masculinity by claiming those two mutts.'

He laughed softly. 'I'm not worried about my masculinity.'

And why would he, she thought, as everything female in her reacted crazily to everything very male about him. It had been a long time since she'd felt such a strong tug of attraction towards a member of the opposite sex. Now it was all she could feel, all she could think about. 'Can I buy you a drink tonight, to thank you?'

Something that looked nearer to shock than surprise flared in his eyes and she winced. Damn, had she sounded too forward? Too much like she was asking him on a date, rather than a simple thank you gesture? *But you have an ulterior motive*, her inner conscience niggled. *You fancy him.*

A loud coughing fit broke the awkward silence and Faith turned to find Chloe staring at them, her eyes like blue saucers.

Oh God, apparently she hadn't just asked a guest out. She'd done it right in front of her impressionable young niece.

'I'm just going to, umm, get myself a drink of water.' Chloe was clearly fighting the urge to laugh. 'You know, for my cough.'

As Chloe sprinted past her, Faith died quietly on the spot.

Adam watched her go, a small smile hovering around his mouth. 'It's good to see her smiling.'

'Yes.' *He's changed the subject*, she thought miserably.

He shifted on his feet, looking uncomfortable, and she braced herself for the excruciating *thank you but no thank you* speech. But then he surprised her. 'Something was troubling Chloe earlier. I hope I'm not talking out of turn, but when I came back to talk to her about the information pack, she was crying.'

Faith's heart lurched, her embarrassment forgotten. 'Oh no, how awful. She had a moment earlier with me, too. I think some of the girls she used to be friends with have started being bitchy to her. I'm sorry.'

He cocked his head, giving her a strange look. 'Why are you apologising?'

'You're a guest. You shouldn't have to get embroiled in sorting out my staff.'

His eyes met and held hers. 'I'm your first guest. I'd like to think it gives me special status.'

She had to swallow before she could speak. 'It does.'

'Perhaps then, after you've bought me a drink, that status will allow me to buy you dinner?'

And boom, just like that, her heart began to thump violently against her ribs. 'I'd like that.'

'I'm not sure of the etiquette of taking a lady to dinner in her own hotel.' His eyes smiled into hers and what felt like a swarm of butterflies broke free in her stomach. 'Shall we meet in the bar?'

She was pretty certain her face was one manic grin. 'Works for me.'

With a nod and another small smile, he walked away, almost bumping into Chloe as she came back through the hall with a glass of water in her hand.

'Well?' Chloe demanded when he was out of earshot.

Faith paused, allowing the happiness to ripple through her. 'I might have just got myself a hot dinner date.' Chloe whooped, giving her a high five, and Faith forced herself to rephrase, for her benefit as well as Chloe's. 'Of course it's not really a date. Just my way of thanking him for his help earlier.' But he was the one who'd added dinner to the agenda. Much as she tried to squash it, the thought kept buzzing happily through her head. There was nothing wrong with a little light flirtation. Nothing at all.

As they strode back to the reception desk, the smile Faith had been so delighted to see on Chloe's face began to slip.

'What is it?' Faith asked.

Chloe shook her head. 'Nothing.'

Concerned, Faith reached for her hand, giving it a quick squeeze. 'I know it's something. Does it involve a boy?'

'Leave it, Aunt Faith. Please.'

Chloe's eyes pleaded with her and reluctantly Faith changed the subject.

Adam dressed for dinner with a lot more care than usual. Scratch that, it made him sound like he went out to dinner a lot. He dressed for dinner with care. Hell, it was enough to say he dressed for dinner, because how many times had he actually done that over the last few years? As he straightened the collar of his shirt, he gazed into the mirror. Even after three years, the bearded face that reflected back sometimes took him by surprise. He'd started growing it because he couldn't be bothered to shave. Then it had become something to hide behind, as if by covering half his face people wouldn't be able to see what he was thinking. Lately he wondered if he kept it because he didn't want a reminder of who he'd been before the beard.

Faith obviously didn't mind it.

She'd asked him for a drink. He felt another surge of nervous adrenaline just thinking about it. Sure she'd done it as a means of thanking him, but the smile she'd given him when he'd extended it to dinner couldn't be faked.

She was interested.

His hand trembled slightly as he reached for his beard trimmer. What had he done? He had no right encouraging a woman when he had no intention of following up on it.

And he didn't have … did he?

Shit, he had no bloody idea where his head was. All he knew was he enjoyed her company. No point overthinking anything beyond that.

Besides, he still had the evening to navigate his way through. Had things moved on since he'd last taken a woman out to dinner? Was holding the chair out for her, picking up the bill, considered too old-fashioned? He couldn't even claim to be out of practice, because that presumed there'd been a time when he'd been *in* practice.

He took a deep breath and told himself to stop being a twit. They'd sat down together in the restaurant only the other evening. He hadn't eaten with her, sure, but he'd managed conversation, a light flirtation, and she hadn't run for the hills.

He tucked the pale grey shirt into his black jeans and slipped on a black jacket. Hopefully it said he'd tried, but not so hard he looked like a prat. As he reached for his phone, it started to ring.

Emma (sis).

Briefly he shut his eyes as a heavy dose of guilt swept through him, dragging at his insides. Then he exhaled sharply, hit decline and headed for the door.

She looked stunning, was his first thought as he spotted Faith by the bar, talking to the waitress – Becky, if he'd remembered correctly. Up until now he'd seen Faith in practical trouser suits but tonight she had on a simple green silk dress. It flowed elegantly over curves that his fingers itched to trace.

Becky shot him a quick smile before moving away, leaving him and Faith alone.

'Am I late?' Mentally he slapped himself round the head. She looked like a million dollars and that was the best he could open with?

She gave him a flash of her warm, wide smile. 'Not at all. One of the advantages of having a meal in the same place you live and work. I cut the journey time right out of the equation.'

Nerves fluttered unhelpfully around in his stomach and Adam tried to settle them. Tried to remember this was the same woman he'd had such an enjoyable evening with two nights ago. 'Which part do you live in?' She raised her eyebrows, giving him a playful smile, and he realised how that must have sounded. 'I didn't mean ... I'm not expecting.' He huffed out a breath and she laughed softly.

'Relax, I know. I have a few rooms at the back of the hotel.' She lightly touched his arm. 'Are you okay?'

Embarrassment flooded through him. 'Nothing a stiff drink won't fix.' He forced himself to take a breath. And then another. 'Sorry, I'm making a total hash of this. Truth is, it's been a long time since I went out to dinner with a beautiful woman. I'm trying to remember my steps.'

Her expression softened. 'If it helps, I'm feeling a little nervous myself.' A slow smile spread across her face. 'You just called me beautiful though, which gives you plenty of bonus points in the bag already.'

'Enough to cover me if I spill my drink over you?'

'As long as it's not the one I buy you, yes. What would you like?'

'A pint of whisky?' he asked dryly. 'But I'll start with a shot and see how I go.'

Becky poured their drinks and they took them to one of the many spare tables – clearly Tuesday nights were slow. Remembering manners drilled into him by his parents, he eased the chair away so Faith could sit down. She looked surprised, but not displeased, so he guessed he hadn't forgotten all of his etiquette.

'So.' She took a sip of her wine and gave him a considering look. 'How does a man who looks like you go for so long without a date?'

A blush – for pity's sake, the last time he'd blushed he'd been thirteen – stung his cheeks and Adam swallowed down a mouthful of his drink. 'I guess I've not seen anyone I've been interested in.' *Until now.* The words were on the tip of his tongue but he stopped them, aware he wasn't ready for anything more than a pleasant evening in the company of a gorgeous woman.

You've imagined kissing her though, his inner voice reminded him. *Imagined her naked.*

He coughed, crossing his legs before he gave away his

thoughts. Clearly, he *was* ready for something more, though quite how much of a something, he wasn't sure.

'How about you?' he asked, keen to steer the conversation away from him and on to her. 'You admitted to being nervous, yet you don't strike me as a woman who lacks confidence.'

She winced. 'Do I come across too strong? I know a few men who'd find it a bit weird being asked out for a drink by a woman. They prefer to do the asking.'

He shook his head. 'I like a woman who isn't afraid to go after what she wants.' When she raised her eyebrows Adam frowned, replaying the words again in his mind. *Shit.* 'I didn't mean to imply you wanted me,' he added hastily, feeling another flush creep up his neck.

'Of course not.'

Her eyes sparkled with amusement and Adam sighed, exasperated with his own ineptitude. 'I'd ask if we could start this evening again, but I can't guarantee I'll be any better the second time around.'

She gave him a considering look. 'You know it might just be because it's been a while since I last had a meal with a man who wasn't a member of my family, but I've got no complaints with this first date. If that's what it is. A date.'

He inhaled sharply, knowing this was the time to push back. To make it clear that though he liked her, he wasn't in the right place for anything more than dinner and conversation. 'I'm hugely attracted to you,' he blurted instead.

A gorgeous smile bloomed across her face. 'And I to you, so there's no need to worry about impressing me. Consider me already impressed.'

His heart was beating so hard he could barely think. He wasn't a stranger to women coming on to him – there was something about height and muscles that appealed to them. But it was rare that he was interested enough to want to encourage it. To want to flirt back. Reaching for his glass again, he swallowed the rest of his drink before setting it down and staring straight back at her. 'Safe to say, the feeling is mutual.'

She gave him another slow, sexy smile. 'Good to know.' She nodded towards his glass. 'Would you like another before we eat?'

He shook his head. 'Better not. I don't think drunk me is great company. Besides, I believe catching your mutts is only a one drink reward.'

She laughed, and he felt a puff of pride at being the cause. 'You deserve one for your quick thinking alone. Then there's the fact that the sight of you with a dog under each arm gave me the best laugh I've had in ages.' Her eyes travelled up his chest, lingering a moment on his lips before meeting his. 'Besides, we both know rewarding you with a drink was just a ruse to get you alone.'

Tingles of awareness shot through him. He felt like a dormouse, albeit a giant mutant version, waking up after a long period of (sexual) hibernation. Disorientated, definitely. Hungry – in his case a fierce carnal hunger – abso-bloody-lutely. His groin was tight, his blood hot, his heart in thumping overload, though his lust was tempered by the knowledge that just talking to Faith had tied him in nervous knots. If they took this to the next stage – and let's face it, the leap from light flirtation to the images burning his brain was a huge one – but say they did. That he managed to convince her, convince himself. What then? Was sex like riding a bike? Would it really all come back to him?

Faith was still watching him, her eyes curious, and he wondered what she was thinking. Was she also imagining them taking the next step? Or was she just keeping her one and only guest happy?

Chapter Eight

Faith watched as a mixture of embarrassment and confusion flickered across Adam's face, at odds with the heat she saw in his eyes. Perhaps she shouldn't have been so direct, but she'd never seen the point of pretending not to like someone. Besides, he wasn't trying to hide his attraction to her either. He just clearly wasn't used to flirting. Who would have thought the giant, macho lumberjack of a man would be so endearingly shy? Though shy was the wrong word, because he certainly hadn't lacked confidence when dealing with Guy Bannister.

Just when dealing with her.

He glanced up from his scrutiny of the menu. 'What wine would you like?' His mouth curved in another of his small, unconsciously sexy smiles. 'On second thoughts, maybe you should do the choosing. It is your place.'

'Only if that masculinity of yours isn't going to take another hit.'

He chuckled, handing her the wine menu. 'Give it your best shot. And while you're at it, tell me what you recommend for the food, too. I eat anything as long as it isn't moving.'

God, but he was gorgeous. Not just the powerfully built body, or the rugged, beautifully masculine face, but his whole self-effacing, slightly reserved demeanour. His dry wit. A hugely attractive male with the body of an Adonis who wasn't cocky, wasn't in love with himself.

Faith gave their orders to Becky, choosing the same meal for Adam as she was having herself. As Becky stepped away, she caught Faith's eye over Adam's broad shoulder and winked, giving her a thumbs up.

Totally unaware of the effect he was having on the

female staff, Adam leant back in his seat. 'So.' He ran a hand through his short hair, letting out a rueful smile. 'I'm trying to remember what we were talking about before … well …'

'Before we both admitted we were attracted to each other?'

'Yes, before that.' He gave her a sweetly awkward smile, but it was his eyes that hers were drawn to. And they looked like they wanted to devour her. 'I think you were telling me why you don't have a boyfriend.'

'I was?'

'At least I hope you don't.'

His gaze was riveted on her and for a long, humming moment they stared at each other. 'I don't. I'm most definitely single.'

What would it feel like to kiss him? She could almost feel the tingle of his lips against hers. The light brush of his beard. The heat from his hands as they cupped her face. The press of his powerful body against hers …

Becky arrived with the wine, breaking up the smouldering eye contact. When she'd filled their glasses, Faith took a gulp, hoping to cool her wayward thoughts. *Focus on the question.* 'For a few years I was in a steady relationship with a guy, Patient Patrick my family used to nickname him. PP, for short.' Adam quirked a dark brow and she laughed. 'Nothing ever annoyed him, and trust me I can be pretty annoying at times. I'd cancel on him at the last minute, sometimes even forget totally because a guest needed sorting out and the evening just vanished. Once I missed his birthday, which I know is shameful. None of it seemed to bother him.'

'Are you sure he wasn't a doormat?'

She laughed. 'Okay, I've made him sound really dull when actually he was a good guy.'

'What happened?'

'I found this place. Eventually even Patient Patrick had been stood up one time too many and decided he'd had enough.'

Adam's eyes – clear grey, framed with dark lashes, they'd be called pretty on anyone under six foot four and less than two hundred pounds – studied her for a moment. 'You don't seem terribly cut up about it.'

Faith paused, trying to remember the day Patrick had dumped her. 'I was upset. We'd been together for a couple of years and I guess I'd grown used to having him around.' She groaned, shaking her head. 'That sounds awful. I think what I'm trying to say is he was a good guy, but he came at the wrong time. My focus wasn't, and still isn't, on my love life. He deserved someone who put him first, but my priority was my career. Now it's getting this place up and running. Mind you, at this rate ...' She trailed off, annoyed she'd started to let her niggling doubts worm their way into the open. They might be flirting, but Adam was still a guest.

A few heavy moments of silence followed, Faith wishing she'd kept quiet and Adam probably wondering what on earth he should say to her.

'My friend Damon and I set up an architecture practice together three years ago,' he said after a while. 'Everyone told us we were nuts. What did a pair of twenty-six-year-olds, with only one year's experience in the real world, know about setting up their own business?' He smiled. 'They were probably right.'

'And there was me thinking you were going to tell me you're now worth millions and you don't regret following your heart rather than your head.'

He shook his head, though his eyes were still smiling. 'We're doing okay, and I don't regret too much of it. What I was trying to say was I understand how tough it is in the early days. It takes a while for word to get around, for reputations to be established.' He gazed quietly back at her.

'You have a great place here. Keep doing what you're doing. You'll get there.'

She wasn't sure whether it was his words, or the calm, steady way he said them, but suddenly her throat felt tight, her eyes pricking with tears. Uncomfortable with her emotional reaction, she tried to hide it with humour. 'I take it that advice doesn't run to keeping Chloe on the reception desk.'

To her mortification, he looked embarrassed. 'She's a good kid and I shouldn't have said anything. It's none of my business.'

'Hey, I didn't mean that as a dig. I actually meant it as a joke. Maybe I should have gone with *I take it that advice doesn't run to my choice in Christmas decorations.*'

His face relaxed, though not as much as she'd hoped. 'I'm sure your other guests will love them.'

'Well, so far that's one family, arriving in two days.' Her eyes flicked up to his. 'That's why I need Guy Bannister's booking so much. Hiring the function room for their private party, plus up to eight couples staying over for two nights. It's worth holding my tongue over.'

'Do you need me on dog duty tomorrow?'

He said it with a straight face but she could make out the curve of his lips beneath his beard. 'Thank you, but my parents have promised to take them out so they don't leap all over Mrs Bannister. My dad's delighted.'

His smile became fuller. 'I like your parents. I've seen them around a few times. Your mum's friendly, your dad seems to have a really dry sense of humour. Are they staying through till Christmas?'

'Yep. They were supposed to head back home for a while before coming back to join me on Christmas Day. I think they want to keep their eye on me. Make sure I'm not cracking under the pressure of running this place.' She hesitated before asking, 'Are your parents still alive?'

'Yes. They live in France. Have done for the last ten years or so.'

It wasn't that he appeared upset talking about them. More ambivalent. 'Do you see them much?'

'No.'

Faith nearly hissed with frustration as Becky chose that moment to arrive with their starters: deep-fried camembert with cranberry sauce. To her surprise though, after taking a bite, Adam picked up the thread of their conversation without any prompting. 'I haven't seen them in a while. Not since …' he trailed off, took a sip of his wine. 'Not for several years.'

Adam kicked himself. Why hadn't he stopped at *no*? He knew exactly how long it had been since he'd seen his parents. Three years and ten days. Even then, they'd barely spoken. Not that there had been any animosity. Still wasn't. It's just they barely knew what to say to each other at the best of times – and his parents had come over at the worst of times, when he'd not been able to speak to anyone.

'I guess they won't be turning up for Christmas, then?'

Faith was watching him with her wide, alert eyes. He knew she was trying to understand his family situation, his dislike of the season she loved so much. 'No.'

She frowned. 'Will you be spending the day alone?'

He let out a strangled laugh, desperate to shift the conversation onto something else. 'Hardly. I'll be here, won't I?'

A look of horror crossed her face. 'But the restaurant will be closed. We were going to open it, but with so few bookings it didn't seem fair on Mario and Antonio. Please tell me I warned you when you booked.'

'You did,' he reassured. 'And as you know, I'm not a fan of Christmas so it's no big deal. I'm sure somewhere will be open. Or I can always microwave something in my room.'

Her nose wrinkled in an expression he could only describe as disgust. 'Sorry, but that's not going to work. No way can I have you eating a microwave meal by yourself on Christmas Day.' Her tongue peeped out from between her soft lips, presumably to capture some unseen crumb. He was so distracted he almost didn't hear her next words. 'My family is coming and we'll be taking over the restaurant. You must join us.'

'God no.' Hurt flashed across her face and instantly he felt terrible. 'Sorry, that came out wrong. I meant I wouldn't want to intrude on your family.' And hell, no way on earth had he come all the way here to avoid Emma's invitation, only to receive a similar one. The guest invited through pity, or some sense of misplaced duty to their fellow man on Christmas Day. He was quite happy being alone and miserable.

An uneasy tension settled between them, and the camembert he'd thought was exquisite only a moment ago was now hard to swallow. Once again Adam cursed this time of year.

'You wouldn't be intruding,' Faith said finally, her voice so quiet he almost couldn't hear her. 'You already know me, Chloe and my parents. The only others will be Hope, with baby Jack and her husband Tom, and Charity with her other half Phil. We're a loud and noisy bunch. We do cracker pulling and joke telling, not deep contemplation and meaningful conversation.'

Anxious not to come across as an ungrateful bastard a second time, he chose his next words more carefully than the last. 'Thank you. I appreciate the gesture, truly I do. I'll see how it goes.'

The waitress came to remove their plates, replacing them with the crab linguine Faith had ordered. In a bid to break the tension that was threatening to suffocate the life out of what had begun as a promising evening, Adam took a big mouthful. 'Excellent choice,' he said after swallowing, relieved he hadn't needed to lie.

Her eyes skimmed over his face. 'You look surprised.'

He gave her a sheepish smile. 'Back to those stereotypes we discussed a few days ago; my go-to meal is meat and two veg.'

'You should have said.'

'I wanted to try something different.' He took another mouthful, giving himself time to consider whether to expand on that statement. 'I've been in a rut these last few years,' he said finally, hoping his honest admission would bring them back to where they'd been before the whole blasted Christmas thing had blown up in his face. 'It's high time I climbed out of it. Experienced new things.' He recalled his wandering thoughts since he'd met Faith. How he'd pictured them naked together. *Please don't let her see how far his mind had taken the whole new experiences theme.*

She made a small humming noise. 'What type of experiences did you have in mind?'

Her eyes were on her plate so he couldn't judge whether she was asking him straight, or whether she was teasing him. Or God forbid, she knew exactly what experiences he'd been contemplating and was angry at him for thinking she was that easy.

'I'm not sure,' he said cautiously. 'I'm just trying to be more open-minded about anything that might come my way.'

Finally her hazel gaze locked onto his. 'Like taking a woman out to dinner?'

'Exactly.' There was more, so much more he'd started to fantasise about since meeting her, but he couldn't just assume they were heading that way.

They ate in silence for a few minutes until Adam finally couldn't stand it any more. 'I'm sorry,' he said when he'd finished his last mouthful. 'I kind of put a damper on the evening which was absolutely the last thing I wanted to do.'

'No.' Then she laughed. 'Okay, yes, you did a bit. But we don't have to let it spoil anything. Besides, you already told me Christmas brings up bad memories for you and yet I mentioned it anyway. It's more my fault than yours.' She sat back, eyeing him under her lashes. 'So, do you want dessert?'

His heart began to race. Was the look, the smile she was giving him, suggesting what he hoped it was?

Or was he heading for disappointment and a tiramisu?

'Dessert sounds … good. What do you suggest?'

'We can ask Becky to bring the menu over. Or …' Her eyes flicked up to his, big and bold and beautiful. 'We can see what I can find in my place.'

Desire flooded through him, reaching a pulsing crescendo between his legs. 'The second option,' he croaked, feeling suddenly very hot. 'Please,' he added, aware it might sound like he was begging, though at this stage he didn't care.

Her smile promised every one of his fantasies.

Chapter Nine

Faith's heart raced wildly as she led the way through the hotel towards her own rooms at the back.

She was being rash. Irresponsible. Inviting a guest back to her private rooms – what had she been thinking? But that was the whole damn problem. *Thinking* hadn't come in to it.

They passed by the huge Christmas tree and she snuck a covert glance in Adam's direction, wondering what he thought as he saw it. Let's face it, there was no missing it.

His eyes were staring straight ahead, as if he was determinedly avoiding any connection with it, and she experienced a small kernel of unease. Something horrible had happened to him around Christmas time, something he clearly didn't want to talk about.

It's none of your business. This, if it happens at all, if neither of us get cold feet after opening the door, is at the most a quick fling.

Adam would be going home in just over a week. She didn't need to know his past. Just that she liked what she saw. And if she wanted to do something about that, it needed to be soon, or the moment was lost.

Her hand trembled slightly as she drew out her key. For all her flirting, making the first move, quick flings weren't her style. She preferred to know the man she was taking to bed.

Then again, she'd never met a man like Adam. A man of such quiet intensity, such raw masculinity. She didn't need to know him, to want him.

Slotting the key into the lock, she was aware of every inch of his large, muscular frame standing behind her. She felt the heat of him down her back, the scent of him enveloping her as she pushed the door open.

There was a moment of pulsing, heavy silence as they walked inside. The door clunked shut behind them and a shiver of lust ran down her spine. She had to clear her throat before she could speak. 'Would you like a quick tour?'

The words were barely out before his lips came crashing down on hers.

Definitely not shy then, was her first thought. Other thoughts were swept away as he plundered her mouth, kissing her passionately, thoroughly, hungrily. Effortlessly he lifted her so their mouths were at the same height, his hard thighs pressing on hers as he eased her against the wall. Now he had leverage, he released one of his hands from around her waist, moving it restlessly up and down her side as his mouth continued its devastating attack. It was as if he wanted to explore further, wanted to slip his hand under her top, find her skin, but was holding himself back.

Finally, on a long, deep groan, he pulled back, his huge chest heaving as he held tight to her hips and allowed her to gently slide down the wall.

'Wow.' It was the best she could manage, though it seemed entirely appropriate.

A hint of a smile touched his eyes, mingling with the lingering heat. 'I've been wanting to do that all evening. I couldn't wait any longer.'

'You won't get any complaints from me.' She ran a hand across his cheek, dipping down to touch his neat beard. 'I expected it to be harsher. More of a scratch than a caress.'

'You've not kissed a man with a beard before?'

'No. I've only been as far as one day old stubble.'

Smoky eyes lingered on hers, feeling as much of a caress as his hands. 'Then I'm honoured to be your first.'

'First guest, first bearded kiss.' She laughed softly, leaning into him, wanting to feel more of those sinfully hard muscles. 'Am I your first anything?'

'Second.' The moment the word was out his eyes slammed shut and he exhaled sharply.

'Second?' He surely didn't mean …

He drew in a ragged breath, taking a step back. 'I don't know why I said that. I wish I hadn't.' He dragged a hand through his hair, then down his face.

He looked so pained, her heart bumped a little inside her chest, as if trying to reach out to him. 'Said what?'

He let out a short, sharp, laugh. 'Thank you.'

Because he looked like he was trying to find his balance, she took him by the hand and led him through to her small sitting room. Unlike the guest rooms in the hotel, she'd left this room much as it might have looked when it was the cottage adjoining a working mill. The inglenook fire was original, though she'd added the wood-burning stove. The bricks on the outer walls and the big oak beams supporting the ceiling had been left exposed. Cosy, was how she'd wanted it and cosy was how it felt. With a nod to the time of year she'd added strings of fairy lights around the fireplace, hung large gold bells along the wall and tied red velvet bows around the beams. She hadn't added a tree, but only because there wasn't enough room for the type of tree she loved.

'Take a seat,' she told him, indicating the squishy deep red velvet sofa. 'Would you like a drink? Some actual dessert?'

Sinking his long frame onto the sofa he cursed under his breath. 'I appear to be an expert at putting a damper on things.'

'No, not a damper.' Inside she was still thinking *second*. Would she seriously only be the second woman he'd been with? Perhaps it was no wonder he was having trouble finding his feet. 'Just a small pause, while we draw breath.' He hung his head, not looking at her. It was almost too much to bear, seeing this giant of a man appearing so vulnerable. 'Don't feel you have to stay.'

His head snapped up. 'I want to.' He shook his head, laughing harshly. 'Shit, this is going from bad to worse.' His eyes finally reached out to her, almost pleading with her. 'I'm exactly where I want to be.'

'Good.'

'Unless you count your bedroom.' That quiet intensity was back, burning its way through her. 'That would be my first choice.'

Her shoulders relaxed and she smiled. 'How about I get us a drink and we work our way from there?'

As he watched Faith leave the room, Adam sagged against the sofa. He was making such a spectacular balls up of this and she was being so ... kind. So patient with him. Still, he felt like an epic failure. A shell of a man. How had he come to this, unable to be with a woman he fancied without making an arse of himself?

And had he really just admitted, if he ever did manage to get her into bed, which was looking less and less likely, that she'd be only the second woman he'd slept with?

He had no time to kick himself further as she was back, two glasses of whisky in her hand. Two tail-wagging mutts by her side. 'Sorry. These two weren't prepared to stay in the kitchen. Said they wanted to say hello again to their would-be owner.'

Adam let out a short laugh and, grateful for the diversion, bent to give the dogs the attention they were looking for. Faith handed him his whisky before perching on the armchair opposite. As the dogs leapt up to snuggle down next to her, Adam took a grateful swig of his drink, feeling it burn down his throat.

'Mince pie? Or does your dislike of Christmas mean you can't stand them, either?'

Oh bugger. He gave her an apologetic smile. 'If mince pies were associated with Easter I still wouldn't touch them.'

She looked almost offended. 'But they're delicious. All that scrummy dried fruit and spices, a hint of brandy, covered with melt-in-the-mouth pastry.'

'Shrivelled old fruit and mixed peel.' He shuddered. 'And don't start me on the suet.'

'I'll keep my mince pies to myself then.' Her eyes met his over the top of her glass. 'You sound like a man who knows his way round a kitchen.'

He thought of Damon and his mickey taking. Should he admit he enjoyed cooking, or did that make him look soft? 'I've been known to follow the odd recipe.' He thought it wise to keep Nigella out of it.

'I admire anyone who can cook, I'm pretty hopeless.' A teasing light entered her eyes. 'I can just imagine you in a pinny.'

As he didn't know quite what to say to that, he took another sip of his drink.

'So.' She let the word hang for a moment and tension knotted his shoulders as he waited for the killer question. 'What do you think of my quarters?'

The breath he'd been holding fizzed out of him and his shoulders sagged in relief. She could have asked anything. God knows, with his inept fumbling every time she mentioned Christmas, and his admission that she would be only his second, he'd opened himself up to a multitude of questions. He saw every one of them in her eyes when she looked at him.

'It's cosy.' Because he was so grateful for the innocuous opening, he expanded where he would usually keep quiet. 'Warm and welcoming. The sort of place you can step into and instantly relax.' The sentiment fitted her, too, but he knew better than to say as much. Cosy wasn't a word women wanted to be called, though he meant it as a high compliment. She relaxed him, made him feel he could actually open up to her. If he ever sorted his head out enough to try.

'That's how I feel about it too.' She sounded pleased and he thanked God he'd got one thing right tonight. 'The original owners plastered all the walls but I asked the builders to go back to the brickwork. It wasn't practical to do all the rooms. Perhaps one day.'

Her eyes took on a dreamy look and he smiled. 'Why do I get the feeling you have further plans for this place?'

'Ah, because you can read me like a book?'

He wished he could. Wished he knew what she was thinking as she made small talk with him in her private quarters. 'What comes next then?'

In what had to be an unconscious movement she leant forward, her face animated. 'The Old Mill is currently L-shaped. I see it being a quadrangle one day, with another wing of rooms on one side and, to complete the square, an indoor pool.' Her eyes glinted with amusement as she glanced at him. 'Maybe even a proper gym.'

'Careful. I might be back.'

Her gaze didn't stray from his. 'I'd like that.'

Immediately his pulse kicked up a gear and his tongue felt like a useless lump in his mouth, unable to form any coherent words. As he'd already made such a mess of things by speaking, perhaps now was the time for action.

Carefully, deliberately, he put down his glass and slowly rose to his feet. Her pretty hazel eyes followed his movements, widening as he walked towards her and held out his hand.

She immediately clasped it, hers feeling so small in his huge palm as he pulled her gently to her feet. The dogs cocked their heads up and gave him a long look, which Adam studiously ignored. 'I want to kiss you again,' he murmured, staring down at her, watching those gorgeous lips part as if on reflex the moment he said the word *kiss*.

'I'd like that, too.' He was relieved to hear the huskiness in her voice. He wasn't the only one feeling this. But as he bent to kiss her, she let out a little laugh. 'I think I need a step.'

It took him a second to realise what she was saying. As soon as he did, he placed a hand under each of her thighs and lifted her. Instantly her legs wrapped around his, placing her core snug against the part of him that was crying out to be touched.

She bit into her bottom lip. 'That works, too.'

'You feel incredible,' he whispered hoarsely, showering kisses across her face, loving the feel of her thighs wrapped around him, the curve of her under his hands.

'I could say the same.' Her hands wandered across his shoulders, down his arms, feeling his muscles. 'I can see the advantages of investing in a gym.'

Laughter spluttered out of him, and with it the last of his remaining tension. Suddenly he didn't feel like a man hopelessly out of practice at making love to a woman. He felt like a bloody God. 'Now I wish I'd had the tour,' he muttered, bending to give her a long, thorough kiss. 'Which way is the bedroom?'

She drew away from him long enough to nod behind her.

With her secure in his arms he walked purposefully through to the back room. He barely noticed the lilac tartan curtains, the further exposed brickwork. The plush purple velvet armchair positioned by the window.

All he saw was the giant wooden bed, topped by a white duvet and a mountain of cushions in various shades of pink, purple and blue.

'Kick the door shut,' she murmured, her lips nuzzling his neck. 'Unless you want a canine audience.'

He shut the door firmly with his shoulder before marching towards the bed, dragging the cushions out of the way before he lay her down. Then he climbed over her and saw nothing but Faith, her eyes sparkling up at him, the sexy smile on her lips. Curls a riot around her face.

'You're beautiful,' he managed, his voice hoarse.

Her smile grew wider. 'That's flattery, but I'll take it.'

His eyes feasted on her as he slid her dress from her shoulders, revealing a pink lace bra and soft, cream-coloured skin. As he touched her warm flesh his hand stilled and for a brief moment he was taken back in time to the only other woman he'd ever touched.

Faith's hand cupped his face, drawing his eyes to hers. 'Are you okay?'

Determinedly he shoved all thoughts of the past aside. 'Better than okay,' he croaked, smoothing his hand over her body, loving the small tremor that shot through her. 'Better than I've been in a long time.'

To stop any questions she might have asked, and because he wanted to more than he wanted his next breath, Adam touched his lips against hers. He tried for gentle, tried for the slow approach, but like a spark in a bone-dry forest, within seconds his passion was burning hot and heavy.

His hands fumbled as he inelegantly undressed her. 'Sorry,' he muttered, wondering where the hell his finesse had gone. He used to have some, once upon a time.

Again, her hand cupped his face. 'If you apologise once more this evening, I'm going to … going to …'

She huffed and he felt a smile creeping over his face. 'Yes?'

Her gaze slid over his large arms, down across the muscles of his chest. 'You might be bigger than me—'

'And stronger,' he cut in.

'And stronger,' she agreed. 'But I'm a woman. We're devious. All those feminine wiles. You don't want to cross me.'

He dipped to plant another kiss on her mouth. 'What I want,' he told her softly, 'is to make love to you.'

He felt the heat of her breath against his face as she let out a gentle sigh. 'I want that too.'

Then her hands were on his shirt, wrestling with buttons, pushing it off his shoulders. Her technique was more energetic than smooth and watching her determination turned him on even more. Suddenly he realised Faith didn't need a sophisticated technique or smooth moves. She wanted an honest, real connection.

And that, he could give her.

Chapter Ten

Faith gaped as she stared at the beautifully ripped body she'd unwrapped. Never, in all her fantasies, had she dreamt up a body to rival the one now braced above her. And though she'd seen a hint of the muscles beneath his clothes, to have them revealed, to be able to slide her hand along the hard ridges and dips, blew her mind.

'Did I tell you what a huge fan I am of weights?' she whispered, running her palm over his biceps, up to his bunched shoulder muscles and then down across his well-defined chest.

His muscles twitched at her touch, and a shiver of arousal ran through her.

'Then all the hours I've put in have been worthwhile.' His heated gaze held hers, the grey eyes darkening as he ground his hips against hers.

She gasped. 'Do that again.' He repeated the movement, sending waves of lust simmering through her, but then his face twisted and he swore. 'What is it?'

'I need to be inside you, but ...' His eyes fell briefly to her mouth, her breasts, then back up to hers. 'Please tell me you have a condom?'

She laughed, reaching over to her bedside drawer and plucking one out. 'I'm a modern woman.'

'Thank God.'

She noticed his hand shake, just ever so slightly, as he tore open the packet. Moments later he was slipping inside her.

His gaze remained on her and every ounce of pleasure he was feeling was reflected in his smoky eyes. 'This is going to be over far too quickly.'

She smiled, her hands reaching up to cup his face. 'We have all night.'

He began moving inside her, his hips thrusting, his eyes fluttering shut, his expression as tight as a drum. 'You feel amazing,' he groaned, increasing the pace, driving her higher and higher towards the place she wanted to be.

She could have said the same – his massive body, his hard muscles, his hot skin all felt beyond amazing. But his mouth was on hers, devouring her with the same intensity his body was taking her, and her brain was becoming a scrambled mess.

Suddenly she was shattering, crying out his name, pleasure shooting through her body and leaving nothing but lethargy in its wake.

With a final thrust, Adam grunted softly, his body shuddering with the force of his climax. Then he rolled onto his back, his face staring up the ceiling, his chest heaving up and down. Just when she started to worry, to think that was it, they were going to enter an uncomfortable silence, his fingers threaded through her hand and he squeezed. Not content with that, he lifted her hand to his mouth and planted a gentle kiss on each knuckle. The gesture was worth more than words. It spoke of delight, of contentment. Of gratitude.

Warmth flooded into her heart and Faith bit into her lip. No, she wasn't going to fall for this man, with his hulking good looks and quiet intensity. His sad eyes. *Not now*.

When his breathing started to normalise he turned onto his side. As those eloquent eyes scanned her face he reached to smooth down her hair, the gesture so tender it squeezed her heart. 'How many condoms do you have in that drawer?'

She let out a strangled laugh. 'More than one.'

His lips curved in a half smile. 'Do you mind if I use up another?'

Feeling giddy, flushed, unbearably turned on even though she'd just reached heights of pleasure she'd once thought were beyond her grasp, Faith shook her head. Before she could ask if he meant later tonight, or tomorrow, his mouth was on hers, his hands running hungrily, greedily, across her body. Caressing and arousing wherever he touched.

Slowly she came back to earth again, her head resting on Adam's chest as she listened to the thump of his heart. No longer racing as it had been a minute ago, it was more of a steady, reassuring beat beneath the huge muscles of his chest.

She glanced up at him, liking how relaxed his face finally looked. It made her realise how much tension he carried with him. He arched a brow and she smiled. 'I take it you didn't plan on ending the evening like this?'

She noticed the moment he understood what she was saying, his expression turning from puzzled to adorably sheepish. 'Ah, the condoms. No. I mean I hoped, I fantasised that I'd end up with you in a bed, sure. I guess I didn't venture to the planning stage.'

Intrigued, she levered herself up a little higher so she could look at him properly. 'You're an enigma, Adam Hunter.'

He blinked. 'I am?'

'You are.' She huffed, sitting up, waving her hand towards his naked chest, the duvet nestled tantalisingly low around his hips. 'You look like a flaming Greek God, you're funny and kind, yet you don't carry a condom in your wallet and you say it's been a long while since you've been with a woman.' She caught his eye. 'Can I ask how long?'

'You can ask—'

'But you're going to tell me to mind my own business,' she cut in. 'And quite right, too.'

His chest rose and fell as he sighed. 'Faith, I don't want to give you the wrong impression here. You're an amazing woman. I find you incredibly attractive—'

'Here comes the but,' she murmured.

He frowned, reaching over to frame her face with his large hands. 'Please, I don't want to hurt you. I'm not in the

83

right place in my life where I can offer you anything beyond my stay here.'

She gave him a wide-eyed stare. 'You mean you're not going to marry me?' He froze, panic flying across his face, and Faith immediately touched her forehead to his. 'Relax, I'm joking. I've got a hotel to get up and running. Do I seem like a woman who wants to start up a relationship with a man at the other end of the country?'

Adam's muscles slowly began to unfreeze and he exhaled the air that had become trapped in his lungs when she'd mentioned the word marry. But even as he smiled with relief at her statement, a small part of him was analysing her words. She wasn't averse to starting up a relationship, just didn't want it to be with someone living so far away.

He imagined her in a few months, in this bed with another man, and felt a wave of unwanted, irrational jealousy.

'Let's enjoy this for what it is,' she said softly, her lips planting teasing kisses along his jaw. 'A Christmas fling. Hopefully it will give us both a bit more spring in our step as we stride into the New Year.'

He thought back to the previous three starts to the New Year and felt a small, green shoot of hope. 'Yes please,' he murmured, turning so he could capture her mouth with his. As he kissed her, he eased her down so they were once again lying on the bed, her supple body draped around his. They continued to kiss for a while and soon he felt the long forgotten, yet now gloriously familiar, stirrings of arousal. Before he pressed her back onto the mattress, he decided he owed her an answer to her question. It might just be a fling, but he wanted it to be a real connection and not just about sex. 'It's been three years.'

Surprise flooded her face. 'Wow. That's a long time.' Her finger trailed across his chest, dipping down to his abs and he bit back a groan. 'Didn't you miss it?'

Now he had this vibrant, sexy woman lying next to him, touching him, Adam couldn't comprehend how he'd endured three days without sex, never mind three years. But if he took his mind out of her bed, and back to his own, he had his answer. 'For a long while I didn't like myself much,' he admitted, shutting his eyes as he fought not to drown in memories he'd spent the last few years trying to push away. 'If you don't like yourself, it's hard to convince others to like you. Harder still to believe them if they say they do.'

When he opened his eyes again, she was gazing at him in sympathy. 'Well, whether you believe me or not, I'm telling you right now. I like you very much, Adam Hunter.' Her hands ran over his chest again. 'And not just for your body.'

He let out a half laugh, half huff. 'I thought women went for sparkling personality?' He watched, unsure whether to be upset or just plain delighted when she peeled into laughter.

'That's a myth. We go for looks first, just like men do. We only dissect your personality if we want you to stick around.'

He felt a twinge of something he didn't want to feel. He wasn't sticking around, so it didn't matter that she didn't want him to. Did it? But then she was straddling him, and suddenly Adam didn't give a toss whether she wanted him for his body or his mind. It was enough that she wanted him.

Three times, he thought to himself smugly as Faith flopped down onto the bed next to him. But even he, with his three years of abstinence, didn't think he could manage another round tonight. So should he put on his pants and hobble off to his own room?

The thought of leaving the warmth of her bed, the warmth of her, didn't sit well with him. He'd never had a fling, though. Maybe that was what he was supposed to do?

Rolling to his side, he ran his hand across Faith's stunning curves, causing her to turn her head. Together with her muzzy sex hair, flushed cheeks and smiling eyes, she looked so bloody amazing his breath left in a rush, and for a moment he couldn't speak. 'Do you want me to go?' he managed finally.

She frowned. 'Why would I want that?'

He gestured towards the bed. 'It's your bed, your place. I don't want to intrude.'

'You didn't seem to mind intruding for the last ...' She glanced at her bedside clock. '... two hours.'

That had been sex, he thought, but felt too uncomfortable to say it. 'I'm not sure of the rules of a fling.'

Understanding dawned across her face and she leant forward to kiss him. 'I'm not either. Why don't we make up our own rules?'

He studied her, appreciating her straightforwardness. 'Then I'd like to stay.'

Her lips curved in a warm smile. 'Consider yourself invited.'

Adam nudged her onto her side and tucked in behind her, his front to her back. He put his arm around her waist and hugged her closer, his nose burrowing into the hair at the back of her neck.

His last coherent thought was he wasn't going to be able to sleep. The body he was cuddling felt delicious – soft, lush – but also wrong. She smelt different to the one he was used to. Felt different, too.

But then he fell into a deep, exhausted sleep.

Chapter Eleven

Five days before Christmas

Her back was resting against a furnace, Faith thought as she started to stir. A hard, solid, hot furnace.

Memories of the evening before raced through her. Adam, his surprising gentleness and his raging, seemingly unquenchable passion. A passion not unleashed for three years.

She released a sigh of sheer contentment. Whoever had screwed him over – it had to be a woman – she was grateful to her.

Lips pressed against her neck and the arm around her tightened, drawing her against him. She felt his heat, the heavy throb of his arousal, the musky scent of him. His hand cupped her breast, teasing, rubbing, and Faith smiled. If she knew the name of the woman who'd hurt him, who'd caused him to bottle up his passionate nature for three long years, she'd send her a Christmas card.

A long while later she stepped out of the shower and walked into her bedroom to find him dressed and sitting on the bed, looking lost in thought. His head snapped up when he heard her and he rose to his feet. 'I didn't want to go without saying goodbye.'

'You're booked until Boxing Day.'

He gave her a half smile. 'I meant I didn't want to slink off while you were in the shower. I know we'll see each other around but, well.' He cleared his throat. 'I wanted to say thank you. Last night was … it meant a lot to me.'

Her heart stirred, and even as she smiled and went to kiss him, fear rippled through her. How was a woman supposed to not lose at least some of her heart to a man who looked so physically commanding, yet had such a sweet awkwardness about him? 'It meant a lot to me, too. I hope we can do it again.'

He cupped her face, his expression serious. 'You promised me a fling.'

'So I did. A Christmas fling, I believe I said.'

He gave her a slightly pained look. 'Except for the obvious timing, is there anything different about a Christmas fling?'

Before he left she was going to get to the bottom of why he hated Christmas so much. But not now. 'I'm sure I can think of something,' she replied teasingly. 'Obviously we'll have to kiss under the mistletoe.'

'I can manage that.'

'And as you don't like mince pies we'll have to find something else to gorge on while we drink whisky.'

'I can push to a piece of stollen,' he said stoically.

'Excellent. How do you stand on eggnog?'

He shuddered. 'You can keep the sugar, eggs and cream. I'll take the rum.'

'Deal.'

He bent, lifting her up so he could look her straight in the eyes. 'Can I see you tonight?'

'I'll have the mistletoe ready.'

As Faith walked towards the reception she felt flushed and breathless, and it wasn't just from Adam's final humdinger of a kiss. Yes, they'd spoken of a fling, but it was one thing to have the word mentioned in abstract. Another to have a firm agreement. To know that in around twelve hours they'd be getting naked and sweaty again together.

She fanned herself as she strode past the huge Normandy fir, her secretive smile turning into a full-blown one when she saw her middle sister, Charity, waiting in the lobby. Trying to calm her fussing four-month-old.

'What a lovely surprise.' Charity looked up and immediately Faith felt a jolt. Charity looked terrible. Huge dark circles under her eyes, face far too pale. Chestnut hair that was usually so glossy, now looking lacklustre and hanging limply around her face. 'What are you doing here so early? Is everything okay?'

Charity gave her a tired smile as she moved Jack onto her shoulder and ran a soothing hand down his back. 'Everything's fine. This one woke us up early. Phil decided he might as well use the time to get some work done, so I thought I'd pop in and see how your new venture is going. I saw Mum and Dad in the car park. They said they were going home to check on things but now they're staying with you till Christmas?'

Faith rolled her eyes. 'So they say. I'm not sure if it's because they genuinely want to, or if they're keeping an eye on me.'

Charity kissed the top of Jack's head as he started to cry. 'Probably a bit of both. They did the same to me when this one was born. Maybe they don't like to think we can manage without them.'

'Well, you've got a child of your own to worry about now.' Faith held out her arms. 'Come on, let Auntie Faith have a cuddle.'

Charity sighed and handed him over. 'He's not hungry, not wet. I don't know what's wrong with him.'

Faith blew a raspberry against Jack's soft cheek. 'Teething?'

'It's early but yes, I guess it could be.' Charity frowned. 'When did you become a baby expert?'

'I'm not, but I remember spending time with Hope when Chloe was about Jack's age. Baby Chloe was really cranky and Hope kept telling me it was down to teething.' Faith looked up after pulling another face at Jack. 'Teenage Chloe can also be cranky, but now it's down to hormones.'

'Ouch.' Charity glanced around the hotel lobby. 'She's not in yet?'

Jack stopped crying and started gurgling. Delighted, Faith kissed his cute little nose. 'She'll be here in a bit. The bus is usually late.' Once again, she studied her sister. 'How much sleep did you get last night? And the night before that?'

Charity made a pffing sound. 'Sleep? What's that?'

Faith's heart ached for her. 'You look tired,' she told her softly. 'Why don't you pop into my place and get your head down for a few hours? I'll mind this one.'

Charity looked like she didn't dare to believe what she was hearing. 'But you're working. I didn't come here to—'

'I know,' Faith cut in, squeezing her arm. 'I'll need to wake you up by 11.30 as I have a meeting with a potential guest. They're looking for a place to hold a small New Year party.' She glanced down at her watch. 'But it gives you almost two and half hours to rest your eyes.'

A gleam of delight crossed Charity's tired face. 'And that's why you're my favourite sibling.'

'You say that to all of us.' Suddenly Faith remembered the previous night, and what had happened on the same bed her sister was about to lie on. She felt her cheeks burn as she rummaged in her pocket for the room key. 'Umm, I hope I didn't leave the place in too much of a mess.'

'Oh, I'm used to messy …' Charity trailed off as she studied Faith's flushed face and her eyes rounded. 'Bloody hell, Faith, you've had a man in there, haven't you?'

'I might have.'

'Well, well, you're a dark horse. Last time I spoke to you about men you said you didn't have time for them.'

'I don't.' Faith had never hidden things from her sister, and couldn't see the point in trying to now. 'This one kind of landed on my doorstep, so to speak.'

If anything, her sister's eyes grew wider. 'You're shagging one of your guests?'

Faith hurriedly checked around her. 'Jeez, why don't you say that a bit louder? I'm not sure everyone heard you.'

Charity blinked, and blinked again, a sly smile creeping across her face. 'If I hang around here a bit longer will I get to meet him? Or is he flaked out in his room recovering from sexual exhaustion?'

Faith shoved her sister towards the hall. 'Go and sleep. I'll fill you in later.' She gently cupped her nephew's head. 'When young ears aren't listening.'

'I'm going to hold you to that.' The tiredness she was obviously feeling crept up on her again and Charity yawned. 'Sadly right now I'm too tired to even talk about sex, never mind consider doing it.' She gave a little wave towards her son. 'Be good for your aunt or she'll never look after you again. And you'll have blown any chance of siblings.'

After watching her sister wearily walk away, Faith looked down into the round, blue eyes of her nephew. 'So, little man. What am I going to do with you for the next few hours?'

Adam allowed the hot water from the shower to pummel his exhausted muscles. He wasn't just knackered from his morning work-out, he thought a touch smugly as he squirted soap onto his body – the same body Faith hadn't been able to take her hands off last night. He'd forgotten how tiring late night sex marathons could be.

As he dried himself off though, he was already wondering how soon he'd feel her hands on him again.

Maybe he could have lunch with her, he mused as he drove the short journey from the gym to the hotel. The phone interrupted his thoughts and he pressed answer on his hands free.

Damon's voice thundered through the speakers. 'I see you're up then.'

'Up, dressed, work-out completed.'

Damon grunted. 'You sure know how to relax on your holiday.'

'I am relaxing.' He thought of how loose his body felt, how he'd even forgotten what day it was.

'You do sound perkier than usual.' A pause, and Adam heard a muffled voice come and go. 'Sorry, that was Anita. She says hello. Well actually she has a long list of questions for you, but I've told her the interrogation will have to wait. So, how is the nice hotel owner?'

Adam swung into the hotel car park and slammed the brakes on a little too forcefully. 'Still nice.'

'Umm. Define nice.'

Adam turned off the engine, exhaling roughly. 'I was feeling relaxed until you phoned.'

'The quicker you tell me what I need to know, the quicker I'll leave you in peace.'

'You gossip like a woman,' Adam muttered before taking a breath and blurting. 'Faith's better than nice and I slept with her last night.'

He heard a rush of air, presumably as Damon almost choked. 'Bloody hell, that Northern air must have done something funny to you. For a minute there I thought you said you'd given up your vow of celibacy and slept with the hotel owner.'

'Now piss off and leave me alone.'

'No, no.' Adam could imagine Damon flapping his hands. 'You don't get to drop a bombshell like that and put the phone down. Details, Hunter, details.'

'You want to know the positions …?'

On the other end of the phone it sounded like Damon was being slowly strangled. 'God no. Just …' He sighed. 'Just tell me you're doing okay.'

He heard both the words Damon was saying, and the ones he wasn't. His friend had witnessed the worst of him over the last few years. Witnessed, empathised with, supported, yelled at in frustration, at times cajoled, at other times manhandled him, kicking and screaming. However bleak his life had become, Damon had been there to pick up the pieces. 'Don't worry about me,' he answered gruffly. 'I'm fine. Get out of that office and home to that saint of a wife who puts up with you. There isn't anything for you to do now that can't wait until next year.'

'You know, as you're so rarely in a good mood, I might just take you up on that while I can.' Damon hesitated. 'Am I allowed to wish you a happy Christmas?'

Adam leant back against the headrest, briefly shutting his eyes. Then he sucked in a shaky breath. 'I don't know,' he said honestly. 'I don't think the words happy and Christmas will ever go together in my mind.' His mind flashed to Faith, her body straddling his, her eyes smiling down at him with promise. 'But I'm working on it. See you next year.'

His mind was full of her when he walked through the hotel door, but the image he had wasn't the one he was faced with. She looked harassed, holding a crying baby while trying to talk to a slender woman with dark hair and a harshly attractive face.

'I wasn't expecting you this early, Mrs Bannister,' Faith was saying, one hand smoothing up and down the back of the squawking, red-faced infant.

'Clearly.'

'I can show you the room.' Chloe, her red hair looking particularly spiky this morning, walked round to the front of the reception desk.

The woman ran her eyes over Chloe's black Dr Martins, her chequered red and black tights and up to her short black denim skirt. 'And you are?'

Chloe frowned at the sharp tone. 'Chloe.'

'Hmm. My husband told me I shouldn't be put off by the teenager on the desk.' Hurt flashed across Chloe's face and Adam itched to intervene but he didn't want to cock this up for Faith. Reluctantly he hung back. 'I presume this child won't be on the desk if we decide to hold our gathering here.'

It was clearly a statement rather than a question and Chloe's eyes flared with resentment. 'I'm not a child.' Thankfully before she could annoy the opinionated Mrs Bannister any further, the phone rang on the reception desk. With a huff, Chloe went to answer it.

And still the baby cried. Faith, who'd taken to pacing up and down, met his eyes. The plea he saw there froze him to the core. She couldn't be asking him … no. It was too much.

He stood rooted to the spot, heart thundering in his chest, as Faith looked helplessly over to Chloe, who was still on the phone, and then to the woman whose business Adam knew she desperately needed.

'You know what, I'm not sure it's even worth me seeing the room.' Mrs Bannister's lip curled in disgust. 'This place seems to be more of a kids' club than the sophisticated hotel it's advertised as.'

Again Faith's eyes pleaded with his. In that moment, Adam hated her for what she was asking him do. He gave his head a small shake.

Her eyes rounded and she glanced down at her grumpy nephew before looking back at him. *Please*, she mouthed silently.

He cursed, equally silently, feeling trickles of cold sweat running down his back. As every one of the muscles that had just felt so loose started to knot, he dumped his sports bag on the floor by the reception desk and strode over to her. 'Give it to me.'

'It's a boy,' she mumbled, handing the squawking infant over. 'Jack, meet Adam. Adam, meet my nephew, Jack.'

Awkwardly he held the boy at arm's length, his heart pounding, his stomach churning so much he feared he might puke right there and then. All over Mrs Bannister's patent black stilettos. What the hell was he supposed to do now?

Faith motioned for him to put Jack over his shoulder. Swallowing down his fear Adam did exactly that, the boy feeling ridiculously small. Too light, too delicate, even though his little body was rigid with temper. 'I'll take him to my room.'

Unencumbered by the two-foot wailing machine, Faith's eyes shone with gratitude before she turned them towards Mrs Bannister and gave her a professional smile. 'I apologise for my nephew. I'm looking after him for a few hours this morning to give his mother a rest. I'd planned to hand him back before your arrival.'

I can do this, Adam told himself as he left them to it and made his way towards his room. But as he jigged the grumpy baby up and down on his shoulder, resentment added to his unease. He wanted to help the woman he'd started to like, really *like*, but he hated feeling forced into it. Especially hated being forced into this, looking after a baby, for Christ's sake.

And while he was at it, why the bloody hell was she looking after her sisters' kids, when she should be focusing on her own needs?

Chapter Twelve

Faith eased the prickly Mrs Bannister away from the lobby and down towards the function room. Dimly, she could hear Jack crying in the background, but the sounds were becoming less angry. Guilt lay heavily inside her as she recalled Adam's look of horror as she'd silently pleaded with him to take her nephew. She shouldn't have done that to him. Men were frightened of babies. Even hulking great giants of men, apparently.

She sighed, knowing she was going to have some major grovelling to do, but she'd panicked. With Chloe on the phone, Charity fast asleep in her rooms at the back of the hotel and her parents out, giving Jack to Adam had seemed the only option to stop Sally Bannister walking out.

'It's a good size,' the woman in question murmured as she cast a critical eye over the room Faith had kept for small functions.

'We'll decorate it for you,' Faith told her. 'We can wind lights round the beams and string them across the ceiling. We have some tables we can set for the meal then push to the back if you'd like a dance floor.'

Sally Bannister's face wasn't giving anything away, Faith noted grimly. She bet the woman played poker in the evenings. When she wasn't scaring small children with her permanent scowl.

'And the bedrooms?' she said finally, once she'd run her finger along the window sill.

It came up dust free. Faith chalked herself up a point and made a mental note to double the housekeeper's Christmas bonus. 'I can show you a couple of rooms. They're all of a similar size and décor, but as it's an old building no two are exactly the same.' She hesitated. 'How many rooms would you be looking at?'

'*If* we decide to proceed.' Her emphasis on the first word left Faith in no doubt who was in control of their little meeting. 'We'd be looking at seven, possibly eight rooms.'

Currently she had only two rooms booked for New Year's Eve. 'We can manage that,' she told her. 'Though of course we're getting enquiries every day,' she added quickly.

Sally Bannister looked at the rooms silently and as they walked back to the reception, Faith had no idea whether she liked them or not.

When they reached the lobby, Chloe was polishing the reception desk. Faith let slip a small smile. She'd given her niece a list of jobs to do when it was quiet, which was pretty much ninety percent of the time. Looks like not everything she said fell on deaf ears.

'My husband told me last time there were dogs running around.'

'Ah, yes. They were accidentally let out.' She kept it deliberately vague, not wanting to lie, yet very aware they'd left Guy Bannister with the impression the dogs belonged to Adam. 'It won't happen again.'

Sally pursed her lips. 'If you can promise that while my guests are staying here there'll be no dogs, no crying babies,' she said, arching a brow in Chloe's direction, 'and no teenagers on the desk, we'll confirm the booking.'

Behind Sally's back, Chloe stuck up her middle finger. If it had been just that, just a rude gesture in response to a nasty comment, Faith would have pasted on a smile, shaken Sally Bannister's hand and done a jig the moment the woman was out of the door.

But there was more than rebellion and temper in Chloe's eyes. There was hurt. It was the second time Sally Bannister had upset Chloe. The first time Faith had bitten her tongue, desperation for the booking overriding her natural instinct to defend her niece.

She couldn't, wouldn't overlook it a second time.

'Chloe is my niece,' she told Sally firmly. 'Unlike many teenagers her age she's not spending the build-up to Christmas lying in bed until midday and then wallowing in front of the TV. She's setting her alarm and coming to work here. I'm proud of her. If she wants to work on New Year's Eve or New Year's Day, I'll be happy to have her here.'

As Chloe gaped, Sally Bannister sucked in a breath, her face looking like she'd just eaten a plate of raw dandelion leaves. 'Then it seems you've just wasted my morning.'

Her heels clattered furiously across the lobby floor as she stalked out.

The heavy door slammed shut behind her.

'I didn't like her,' Faith said calmly into the silence, though inside her stomach was a churning, knotting mess. Holy crap, she'd just thrown away eight bookings, plus the room hire. Plus the meals.

Chloe began to snigger. 'Me neither. She was a total bitch.' She wrung her hands together, glancing once more at the door before meeting Faith's eyes. 'I don't mind not working New Year though. I might not be around, anyway.'

'I don't expect you to work it,' Faith reassured her.

'Then why…'

Understanding slowly dawned on Chloe's face and Faith walked over to her and placed a hand on her cheek. 'I wasn't going to have that woman badmouth my beautiful niece.'

Chloe huffed, her eyes darting away. 'I'm not beautiful.'

'Yes, you are.'

Her gaze flickered back to Faith's. 'You're biased, you're my aunt. Boys don't think I am.'

'Then you're mixing with the wrong sort of boys. Stupid boys.' Chloe snorted and moved away, but as she returned to her polishing, Faith was sure she caught the glimpse of a smile. 'What was the phone call you took?'

'A party of four wanting to eat in the restaurant and book two rooms for the night.' She smirked. 'New Year's Eve.'

'Who needs Sally Bannister?' Just as she was starting to relax though, Faith experienced a dart of alarm. 'Please tell me you took down their details?'

Chloe raised her eyes to the ceiling. 'Of course. I'm not completely stupid, you know. I said you'd phone them back to confirm.'

Exhaling in relief, Faith gave her niece's slim shoulders a quick squeeze. 'I meant what I said, you know. We had a few wobbles at the start but you've been a huge help, Chloe. Thank you.'

'Duh, you're paying me, you don't have to thank me.' The flush in her cheeks and the pleasure in her eyes said otherwise.

'Right, if you're okay to stay here a little longer I'd better go and find my nephew.' Last seen in the arms of one of my guests, she thought with a fresh rush of guilt. One who was paying her, rather than the other way around.

Her stomach fluttered nervously as she knocked on Adam's door.

'It's open.'

She wasn't sure what to expect when she opened the door, though at least it was blissfully quiet. As she stepped cautiously inside, the sight of the huge strapping man lying on the bed, a sleeping baby curled up on his chest, tugged at her heart. About to say something soppy and sentimental, she stopped short when her eyes met Adam's. He was angry.

'I'm sorry,' she said softly, anxious not to wake her sleeping nephew.

'Why?' he asked. When she gave him a confused look he shook his head. 'Why were you looking after your sister's baby? You're already looking after Chloe.'

She was taken aback by the vehemence in his tone. 'Charity is shattered,' she said stiffly. 'Why wouldn't I offer to look after Jack for a bit?'

'Because you have a business to run? A potential guest to show round?'

'Charity's sleeping in my bed. Not that it's any of your business. I'd planned to take Jack back to her in time for the meeting. Sally Bannister was early.'

He heaved out a sigh, causing Jack to bob up and down on his chest. 'Okay. It just strikes me that you have to learn to say no to people. Business reputations can be made and lost in the first few months.'

He was making her sound like a naïve, incompetent fool. 'Any more advice you want to give me?' She asked coldly.

'Don't offer to help and then shove the burden of doing it onto someone else.' His tone was equally cool.

She bit her lip, feeling the prick of tears and hating it. 'I said I'm sorry. If Sally Bannister had been on time there wouldn't have been an issue.'

Adam heard the tremor in Faith's voice and cursed silently. Why was he being such a git to her? She didn't know he'd been a gibbering wreck the moment he'd seen the baby. How could she, because every time he'd had a chance to talk to her about anything personal, he'd ducked the issue.

'I'm sorry, too,' he said quietly. 'I'm not good with babies. It freaked me out a bit.' It was the closest he could come to admitting how shaken up he'd been.

Her eyes strayed down to the sleeping bundle on his chest, and back up to his. 'The evidence would suggest otherwise.'

'He was just exhausted from all the crying.'

'Maybe. Or maybe he found that a big, warm chest makes a very comfortable pillow.'

Something flickered in her eyes and he wondered if she was remembering how she'd slept part of the night on him last night, too. 'I'm all for being slept on. It's just I prefer the person doing the sleeping to be female and twenty-seven.'

He stared straight at her. 'Curly brown hair and pretty hazel eyes are another strong preference.'

A glimmer of a smile crossed her face. 'Does that mean I'm forgiven?'

'Only if you forgive me for shoving my nose in your business.'

She sighed and sat on the end of his bed. 'Hard not to, when I know you're right.'

He stilled, running his hand over the baby's back in an unconscious movement. 'Didn't you get the booking?'

'Oh, I got it, provided I didn't have Chloe working when the Bannisters' precious party was here.' Annoyance threaded tightly through her voice. 'As if I'm going to let Sally Bannister dictate whether my niece works that day or not.'

'I noticed she was rude to Chloe.'

She turned to him, her eyes serious. 'Tell me honestly what you thought when you first saw Chloe on the reception desk.'

He winced. 'Stroppy teenager? Not sure what it says about the professionalism of the hotel? But the second time I saw her I revised my opinion,' he added hastily. 'I thought she was a troubled teenager, not a stroppy one.'

'Yes, I think she is. I also think working here, not having too much time to obsess about what her friends are up to, is doing her good.'

'And that's more important to you than anything, isn't it?' he asked gently. 'Even more important than your hotel?'

'She's family.' She gave him a wry smile. 'You don't understand that, do you?'

'No,' he said honestly. 'But I think Chloe is lucky to have an aunt who does.'

Faith smiled, and as she shifted further onto the bed, the neat black skirt she wore rose up a fraction, giving him a glimpse of her thigh.

'Chloe's mother, my sister Hope, is a great mum, you know,' she said, clearly oblivious to the effort he was making to not look at her legs while he had a baby sleeping on his chest. 'Up until the last few months Chloe's been a normal, happy teenager.' He tried valiantly to focus on what Faith was saying. 'It's just Hope's freelance writing work has really taken off, so recently she's been really busy. I think maybe Chloe's missing their connection. Missing someone she can open up to.'

His eyebrows shot up. 'You're busy, too.' Jeez, could the woman not see how much she was taking on?

'That's just the point, I'm not, am I?' Faith let out a deep sigh, her expression turning so sad he felt a pang of long forgotten emotion. 'And if I carry on like this, I won't be busy any time soon, either. I mean, I've just thrown away a huge booking I couldn't afford to lose. Maybe I'm not ready to have my own business yet.' Before he could say anything, she jumped up from the bed, flapping her hands. 'Oh God, I shouldn't be moaning to you about this. You're my only paying guest right now.'

Though true, the statement hurt. 'I thought we'd moved on from that.'

For a moment she was silent, frowning down at her hands before finally meeting his eyes. 'Sorry. We never did firm up our rules for …' She gestured between them. 'This. If it *was* the start of a relationship I'd want to share things. But as it's not …' She trailed off, shrugging her shoulders, looking as uncomfortable as he felt.

Jack must have picked up on his tension because he started to wriggle. Unsure what else to do, Adam placed his hand on the baby's back. Much to his astonishment, Jack quietened instantly.

Faith started to laugh softly. 'You've got the touch.'

He stared at his big hand on Jack's tiny frame. 'I'm terrified I'll squash him.'

'You won't. You're far gentler than you think. I've also dumped him on you for longer than I'd intended. Here, hand him to me and I'll take him back to his mum.'

Jack made a few disgruntled noises as he was passed over, but settled again on Faith's shoulder. Adam was surprised how much he missed the warmth of the little body snuggled up against him. He suddenly realised he'd gone from being terrified of the mite, to being soothed by him.

'I'll see you later?'

Her eyes met his and desire surged through him at the promise he saw there. 'Absolutely. I'm around all evening.' She smiled and as she turned to leave he bolted up from the bed and went to open the door. 'About the hotel.' He cupped her chin, tilting her face towards his. 'Don't lose confidence in yourself. You'll make it work, and you'll do it the way that's right for you.'

She beamed with gratitude, reaching up to kiss his cheek. 'Thank you.'

'And as for what you said about us,' he added, 'I've never had sex for the sake of sex, so let's not overthink this. I like you. I enjoy your company both in and out of bed.'

Her cheeks flushed a little. 'Me, too.' Then she rolled her eyes. 'I mean I enjoy your company, too.'

Once she'd left, Adam sank back on the bed. For a man who'd spent most of his life overthinking absolutely everything, it was a shock to find he was now willing to take one step at a time. With no clue as to the direction he was travelling.

Chapter Thirteen

Four days before Christmas

Heaven help her, she was humming. Faith quickly checked there was no one outside her small office who could overhear. Thankfully Chloe hadn't arrived yet, so it was just Faith, and her thoughts.

Last night had been even better than the night before, she thought with a rush of delight. Adam had been more at ease, more flirty. And the sex had been off the scale. A warm flush settled through her and Faith couldn't form her mouth into any other position than a wide, inane grin. Adam Hunter was built like a Greek God and made love like a sex God. With a voracious appetite.

Following another hum of pleasure, she focused back on her marketing plan. The major areas were already covered; she had a snazzy website, ads on all the major travel sites, the hotel name in the Lake District tourist information books and leaflets. Now it was time to think more creatively. Maybe link up with some of the local businesses. Advertise her function room to firms who might be looking for off-site retreats.

She needed to drum up bookings from somewhere.

For the next few hours she worked steadily, only dimly aware of Chloe arriving, of her saying hello to Adam as he went off for his daily gym session.

'Aunt Faith?' Chloe's voice startled her. 'There's a man here to see you. Think he's that guy you used to go out with.'

Faith looked past Chloe and gasped in surprise. 'Patrick. What are you doing here?'

The tall man with fair hair, a pleasant looking face and calm blue eyes smiled back at her. 'Thought I'd see how you were doing.'

With a rush of affection she rose from her chair and went to hug him, his slim frame feeling oddly unfamiliar. It had only been two days but already her hands had become used to feeling wider shoulders, a broader chest.

'So, this is it?' His eyes darted round the lobby. 'Very nice. Have you time to give me a tour?'

She thought of the unfinished letter she'd been drafting to local businesses. Then thought of all the times she'd let Patrick down. 'Of course. As long as that's okay with Chloe?' Chloe gave the usual shoulder shrug, and Faith led Patrick away, towards the hall.

'Got your family working for you then.' Patrick nodded over to where Chloe was still watching them.

'Only my niece.' On an impulse, she asked him, 'What do you think of her on the reception desk?'

He shrugged. 'Your hotel, your business. I wouldn't dream of putting my nose in it.'

Funny how two years ago that response would have pleased her, yet now it made her feel he wasn't interested. It was such a stark contrast to Adam, who despite not really knowing her, had pushed his nose into her business several times since he'd first arrived. And each time it had been through concern for her.

As she showed him around they caught up on each other's news. Patrick made all the right noises, said all the right things, but Faith was left feeling flat. There was no sizzle, no sparks. Not even any angst.

She'd experienced all three with Adam.

'I was wondering,' Patrick said as they walked back to the lobby. 'Are you free for dinner tonight? I could take you away from this place for a few hours?'

'What's wrong with this place?'

He laughed, the noise sounding forced. 'Nothing, of course. I just thought you might like a change.'

Stop being so touchy, she told herself. 'I'm afraid until my deputy manager starts next year, I need to be here.'

'So we can't have dinner together?'

Her mind flashed to Adam, to the last three evenings they'd shared. Two of which had ended back at her place.

In days he'd be gone, though.

'Perhaps next year,' she said lightly, not quite sure what Patrick was really asking. Not sure how she felt either, other than wanting to enjoy Adam for as long as she could. 'It's been lovely to see you though,' she added quickly, honestly. She'd meant what she'd said to Adam. Patrick was a good guy.

As she kissed Patrick's clean-shaven cheek she was dimly aware of the front door opening.

'Hi Adam.'

Faith jerked guiltily away from Patrick as Chloe greeted their one and only guest. Though why she felt guilty, she didn't know. She'd only kissed Patrick on the cheek, for goodness' sake. And she and Adam weren't even a couple, not in the proper sense of the word. Yet as she glanced over at Adam she saw his confusion, his hurt. And a flash of something fierce and possessive in the smoky grey eyes staring back at her.

The particulars didn't matter, she realised. She'd have felt the same hurt and confusion, the same jealous possession, if she'd seen Adam with another woman. 'I ... hello Adam.' Her heart bumped madly in her chest. 'Did you have a good work-out?' she added, noticing his gym bag, his damp hair. The smell of his body spray which she knew, from the last few evenings, clung to his skin and did crazy things to her hormones.

Whatever thoughts he'd had when he'd first seen her were now firmly masked. 'Thanks, yes.'

Very aware of the way Patrick was watching them, Faith made some awkward introductions.

When she mentioned Patrick's name, Adam's jaw tightened but he said nothing, merely nodded in Patrick's direction.

'Adam's our first guest,' Faith murmured, finding the need to fill the gaping silence.

'Oh, right. I guess that means he gets special attention.'

Patrick meant nothing by his remark but Faith wanted the ground to swallow her up. When she dared to look at Adam, a hint of amusement crept into his expression.

'I can fully vouch for the service here.' His eyes sought out hers, searing her with their intensity. 'My every need has been catered for.'

A hot flush stung her cheeks and as he strode off towards his room, she flung a few mental daggers his way.

Once she'd ushered Patrick out of the door, Faith took in a deep breath.

'Wow, what was all that about?' Chloe asked.

She feigned innocence. 'All what?'

'All that stuff between you and Adam. *My every need has been catered for.*' She mimicked Adam, puffing up her chest in a fairly accurate impression of male posturing.

'I'm not sure.'

Chloe narrowed her eyes, staring at her. 'Are you and Adam hooking up?'

Oh help. 'Please, keep your voice down,' she hissed.

'Why? It's not against the rules. You're both single, right? Patrick seems like he's forgotten he dumped you, but Adam's way better than him, anyway.'

'He is, huh?' Faith gave up trying to be the sensible aunt and started to laugh. 'Okay, okay. We can only discuss my love life if we talk about yours, too.'

Immediately the laughter drained from Chloe's face. 'I haven't got one.'

Faith knew she was about to tread on eggshells but whatever was upsetting Chloe, she had a strong feeling it involved a boy. 'You're a bit young to have a boyfriend, but not too young to have a crush,' she ventured cautiously. 'When I was fifteen I fancied the boy I sat next to in maths. I can still remember him. Dreamy brown eyes, dark hair and pale skin. I thought he looked so romantic.'

Chloe snorted. 'Sounds like a weirdo.' She dipped her head and began to chew at one of her chipped nails. 'Michael's got blond hair and blue eyes. He's going out with Alice. They were kissing at the Christmas party.'

A rush of understanding, of tenderness, welled inside Faith. 'So that's why you're upset.'

Chloe shook her head. 'No. I mean, sure I hate that he likes her instead of me, but it's not just that. I …' She trailed off, looking down at her boots.

Faith put an arm around her, hugging her close. 'What, Chloe?'

'I'm the only one without a boyfriend,' she blurted, not looking at her. 'Tamsin has Rory, Alice has Michael and I've got a big fat nobody.'

'Oh Chloe, darling, your time will come.'

She wriggled away from Faith's hold. 'You don't understand. They're making fun of me, saying I'll never get one.' Chloe inhaled a deep, shuddering breath. 'Boys don't fancy me.'

Tears began to stream down her face and as she started to move further away, Faith clutched at her arm, bringing her back.

Moments later Chloe was gripping onto her, and sobbing into her arms.

Back in his room, Adam debated long and hard whether to hunt Faith down and confront her, or get in his car and drive miles away from her.

He hated feeling this way. Angry, jealous. Hurt. It wasn't even as if she'd done anything wrong. There was no reason why she couldn't see her ex, kiss him even.

Another burst of jealousy snaked through him. Damn it, this was supposed to be simple. Flirtation, fun, sex. Something to take his mind off the time of year. What had Faith said? To help them start next year with a spring in their steps.

Picking up his jacket, wallet and keys he stalked towards the door. He'd go for a hike. Have a pub lunch somewhere. Windermere wasn't far and he hadn't been there yet. Plus snow was forecast in a couple of days, so he should make the most of getting out while he could. A walk by the lake would calm him, help release some of this angst, this tension that was tying knots in his stomach.

As he walked by the reception desk though, his resolve crumbled. He couldn't ignore the woman with her arms wrapped around the quietly sobbing red-haired teenager.

When he cleared his throat, both their heads snapped up. 'Everything okay?' He gave himself a mental slap round the face. 'Let me rephrase. Anything I can do?'

Faith smiled sadly. 'Not unless you can convince my beautiful niece that not all boys are blind and stupid. Only the ones she's at school with.'

Chloe made a noise that sounded like part sob, part hiccup with a hint of a laugh.

'Not all boys are blind,' he confirmed. 'As for stupid, I'm afraid we usually are. You girls are a lot smarter. Though you can be a lot bitchier, too,' he added, his eyes on Chloe.

As she straightened up, Chloe gave him a glimmer of a smile before accepting a tissue from Faith. 'I should have done what you said. Shut the Facebook account.' Faith shot him a surprised look as Chloe wiped her eyes. 'I tried to once, but then I was like, what about my other friends? How do I keep up with them? And I kept thinking maybe they'll say some nice stuff soon. Stupid.'

He should go, he thought. Walk away, because he found it hard enough making normal conversation, never mind discussing stuff like feelings. Emotions. Yet there was something about the trusting way Chloe was looking at him, the brave way she'd opened up, that stopped him. 'A few years ago I went through a tough time.' He was aware of Faith's look of shock at his admission. Of Chloe watching him carefully. 'Somebody whose opinion was very important to me made me feel really bad about myself. I'm not going to say I have a magic cure, but that's when I started exercising, doing weights.' He glanced down at his hands, now bunched into fists, and consciously forced them to relax. 'It helped me channel some of the anger I was feeling into something positive. The more I worked out, the more I began to like at least part of myself again.'

He met Chloe's eyes, stunned when the girl with the crazy red hair, clunky black boots and teenage attitude gave him a smile that lit up her face. 'Cool, will you show me?' As if aware she'd lapsed into keen, she added her usual shrug. 'Just some easy stuff. You know, with small weights. Nothing heavy. I don't want to be big like you. Not that you don't look sick, you know. For a guy.' Her face grew slowly redder the more she talked.

He laughed softly. 'Thanks, I think. I'd be happy to show you a few routines, just let me know when your aunt can spare you. We can use the pretty dumb-bells in the exercise room here.' He flicked a glance towards Faith.

'It would be nice to see them being used for something other than a dust magnet.' Faith reached down to grasp her niece's hand, giving it a quick, supportive squeeze. 'What size feet are you?'

'Six.'

'Me too. Why don't you borrow my trainers, and anything else you need, and have a session with Adam now? If that's okay with him?'

Two pairs of eyes stared back at him and Adam nodded, wondering how he'd gone from a lake walk and a pub lunch to showing a teenager some exercises.

Wondering, too, why he actually preferred the thought of helping Chloe. He wasn't going to kid himself he'd turned into a saint. Though he liked the girl, felt he even understood her a bit, if he was honest with himself, it was pleasing Faith that gave him the biggest buzz.

Chloe raced off to Faith's quarters to change, and Faith placed her hand on his arm. A gentle touch, yet it scorched through his shirt.

'Thank you.'

'Thought it was about time your snazzy room was used.'

She smiled, such warmth in her eyes he felt it seep all the way to his heart. 'I appreciate it, but I wasn't only thinking of your offer to help her with the exercises. I hadn't realised you'd advised her about Facebook?'

He shrugged. 'Just told her she didn't have to read all that shit.'

Faith's eyes remained on his, studying him, as if she was trying to understand him. 'That stuff you said about feeling bad about yourself.'

'Ah.' He shuffled his feet, suddenly uncomfortable.

'It's okay, I'm not going to pry. Just know that if you want to talk about it, I'm here for you. Otherwise, what happened in the past can stay in the past.'

'Speaking of things past.' He willed himself to keep his tone mild. 'What did Patrick want?'

She scrunched up her face. 'You know what, I'm not absolutely sure. He asked me out to dinner.'

Something reached inside him, grabbed his heart and squeezed it tight. 'Tonight?'

She shook her head. 'I said I couldn't. Maybe next year.'

When he wouldn't be here. The answer didn't please him a hell of a lot more than if it had been tonight, though he could hardly complain. He was the one who'd told her he wasn't ready for another relationship.

What if he was, though? Would she be interested in meeting him halfway now and again? If he could somehow manage to put the last few shitty years behind him. And if she no longer had feelings for her ex. Was it possible they could give a cross-country relationship a try?

He felt the warmth of her hand on his face as she eased his head down to meet her eyes. 'I didn't want to have dinner with Patrick, Adam. I want to spend any spare moments I have with you, before you leave.'

The air left his lungs in a rush and he hauled her up against him, kissing her until they were both hot, panting and breathless. 'Have dinner with me again tonight,' he murmured against her lips. 'Then let me show you how grateful I am that it's me you chose to be with.'

Chapter Fourteen

Three days before Christmas

He flustered her, Faith thought as she slipped on her blouse the next morning, trying to act as if it was perfectly normal for her to get dressed while a hunk of man sat on her bed, watching her with hungry, grey eyes.

'I could get used to this,' he said quietly, hands behind his head, eyes not leaving hers.

'Watching me dress?' Her heart bumped a little beneath the buttons she was fiddling with. 'Wouldn't you prefer me undressing?'

His mouth, capable of giving such pleasure, curved upwards. 'I enjoy that, too, but there's something very satisfying about watching you slip on clothes I'll be taking off later tonight.'

Desire flooded through her and she fumbled with the last, errant button. 'I think your inner caveman is coming out.'

He chuckled softly. 'Perhaps.'

She wanted to tell him she could get used to this too, being the sole focus of attention of a beautiful man. Knowing that he was watching her every move, listening to her every word. Two years spent with Patrick, yet she'd never felt this important to him. With a flash of insight, she realised her ex hadn't been patient, he'd been indifferent.

'What would you do if I forgot to turn up tonight?'

Adam arched his brow. 'Are you trying to tell me something?'

'No. Just wondering how you'd react.'

'I'd be hurt. Then angry. Then I'd hunt you down and remind you of your promise.'

That, she thought with a rush of delight, was exactly

the answer she'd wanted. Fastening the zip on her skirt she strode over to him, and wrapped her arms around his neck. 'I can't imagine I would ever forget a date with you, but I'm glad you'd care enough to be hurt and angry.'

'I have ways of making sure you don't forget me.'

'Oh yes?' Her lips teased his. 'What ways are those?'

'I don't think I can tell you,' he murmured, returning the kiss. Notching up the heat. 'I think I'd have to show you.'

Breathlessly, reluctantly, she pulled away. 'I look forward to it, but sadly right now I have to get downstairs.'

'Ah yes. I forgot one of us has to work.' He shifted off the bed, picking up his room key from the bedside table. 'Don't you have some more guests arriving tomorrow?'

'A couple with two kids. Yes.' For a beat she just stared at him. 'You remembered?'

'Of course. I feel like I'm part of this hotel now.'

Her heart flipped slowly and Faith put a hand over it to steady herself. All this talk, him getting used to watching her dress, feeling like he was part of what she was doing here. It felt almost too much. Too deep, for something that was meant to be a fling.

She was starting to fall for him, she thought in a panic. Yet in four nights he'd be checking out and going home.

Suddenly his big body wrapped around her. 'You okay?'

She drew in a breath, told herself to stop being daft. It was impossible to fall for a man she'd only known a few days. She liked him, that was all. It would be a wrench to see him go but the hotel was her focus now.

'Just thinking how I'm not looking forward to saying goodbye to you,' she admitted, turning in his arms so she could bury herself in his chest.

He kissed the top of her head in a gesture that brought a lump to her throat. 'It doesn't have to be goodbye,' he said quietly.

Her heart missed a beat. 'We live at other ends of

the country. You said you're not in the right place for a relationship.' She tried to dampen down the surge of crazy hope. 'I've got a hotel to run.'

She felt his breath ruffle her hair as he sighed. 'I know. Let's enjoy the time we have left without thinking too far ahead.'

But that time was fast disappearing. Swallowing down her emotions, she stretched up to kiss him. 'Deal.'

As she drew away he tugged her back, lifting her into his arms so he could kiss her properly, deeply.

By the time he put her down she was aching, panting. And late. Rushing them both out of the bedroom, she almost tripped over Nip and Tuck. 'Damn. Sorry boys, I forgot to take you out this morning.' How had she lost her mind so much she'd forgotten her gorgeous boys?

'I'll take them.' Faith did a double-take, unsure whether she'd heard Adam correctly. He shrugged, as if his offer was no big deal. 'Thought we'd agreed they were mine, anyway.'

'Really? You don't mind?'

'Only thing I have planned for today is a work-out with Chloe at lunchtime. Think I can just about squeeze in some time to walk a pair of wild mutts.' He bent to scratch them behind their ears. 'It's not like they're going to want to go far on those stumpy legs.'

Gratitude swept through her, though it wasn't only his offer to help with the dogs that had her heart melting into a gooey mess in her chest. He was helping her niece, too. 'Thank you, thank you, thank you. Their leads are hanging in the kitchen. The back-door key is in the lock. I'll be downstairs in the office if you need me. Oh, and the poop bags are in the cupboard under the sink.' His face paled and she had to bite back a grin. 'You're okay with picking up dog poo?'

His Adam's apple moved up and down as he swallowed. 'No problem.'

The feeling of her heart shifting, filling, somersaulting, happened again. 'God, you're gorgeous,' she murmured, mostly to herself, before darting out of the door before she said anything more incriminating. Like *I think I'm falling for you*.

It didn't take Adam long to find the leads. Longer to clip them onto the dogs who refused to sit still, despite his repeated attempts to ask them to, first nicely, then with what he thought was authority. Finally he gave up and hauled them onto his lap, wedging their wriggling bodies under his arm as he fastened the leads.

'No crazy stunts,' he told them as they gazed up at him, their faces looking like he felt. Dazed, confused. Eager to get going.

Only for him the eagerness wasn't about the walk. It was all about the woman whose dogs he'd be walking. He *could* get used to all this, he thought with a burst of nervous excitement. For so long he'd been numb to life, frozen on a moment three years ago and unable to move from it. Since arriving here it had been like someone had put him next to a warm fire. He'd started to defrost, life seeping back into him, enabling him to take pleasure from things he'd forgotten he enjoyed. Walks in the fresh air, conversation, helping others. The smell, taste and feel of a woman as she lay beside him. Even something as simple as holding somebody in his arms.

It wasn't a warm fire that had defrosted him though. It was Faith. And while she wasn't looking forward to him leaving, he was dreading it. Now he'd had a taste of feeling alive again, he was loath to return to his old life.

He felt a tug on the leads and looked down to find the dogs trying to pull him towards the back door that led out to Faith's small garden, and the fields beyond.

'Okay, okay. Enough of the introspection, I get it. Let's go.'

The dogs barrelled out, yanking on their leads, yapping away.

'Quiet,' he told them, locking up the door. 'You'll wake the neighbours ...' He trailed off when he realised why, or rather who, they were barking at.

Shock registered on the faces of Faith's mother and father as they stood on the footpath, staring at him. 'Umm, hello.' He could feel a telltale blush creep up his neck and suddenly felt like his teenage self, caught sneaking out of his then girlfriend's bedroom. Stupid, because he towered over both of them.

It was Faith's mother who recovered first, giving him a tentative smile. 'We came to see if Faith wanted us to walk the dogs.'

'I've got that covered.' *You've got the flaming leads in your hand, Hunter. Talk about stating the bleeding obvious.*

'So I see,' her father remarked dryly.

He was a twenty-nine-year-old man, Adam reminded himself. A guest at their daughter's hotel. He shouldn't be feeling so wrong-footed. 'Unless you want to walk them?'

'Oh no.' Her father let out a sharp laugh. 'You're not getting off the hook that easily. We'll leave you to it. We might go and have a little chat with our daughter, instead.' He levelled him a look. 'I presume she's left already?'

Adam swallowed, then swallowed again, his neck and cheeks feeling uncomfortably hot. 'I think she went to her office.' *After we had sex in her shower.* The way her father was scrutinising him, he'd like to bet he knew exactly what Adam had been doing with his precious daughter.

He started to walk, desperate to get away, but her mother spoke again. 'How long will you be with us, Mr Hunter?'

Was it a pointed question, he thought frantically? Was she testing out whether he was the sleep-and-ditch type? Or was she just making conversation, one guest to another?

'I check out Boxing day.' It sounded better than *I leave*. Less final.

'So we'll see you on Christmas Day?'

He froze, every muscle tensing. 'I'm not sure.'

'Are you visiting family in the area?'

He cursed long and hard – and silently. If he hadn't faffed around with the damn leads for so long he would have missed this interrogation. The dogs were looking at him as if to say *come on, you promised us a walk. Stop talking to the oldies.* 'No family, no. My parents live in France. I have no brothers or sisters.'

'Friends then?'

He looked desperately over at the dogs, pleading with them to start barking, damn it, even to take a dump. Anything to provide a distraction. The traitors just stared at him, a couple of mop heads with big brown eyes and lolling pink tongues. 'No friends in the area, no. I came here to get away for a few weeks.'

'Then you must join us for Christmas lunch.' Hell, Faith's mother was just like her daughter. 'Faith closed the restaurant for the day so the chefs could spend it with their families. Her sisters are coming with their children and Faith and I will be doing the cooking. Though mainly it will be me, knowing my youngest daughter's tendency to overcook everything.' She beamed up at him. 'It will be turkey with all the trimmings.'

'They've not knowingly poisoned anyone yet,' her father added helpfully.

'I … that's very kind of you.' It was his worst nightmare, he thought despairingly. He'd come to get away from the day. Not be shoved into it, forced into polite conversation and false Christmas cheer. Feeling the first ripples of panic he nodded over to the dogs. 'I'd better be going.' Without waiting for them to ask him anything further he strode off down the path, hunched against the cold wind. Maybe he should check out on Christmas Eve, he mulled as the dogs scampered ahead of him.

But that would mean only two more nights with Faith.

He clattered into a fence post, stubbing his toe and yelping out in pain. Funny though, it was his chest that hurt more. Specifically, the part near his heart.

Chapter Fifteen

On hearing the tap on her door, Faith looked up with a start before breaking into a wide smile. 'Hey there. You two are up and about early.'

Her parents shuffled inside the small office. 'We're popping into Kendal to buy the turkeys. We were going to offer to take the dogs, but it seems we were beaten to it.'

Faith saw the twinkle in her mother's eye and groaned. 'You came across Adam, didn't you?'

'We tried your front door, got no response so went round the back. There we found a very large man walking up your path with two tiny dogs.'

Faith's lips twitched. 'Quite a sight.'

'Mmm, quite a sight indeed.' Her mother glanced at her dad. 'Maybe your father should put his hands over his ears because I'm about to ask my darling daughter a very direct question.' She turned back to her, a soft expression in her eyes. 'Did the rather splendid Mr Hunter spend the night with you?'

Her father grunted. 'It's none of our business.'

'Of course it's not.' Her mother pressed her hand to Faith's cheek. 'But my daughter's happiness is. I'm only going on appearances and a very short, awkward conversation, but I've rather taken a shine to the gentle giant. I wondered if she had, too.'

Her heart fluttering, Faith clasped her mother's hand. 'I have. A little bit more than a shine, if I'm honest.'

Though pleasure bloomed on her mother's face, there was also a trace of worry in her eyes. 'He leaves in a few days, doesn't he? Have you made plans to see each other beyond his stay here?'

Emotion balled at the back of her throat and Faith sadly

shook her head. 'It was only ever intended to be a fling. He lives down south. I've got the hotel. Plus,' she sighed. 'Plus something happened to him a few years ago that means he doesn't want a relationship.' She recalled the look in his eyes that morning when he'd told her his leaving didn't have to mean goodbye. Maybe the door was no longer so firmly shut.

Which still left them with the problem of two busy careers and two businesses in opposite ends of the country.

'People change their minds,' her mother said, patting her cheek. 'I invited him to have Christmas lunch with us.'

Faith cringed. 'Oh dear. He's got this thing about Christmas. Whatever happened to him a few years ago must have happened around Christmas.' She was almost too scared to ask. 'What did he say?'

Her mother smiled. 'He was a bit hesitant, but he said he'd come.'

Her father coughed. 'No. He said, and I quote, *that's very kind of you.*'

'That's the same thing,' her mother insisted.

'To a woman, maybe. To a bloke it means I don't want to offend you by turning you down but there's no way in hell I'll be there.'

When her mother opened her mouth to disagree, Faith stepped in. 'I'm afraid I have to agree with Dad. I invited him a few days ago, before we … umm … got together.' Heaven help her, she could feel herself blushing. 'He told me, *thank you. I'll see how it goes.*'

Her father let out a triumphant sounding noise. 'Another way of saying no way in hell I'll be there.'

Though Faith knew he was right, it saddened her to think Adam was going to be spending the day on his own. She wanted him with them, not for his sake but for hers.

'I'm going to buy an extra turkey,' her mother said primly, noting something down in the small notebook she was carrying. Presumably her shopping list. 'I think he'll come and he looks like he eats a lot.'

Faith spluttered out a laugh but before she could argue that Adam was hardly going to eat a whole turkey to himself, there was another knock on the door.

Chloe popped her head round. 'There's a Mrs Leighton on the phone.'

Faith's heart fell. 'Oh no, she's the party of four arriving tomorrow.'

'Oh my, I'd forgotten you had that booking.' Her mother's pen hovered over her notebook. 'Do I need to buy a turkey for them, too?'

'No!' Faith tried to keep the exasperation out of her voice. 'I warned them in advance there would be no restaurant on Christmas Day and they're fine with that. They're visiting family. At least I hope they still are, and they aren't phoning to cancel.'

'Don't think so.' Chloe smirked. 'She's banging on about Father Christmas, like he's real. Wants to know if we can arrange for her kids to see him 'cos she hasn't had a chance to take them yet.'

'Oh God, it's a bit late for that.'

'That's what I thought. I can always tell her he's back at the North Pole.'

It was the easiest option, but if Faith had wanted easy she wouldn't have bought a hotel. 'I'll ring round. Tell her I'll call her back, will you?'

Her parents quietly disappeared and Faith spent the next hour googling frantically and making numerous phone calls, trying to pin down a place that still had a visiting Father Christmas.

'I can find one at a department store in Penrith,' she told Mrs Leighton, who sounded pleasant but frazzled.

'Oh dear, that's so far away. We'll already have been four hours in the car.'

'We may be able to find a more local one if we ask around, but they might be …' She hesitated over the word. 'A bit tacky?'

Mrs Leighton sighed. 'You're right, of course. Better they don't see him than see one who looks fake.'

Faith hesitated, an idea forming in her mind. 'Leave it with me a little longer,' she told her. 'I have one more thing to follow up on.'

Adam walked the damn dogs further than he'd intended. Turns out the dopey mutts were okay company. It meant his work-out session at the gym was shorter than usual, something that would have stressed him out a few weeks ago. These last few days the need to drive himself into exhaustion had lessened. He still enjoyed the exercise but now he found he was happy to lift and bench his usual weights, not pushing himself to go beyond them. He went to the gym out of habit, and yes, out of vanity – Faith's frank admiration was still etched in his memory. He no longer went out of need.

When he finally drove into The Old Mill car park he was only five minutes behind schedule. Hopefully Chloe wouldn't think he'd forgotten her. He'd enjoyed taking her through some routines yesterday. Not just her company, though the girl had turned out to be surprisingly giggly once exercise had lowered her defences. He'd also enjoyed knowing that what he was teaching her would boost her self-confidence. Help her to like herself more.

Just as it had helped him.

She was there on the desk when he strode in. 'Sorry I'm late.'

'No sweat.' She gave him an oddly secretive smile. 'My aunt wants to talk to you before we go.'

His heart gave a quick jump. 'Right.' Chloe still had that funny smile on her face. 'Should I be worried?'

The smile reached her eyes and she bit into her lip, clearly trying not to laugh out loud. 'Depends.'

He winced. 'On what?'

'How much you like dressing up.'

Before he could quiz her further, Faith walked out of her office and smiled at him. Hers was less secretive, more … cunning? His pulse began to pick up pace as he went from mildly curious to slightly panicked.

'Adam.' She reached for his hand and tugged him towards her office.

As the office door closed behind him, a dart of hope pushed away at the anxiety. Perhaps he'd been wrong about the cunning. Perhaps her smile said let's have a sneaky lunchtime make-out session? Something he definitely wasn't averse to. On a rush of desire he lifted her onto the desk, easing her legs apart so he could wedge his thighs between them. Then he kissed her; deeply, heatedly. Thoroughly.

Her cheeks were flushed when he drew back. 'Wow. I'll have to haul you into my office more often.'

'Works for me.' He started to move towards her again, his hand snaking under her blouse, when she drew back.

'Umm, I'm not sure what you thought I brought you in here for, but I've a feeling you're going to be mightily disappointed.'

She no longer looked cunning, or teasing. She looked awkward and uncomfortable, which had the same effect on his libido as a bucket of cold water. 'Not office sex then.'

She laughed but it held none of the richness he was used to. It sounded … hell, he'd go as far as to say *nervous*. 'Can we take a rain-check on that?'

Her answer relaxed him slightly. If office sex was still on the table sometime in the future, whatever she had to say to him couldn't be that bad. 'Sure.' He perched on the desk next to her. 'I'm all ears.'

His worry cranked up a notch again as he watched her fiddle with her hands. The Faith he knew was gloriously, sexily confident, but this Faith was on edge. He placed a hand over hers, stopping her fidgety movements. 'Talk to me.'

She avoided his gaze, which further troubled him. 'The guests coming tomorrow have two kids, a boy of five and a girl of four. They've been asking for weeks to see Father Christmas but the parents both work and they've been too busy to take them. The mother asked if there was a Father Christmas round here but I checked and the only decent one I could find was in Penrith and she said that was too far, which is reasonable considering—'

'You're rambling,' he cut in, concerned. 'You don't ramble. Cut to the chase.'

'Would you dress up as Father Christmas for the kids?'

Dread sliced through him and he jumped to his feet, distancing himself. He'd thought she was going to talk to him about her mother's invite for Christmas lunch. Not dressing up as flaming Santa. 'No,' he said bluntly, the familiar panic rising inside him. There were three hundred and sixty-five days in a year. Why was so much emphasis put on ruddy Christmas Day? It was spoken of for months before, and often in irreverent tones, as if it was something special. A day when great things happened.

It was lies, the lot of it. Shit happened at Christmas, just like it did every other day of the year.

She looked like he'd slapped her. 'I know you have a hang-up about the day,' she said quietly. 'I was hoping you could put that aside to help me out. Unreasonable of me, I know, because you've already gone out of your way for me on numerous occasions.' She paused to take a breath. 'If you can't do it for me, perhaps you could do it for these kids?'

'Why me?' He felt as frantic as he sounded. 'There must be other men you know who could do this. Your father, for one.'

'I thought of Dad first, but when I went to pick up the costume they only had one in extra large. It would drown him.'

'What about the guys in the restaurant? Other people in the village?' He was going to clutch at every damn straw he could think of. 'Maybe the kids' father could do it.'

She took a step towards him and rested a hand on his cheek. 'Don't worry. Forget I asked. I'll think of something.'

The sympathy in her eyes, the sad but understanding smile – he felt like a total bastard. With a sigh he perched back on the desk, rubbing a hand across his face. 'I'm sorry.' How inadequate were those two words?

'I should be the one apologising. I shouldn't have asked.'

'Of course you should.' He was spending every evening, every night with this woman and he couldn't do her a simple favour? And it wasn't even for her. It was for a couple of kids she didn't even know, but wanted to please. 'I'll do it,' he found himself saying.

Her eyes widened with shock. 'Seriously?'

His heart lurched and he curled his fingers round the edge of the desk while he took a few deep breaths, annoyed at his overreaction. Christmas might not be magical, but he had to stop making it into something evil. 'Put on a red suit and say ho ho ho? How hard can it be?'

Faith could see the tension in his face, the way his hands clutched at the desk, and felt terrible. He hated Christmas. Of course putting on a Santa suit, pretending to be Mr Christmas himself, was going to be hard for him. Yet he was going to do it anyway. For her.

Feeling equal parts guilty and touched she reached for one of his hands, unfurling the rigid fingers and clasping it in hers. 'Please only do it if you're sure. I won't hold a grudge if you say no.'

He let out a frustrated huff. 'I'm sure.'

She sensed making a big deal out of it was only going to make things worse so she kissed him softly on the lips instead, hoping he could feel her gratitude. 'Why don't you come over to my place later and try the suit on?' She waggled her eyebrows suggestively. 'If you behave, I might even sit on your lap.'

Some of the tension left his face. 'That's an offer I don't get every day.' His eyes dipped to the floor and he drew in a deep breath, letting it out slowly before looking back at her. 'Thank you.'

'For?'

'Not asking me what happened at Christmas.'

She was still holding his hand and she lifted it to her lips, kissing his knuckles in the same way he'd once kissed hers. 'I can't say I'm not interested, but I figure you'll tell me if you want to. Otherwise it's none of my business.'

'I want it to be your business.' He spoke the words so quietly she almost didn't hear them. 'It's just ...' He shook his head, turning away from her. 'I've enjoyed putting it behind me. Enjoyed rediscovering the man I think I was before ...' He trailed off, inhaled a shaky breath. When his eyes met hers again they were unbearably sad, the gentle plea in them almost undoing her. 'I'd rather we kept it that way, if it's okay with you?'

Because he was perching on the desk and she was standing, it made it easy for her to put her arms around his neck. To kiss him fully. 'Whatever you want,' she whispered. 'But know that if you do ever want to tell me what happened, it won't change how I think of you.'

His eyes slammed shut and his big body stilled. As she moved to hug him again she heard him mutter under his breath, 'I'm very much afraid that won't be the case.'

Chapter Sixteen

Two days before Christmas

Chloe had a small bounce in her step as she walked back over to the reception desk after her lunchtime work-out session. Faith smiled affectionately at her.

'You look like you're in a good mood.'

Chloe frowned. 'What do you mean?'

Okay, so probably best not to point out to her that she was looking happier than she had when she'd started a week ago.

A week. That's all the time you've known Adam. When she thought of how little she knew him, how tightly he gripped to the secrets that haunted him, a week seemed about right. When she thought of how much her heart knew him, how important he'd become to her, a week seemed ridiculously short.

Chloe was still staring at her. 'Did you have a good work-out?' Faith asked, changing the subject.

'It was okay.' Chloe moved round to the other side of the reception desk and dumped her bag in its usual place by the stool.

'Are you out lifting Adam yet?'

Finally, she smiled. More than that, she started to giggle. 'As if. His arms are massive. He's like Thor.' When Faith looked at her nonplussed, she rolled her eyes. 'You know, Chris Hemsworth.'

'Mmm, yes he is.'

Chloe's smile turned into a smirk. 'When did you see his arms?'

Jeez, please don't let her blush again. 'I can see enough through his shirt sleeves.'

Chloe burst into laughter. 'You're so sleeping with him.'

As Faith made a hasty scan of the foyer, Chloe laughed even harder. 'Why are you being all secretive and stuff? I'd be well happy to have a boyfriend like him.'

'He's not ... we're not.' She sighed. 'He goes home in a few days.'

Chloe's face lost its laughter. 'Yeah, I know. I guess that sucks for you.' She lifted her shoulders. 'Sucks for me, too. He said he's gonna write all the routines down for me so I don't forget them.'

A wave of sadness washed through Faith. There was no need for her to write anything down – she knew she wouldn't forget a single moment from her time with Adam. An image from last night burst into her mind. Who'd have thought sitting on Santa's lap could have led to *all that*?

'When do these new people arrive?'

Chloe's question cut through her smutty thoughts. 'They said around two. I've freshened their rooms and stocked the minibar. Just a question of keeping an eye out for them now.'

Chloe glanced at the computer. 'Mr and Mrs Leighton, plus two kids.'

'Sally and Robert.'

'They're the ones Adam's dressing up for?'

'Yes.' Behind her back, Faith crossed her fingers. Last night he'd been up for it. This morning, when she'd gone back to say hello to the dogs, the Santa suit was still thrown over the sofa where they'd left it last night. Had Adam forgotten to take it back to his room, or deliberately left it there?

She'd popped it back in his room this morning after he'd gone to the gym, attaching a note to it. *Please put me on when Faith calls you.*

By three o'clock, the Leightons were settled in their room – actually two rooms with an interconnecting door allowing the kids and parents to have their own space but still be together.

'It's perfect,' Ivy Leighton told her as she popped back to

the reception desk. 'Such a lovely space.' Her eyes flickered towards the tree in the hallway. 'And what a magnificent tree. The kids can't stop talking about how it's the biggest one they've ever seen.'

Faith felt a flush of pride, and a smidgen of smug amusement. 'I'm glad they like the tree. It hasn't been to everyone's taste.'

Her guest looked at her in amazement. 'Why ever not? It's everything that's fabulous about Christmas. Joyful, beautiful, full of promise. And it smells exactly like you want Christmas to smell; pine and cinnamon with a hint of ginger.'

Delighted with her guest, Faith grinned. 'I hung cinnamon sticks and gingerbread men on the tree. You're the first to notice.'

'That's probably because I'm like a big kid at this time of year. I love everything about it. We usually spend it at home so I can go mad on the decorations, but my dad had an operation a few weeks ago so can't travel. The family are all coming to him, instead.'

'So you definitely don't need the restaurant open on Christmas Day?' Faith held her breath. She'd checked at the time of the booking, followed up with an email, but guests couldn't always be relied on not to change their minds.

'Oh no, we'll be eating at my parents'.' Relief washed through Faith as Ivy continued to talk. 'My brother's wife has offered to make it and she's such a good cook. And what with that, and your amazing tree, I don't think I'll miss being at home this Christmas. My only worry is I haven't had time to take the kids to see Father Christmas.'

'Don't worry. He's going to come to you.' Faith gave Ivy a confident smile, but behind her back she kept her fingers firmly crossed. 'I told our Santa I'd call him when you were settled. I was going to put an armchair in the hall so he could sit by the fireplace, hidden by the tree until Sally and Robert pop their heads round.'

Ivy clapped her hands together. 'Perfect. We're ready whenever you are. Just let me know when to unleash the little terrors.'

When she'd gone, Faith turned to Chloe, who was putting the finishing touches to the information packs she'd been working on. 'They're looking really good, Chloe. You've done a great job with them.' Chloe lifted her shoulders in that I-don't-care shrug of hers, but there was a definite blush to her cheeks. 'Umm, did Adam mention anything to you about dressing up as Father Christmas today?'

'No, why? Worried he's gonna back out?'

'Of course not.' *Liar.* 'I'll just go and knock on his door.'

But when she tapped, and then thumped, on the door of his room, there was no reply.

Adam eased himself out of the under-stairs cupboard and shook his head. 'Sorry mate. I can't see anything obvious, and obvious is the limit of my electrics expertise.'

Giles, the elderly sheep farmer who lived opposite The Old Mill, gave him a wry smile. 'That'll be one step up from mine. At least now when the electrician comes I won't look like a prat. Give me a sick sheep and I'll tell thee what's wrong. Electrics go off and I'm up shit creek without a paddle.'

Adam glanced at his watch and grimaced. 'I'd better be getting back. Faith's going to be wondering where I am.'

'Got her guests on a tight lead, has she?'

Adam smiled, hoping it would do in place of a reply. He wasn't about to divulge his sleeping arrangements with a guy he'd only met an hour ago. They'd met on the way back from his walk. Despite working out this morning, and the training session with Chloe, Adam had felt restless sitting in his room. Sitting led to thinking. Today he was dressing up as Santa, tomorrow it was Christmas Eve ... nope, thinking was off-limits. To empty his mind he'd set off for a brisk three-mile walk, ending with a trip to the corner shop to buy more toothpaste. There he'd met Giles, who'd been buying candles because his electricity had gone off. Adam had offered to go back and see if he could fix it.

A few months ago, he wouldn't have offered. He'd have kept his head down, not wanting to talk. The friendly nature of the place was getting to him. Or maybe what he'd said to Faith about rediscovering himself wasn't just a hopeful whimsy. If he could manage to push past the last three years, learn to move on, perhaps he could start to live again.

Then again, if he didn't get back to the hotel fast, Faith was likely to kill him before he had the chance.

Bidding Giles a hasty goodbye, Adam dashed over the road and across the gravel car park. As he pushed open the door he looked over to the reception desk where Faith was talking to her father in an agitated manner. He reckoned he knew what that was about.

He cleared his throat. 'I'm here.'

Her gaze flew up to his, relief flooding through it. 'Thank God.' Then her expression tightened and she frowned. 'Are you still happy to do this?'

'Dress up? Can't wait.'

She smiled, rolling her eyes. 'Okay, let me rephrase. Are you still prepared to do this? Because Dad said he will, if you've changed your mind.'

Her father slid him the type of look that made no words necessary. He might have muscle mass and age on his side, but he had no doubt Faith's father could make his life hell if he chose to. 'I've not changed my mind.'

Her father smirked, victory shining in his eyes. 'I'll leave you to it then.'

As she watched her father walk away, Faith sighed. 'He kind of made you say yes, didn't he?'

And now his masculinity was affronted. 'You think I'm scared of a pensioner?'

'Sneaky pensioner,' she corrected. 'We haven't got time for

this conversation though. We need to get you into the Santa suit pronto.'

'I prefer it when you're getting me out of my clothes,' he murmured, lowering his voice, his pulse quickening when she shot him a heated look.

'Me too.' She rose onto her tiptoes and gave him a sedate kiss. 'But right now I need you to drop the sexy and get into character.'

He cupped the back of her head, deepening the kiss before huffing and pulling back. 'I left the suit in your room.'

'I put it back in yours.'

'Worried I'd left it on purpose?' Her eyes refused to meet his and he scowled, only partly in jest. 'When I say I'll do something, I do it. I'm a man of my word.'

'Even when the thought of doing it worries you so much you've kept yourself deliberately busy all day?'

Wow. He shook his head, amazed at how well she seemed to know him already. 'You're scary, you know that? Though I should point out I'm not worried, just anxious not to let them down.'

Her eyes softened and she gave him a smile that brimmed with confidence, with belief. 'You won't.'

As he sat on the big red armchair Faith had asked him to move next to the fire, Adam feared her belief in him was misplaced. He might look the part – black boots, red velvet suit with a heavy black belt, a false white beard that rubbed against his own and a red hat that kept sliding into his eyes. But what the hell did he know about the spirit of Christmas? How was he supposed to instil magic into a day he hated?

The smell of pine wafted up his nose and Adam stared broodingly at the bloody great fir in front of him. How ironic that he'd come here to escape Christmas, and ended up dressed as sodding Father Christmas, surrounded by fairy lights, bells and a herd of flashing reindeer.

The sound of excited chatter echoed down the corridor and he sat up straighter, trying to change his expression from what he knew must be a scowl into something more pleasant. A glance at his hands found them gripping the arms of the chair as if it was the last life-raft on a sinking ship.

Relax, damn it.

He was starting to inhale a deep breath when Faith's head popped round the corner. She looked at him in alarm – clearly his more pleasant expression was still way off the mark.

Before he could practise anything further though, two small bodies appeared from behind her. It was almost comical the way they froze, jamming their small hands over their mouths.

'Father Christmas,' the girl said in an awed whisper.

Adam opened his mouth to speak, but his throat was so tight he had to cough and start again. 'You must be Sally.'

Her eyes grew huge. 'Yes.'

'Do you know who I am?' Inwardly he cringed. Of course she bloody did. She'd just said it.

Thankfully Sally didn't seem to think his question was odd. 'You're Father Christmas.'

'That's right.' He held up his gloved hand and pointed towards the boy standing next to her. 'Is this your brother, Robert?'

Both of them nodded, staring at him as if he was something incredible. He wasn't.

A red suit couldn't change what he'd done.

Nausea rose into the back of his throat and Adam fought to swallow it down. Fought to focus not on himself but the two bright-eyed kids in front of him. Christmas might be forever tainted for him, but he had a shot at making it special for these two.

He beckoned them closer and when he saw the excitement burst through their eyes he didn't have to force his smile. 'So, what would you two kids like for Christmas?'

Chapter Seventeen

The day before Christmas

Christmas Eve morning. Faith stirred, her heart lifting when she felt the heavy weight of Adam's arm around her. Clearly sensing her movement, he tightened his hold, moving her back closer to his chest.

She sighed, keeping still, wanting to prolong this moment when everything felt so perfect between them. When there were no barriers separating them.

All too soon he'd be fully awake, and though his seemingly inexhaustible libido would keep the physical barriers at bay, the mental ones would go straight up. She'd look into his expressive eyes and know he was holding things back from her. Things that upset him, that made him sad.

When she'd watched him with Sally and Robert last night, her heart had ached. The Leightons would only have seen their kids, and the expressions of delight on their faces. Faith had been watching Adam, his own face going through a myriad of different emotions. First fear, which had stopped her in her tracks, though thankfully hadn't put off the kids. As he'd started talking to them he'd looked worried, clearly fretting he was going to ruin their big moment. It had been the anguish she'd seen when the kids had said goodbye though, that had ripped her in two. In that moment, she'd hated herself for what she was unwittingly putting him through.

As the sounds of Sally and Robert's excited chatter had drifted down the corridor, Faith had taken Adam's hand and led him quietly up to her room, all the time regretting her promise not to ask him about his past.

Behind her Adam nuzzled her neck. 'Morning.'

His hand moved from her waist to her breasts, his mouth planting teasing kisses along her back.

Faith pushed out her thoughts and relaxed into the moment.

Later, as she got dressed, she heard a buzzing coming from the sitting room. After slipping on her jacket, she went to hunt down the noise.

She found a mobile phone under the coffee table. It must have fallen out of Adam's pocket last night.

A glance at the caller ID showed *Emma (sis)*.

She frowned, sure that when she'd asked if he had any family, he'd said not really. The sister, because surely that's what "(sis)" meant, must be estranged. In which case the call might be urgent.

And Adam had taken the dogs for a walk.

Heart thumping, she pressed answer.

'Adam? I can't believe you've finally picked up.'

'Umm, it's not Adam.' She heard the swift inhale at the other end and rushed on. 'I'm Faith Watkins. I own the hotel where Adam's staying. I ... found his phone ringing so I picked it up.'

'Oh, right. His work said he was on holiday. Well, when you see him, please can you tell him Emma phoned? Perhaps you could also add that this time she's expecting her call to be returned. I can't tell you how many messages I've left him. Anyone would think he's avoiding me.' Faith was about to press disconnect when Emma added. 'Where is your hotel, by the way?'

'The Lake District.'

'Ahh, such a lovely part of the world. What's the hotel called?'

'The Old Mill. We're a new boutique hotel.' As Faith switched automatically into marketing mode, giving Emma a quick run-down of where they were and what she could expect to find, she started to feel a ripple of unease. Maybe she shouldn't have told Emma where the hotel was? Maybe there was a reason Adam was avoiding his sister. And a reason why he'd lied about not having one. 'We hope to welcome you here soon,' she ended, hoping to God she hadn't just made one humdinger of a mistake.

She was on the reception desk when Adam came up to her, his cheeks flushed from walking outside in what looked to be Arctic conditions. Snow was forecast later in the day. Robert and Sally were going to be delighted. It would be a white Christmas.

'Did the dogs behave for you?'

He grunted, though she was sure there was an edge of affection in his voice when he replied. 'If you call yanking on the lead, yapping at every passerby and trying to chase birds behaving, then yes. They're back at yours, flaked out.' He scratched at the back of his head. 'I saw Giles on the way back. His electricity still hasn't come on. The electrician said he's fully booked and can't come out till Boxing Day.'

Faith looked at him in surprise. 'I didn't know you'd met the neighbours.' She could have added, *then again, there's a lot I don't know about you.*

He gave her a small smile. 'Been here nine days. I'm getting to be part of the furniture.'

But in two more, you'll be going. The thought sent a nasty twist through her chest. 'Thanks for letting me know. I'll pop over and see Giles when Chloe gets in.' She hesitated, feeling suddenly nervous. 'While you were out you had a call on your mobile.' He frowned, patting at the pockets of his jeans. 'I found the phone under my coffee table. The call was from your sister.'

His big body froze and she could almost see each of his muscles tensing. 'I don't have a sister.'

'Emma?'

Anger flashed in his eyes. 'You answered my phone?'

She felt a ripple of irritation at his accusation. 'Only because I thought it was your sister. It said Emma (sis).'

'I know more than one Emma. That one's my sister-in-law.'

Her heart jumped into the back of her throat. 'You're *married*?'

'No.' He stared at her, exhaling sharply. 'I was. She left me.'

'Oh, I'm sorry.' It explained a great deal, she thought as his words slowly began to sink in. 'Did she leave you around Christmas?' she asked softly.

He nodded curtly, sticking out his hand. 'Can I have my phone back?'

His tone was that of a stranger and Faith had to force back the hurt that threatened to swamp her. He hadn't wanted her to find out about his divorce, she reminded herself. He's just reacting. 'I'm sorry for answering it,' she said quietly, handing it over. 'I didn't do it to be nosey. I just thought it might be important.'

His eyes narrowed, his expression so horribly guarded. 'Did she say what she wanted?'

'Just for you to return her call. She sounded very friendly.' In a bid to lighten the tension, Faith added, 'I might have persuaded her to pay the hotel a visit.'

He gave her a look of what she could only describe as horror. 'You didn't tell her where I was?'

Oh bugger. 'I'm really sorry. I didn't think it was a secret.'

'Bloody hell.' Grey eyes flashed with more than anger now. He looked livid, the veins on his neck bulging as he struggled to control his temper. 'It wasn't your place to answer my phone. It certainly wasn't your place to let the caller know where I was.'

'It didn't happen like that.' He was making her feel terrible and she didn't like it one little bit. 'We just got talking about the hotel because she likes the Lakes. She sounded anxious to hear from you,' Faith added pointedly. 'Said she'd already left you lots of messages.'

Faith's accusing stare, the truth of her words, took the wind out of Adam's self-righteous anger. He was still annoyed though, not so much with Faith, but with the circumstances. He felt as if his bolt-hole had been violated. His chance of leaving Faith without her knowing the type of man he was detonated into a million sharp fragments.

Why was Emma hounding him like this? Hadn't she taken the hint by now? He didn't want to see her. Didn't want to see her family. Didn't want any reminders of that part of his life.

Faith was staring at him, hurt and confusion in her eyes. 'Why are you avoiding your ex-wife's sister?'

Adam felt his life closing back in on him. All he'd wanted was a break, a chance to get away from the shitty season and be someone different for a while. That chance was rapidly disappearing down the plughole. 'That's my business, don't you think?'

Tears welled in her eyes and Adam instantly felt like the prick that he was. 'Sorry. I didn't mean it to come out the way it did.'

She bit into her lip, lowering her eyes so he couldn't see into them. 'You're right. I apologise for overstepping my mark. It won't happen again.' She turned away. 'I hope you have a pleasant day.'

The finality in her tone almost crushed him. He wanted to reach out to her. Tell her he was a stupid git who'd panicked at the possibility of being forced to face the woman he'd been avoiding for so long. But that would mean him having to explain himself further. Having to tell her why Ruth had left him.

Reluctantly he took a step away. And then another one.

And then another until he was striding away from Faith towards his room.

Once there he slammed the door shut and sank onto the bed, shoving his head in his hands. What the hell did he do now? He could remove his SIM card. Pretend he hadn't got the message. That his phone had died.

Even he wasn't that much of a cowardly bastard. Was he?

He cursed, aware he was overreacting. So, Emma knew where he was. It wasn't like she was going to drive all the way up here to see him.

Fingers shaking, he put the phone onto the bedside table. He'd call her back later, after he'd been to the gym. And after he'd rehearsed what he wanted to say.

Thankfully Faith was in her office when he slipped past the reception. The gym was deathly quiet. Clearly most people had better things to do on Christmas Eve than work out. Adam ran on the treadmill for a few miles before going through a vigorous weights routine, taking solace from being able to focus on the pain in his exhausted muscles, rather than the mess in his head.

When he left several hours later, his body energised, his mind calmer, he was shocked to find himself walking into a blizzard. Snow was blanketing down, covering the car park in a thin layer. Instantly his head filled with images from three years ago and he swore, throwing his gym bag into the back of his four by four, kicking at the tyres. Tears pricked as he jumped inside and slumped over the wheel, holding his head in his hands.

Leave me alone, he wanted to scream. First Emma, now the snow. He'd had it with fucking reminders.

Inhaling a deep, shuddering breath he forced himself to sit up. Crying in a car park wasn't going to help. He had to get back to the hotel before the roads became impassable.

His heart was pounding as he set off, wipers swishing the

splatters of snow from side to side, hands clenched tightly round the steering wheel.

Three miles, that was all he needed to get through. Three miles and he'd be back at the hotel. It was eerily quiet on the roads. Eerily quiet in the car, too. He didn't put the radio on, not wanting anything to distract his attention from the dangerous conditions.

Don't think about anything but the here and now, he told himself, repeating it as a mantra as he crept along the slushy road. His shoulders began to relax as he saw the hotel.

But then they froze again, his heart lurching, as the car in front of him skidded round the corner, into the ditch.

He was acting on autopilot. Adam knew it, and was immensely grateful for it. As he helped the shaking lady into his car he refused, even for one second, to allow his mind to dwell on the fact that she was pregnant. No. He wasn't going there.

'I'll take you to the hotel I'm staying in,' he told the family as he set off, hands gripping the steering wheel so hard his knuckles turned as white as the snow he was edging across. In the back seat the husband had his arms around his wife. Next to him in the passenger seat, the teenage boy sat quietly, his face pale. 'You can phone the breakdown services from the hotel.'

The man nodded, eyes fixed on his wife. Adam's heart began to thump violently and he clutched even tighter to the wheel. *Don't go there.*

'Where were you heading?' he asked, not because he was interested but because they all needed some normal conversation to divert them from the what-if scenarios racing through their heads. What if the baby is hurt? What if we'd hit another car instead of a ditch?

What if we'd stayed at home …?

'Ambleside.'

The answer came from the boy. It forced Adam's thoughts back to the present, where they should be. Away from the past, where he didn't want them. 'Visiting relatives?'

'My grandparents.'

Adam nodded, carefully turning into the hotel car park. He doubted the boy would get to see his grandparents today. Not if the snow kept coming down like it was.

He stopped the car right outside the hotel and jumped out, staggering as his feet hit the snow-covered gravel. Shit, his legs felt like blancmange. Hands on his knees he bent over and took in several steadying breaths. When his legs felt like part of him again, he slammed the car door shut and started towards the hotel.

Chapter Eighteen

From having a quiet hotel, Faith was suddenly inundated with guests. First had come her neighbour Giles and his wife Margaret. For all that she was still cursing Adam from their altercation earlier, she was grateful he'd let her know the pair were suffering with no electricity. Although they'd insisted they were fine, Faith had practically pushed them over to the hotel.

'Nae lass, we don't want to be a bother to thee,' Giles had told her in his broad Cumbrian accent.

'Then you need to come and stay with me until your electricity is fixed,' she'd insisted. 'Otherwise I'll spend my Christmas worrying about you. And I don't charge my neighbours,' she'd added, in case it was the financial side putting them off.

Giles had grinned, displaying a set of bottom teeth that looked uncannily like those of his sheep. 'We don't accept charity. Though we're not averse to a bit of neighbourly discount.'

Within an hour she'd had them settled in a room with a view of their farm.

Then the snow had started to fall.

And fall.

She'd turned helplessly to Chloe. 'I'm not sure the bus is going to get through that. You might be stuck here tonight.'

Chloe had done her usual shoulder shrug. 'I don't mind. We're having lunch here tomorrow anyway, right?'

The realisation had pushed Faith into action and she'd quickly called Hope and Charity. Within an hour of her call, they'd arrived with their respective husbands, their overnight bags, and baby Jack, who'd been in a far better mood than his previous visit.

No matter what the weather decided to throw at them from that point on, Faith knew her family – minus Jason who'd be with his in-laws – would be together tomorrow.

It was then her mind had turned to Adam. She knew he'd gone to the gym – Chloe had told her she'd seen him leave with his sports bag. She also knew he had a four-wheel drive, so he'd be fine. As she'd watched the snow flurry turn into more of a blizzard, the green fields – and roads – slowly turn white, she'd repeated those words to herself.

And the more she'd worried, the angrier she'd become with herself. He'd made it quite clear his life wasn't any of her business.

How foolish of her then, how utterly stupid, to have fallen for him. Oh, she knew it had only been nine days. What were days crossed off on a calendar though, when it came to matters of the heart? What she felt for Adam far eclipsed anything she'd ever felt after two years of dating Patrick.

Feeling miserable, frustrated, hurt and horribly sorry for herself, Faith had been relieved when the phone had rung.

When she'd ended the call, she'd found herself with another two bookings for the day.

And another reason for Adam to be angry with her.

Her heart jumped as the man himself rushed through the door, his huge frame brimming with an urgency she'd not seen in him before. Snow had settled on him, a bright white dusting against the dark of his hair.

'I've got a pregnant lady, her husband and a teenage boy outside.' His quiet, normally mild voice was edged with panic. 'Their car skidded into a ditch so they need somewhere to sit while they wait for the breakdown service.'

He looked wild, she thought with alarm. His usually calm grey eyes were like a stormy sea, his face pale and tense. 'Are you okay?'

It was a stupid question, considering he was the one who'd come to the rescue of the others. Unsurprisingly, Adam gave her an odd look. 'You mean are they okay and yes, I think so. But the woman is pregnant ...' He trailed off and shoved a hand through his hair, sending snowflakes flying. She didn't miss the way his other hand clenched into a fist by his side.

Faith snapped to attention. 'Right, let's get them into the warm.'

Half an hour later, the Templetons – Mary, Joe and Joe's son Stuart – were sitting in the restaurant and drinking hot chocolate. Adam was pacing up and down on the phone, trying to get a doctor to come out and check on Mary.

'He doesn't need to worry.' Mary ran a hand over her heavily pregnant stomach. 'I can still feel him kicking.'

Faith glanced up at Adam, at the rigid set of his shoulders, the clenched jawline. 'I think he just wants to be sure.'

Joe, the husband, wasn't faring much better in his efforts to get a breakdown truck out to them. 'They say they can't send anyone at the moment. All the trucks are already out and the roads are getting worse. Because we're safe and warm, we aren't an emergency.'

Stuart, Joe's son, sighed as he clattered his phone onto the table. 'The thing's just died on me.'

Faith eyed him speculatively. He looked to be about Chloe's age. A good-looking boy, in that skinny, overly long-haired way that teenage girls seemed to love. 'My niece will have a charger. She's on the reception desk. Why don't you go and ask her?' As he stood up, she smiled at him. 'She's called Chloe. I'm sure she'll be glad of the company of someone her own age, as she's stuck here, too.'

When he'd ambled off, she turned back to the couple. 'We have room here if you need to stay the night so please don't worry.'

Relief shot through Joe's eyes and he hugged his wife towards him. 'I think we might just have to take you up on that.'

Faith rose to her feet. 'Then I'll go and prepare two rooms

145

next to each other.' She squeezed Mary's shoulder. 'I think this lady could do with a lie down.'

As she walked down the corridor, Adam came up behind her. 'I can't get a doctor to come out.'

Panic still lingered in his eyes and there was a restless, agitated look to him that troubled her. 'She says she can feel the baby kicking, so she's not worried. According to Joe they slid slowly into the ditch. The airbags didn't even inflate.'

'But she's pregnant,' he said, as if she was so dumb she hadn't realised. 'She needs to get checked out. Is there a doctor that lives locally? A house I can bang on to see if anyone's home?'

Faith could see he wasn't going to be persuaded. 'The lady who lives at number four is a retired GP.'

'Right.'

He started to stride purposefully away from her but Faith put a hand on his arm. Immediately she felt the connection all the way through her body. It seemed even when she was supposed to be angry with him, she wasn't immune. 'Dr Ferguson is seventy-eight. It's not a good idea for her to come out on an afternoon like this. Or for you to be driving in this weather.'

Adam glanced down at her hand, then into her eyes. So much emotion, she thought, staring into the tumultuous grey depths. She couldn't begin to work out what he was thinking, feeling. 'I'll take care of her.'

Then he was walking away, his long strides taking him past the reception desk, where Chloe was laughing at something Stuart was saying to her, and out through the door.

Adam felt queasy as he parked up outside the doctor's house. A combination of coming down from the adrenaline high he'd been on for the last few hours, and disgust with himself for dragging this lovely old lady out into a blizzard.

'I'm sorry to have put on you like that,' he told her again as he helped her back inside.

'You've said that four times now, dear.' She patted his arm as she shook off her coat. 'I didn't mind. I could see you were anxious.'

Anxious was putting it mildly, he thought grimly. He'd been almost manic by the time he'd driven the two miles through the snow to her door.

'She'll be fine,' Dr Ferguson reiterated. 'The baby has a good strong heartbeat. I suspect it will be due in the next few weeks.'

When he finally drove back into the hotel car park, Adam felt exhausted. It was the stress of the last few hours, on top of the rigorous work-out he'd put his body through at the gym. He was ready to collapse onto his bed.

Just as he was about to heave his weary body out of the car, his phone pinged, signalling a text from Damon.

I'm not worrying about you. That would be a girl thing to do.

A second message followed.

But text me back some reassuring words about life in the Lakes or I'll be phoning you.

Adam sighed, letting his head fall back against the headrest. Reassuring words? He'd rowed with Faith, had a meltdown over a small car accident and been pushed into a corner over calling Emma.

Girl? You feel like my ruddy mother. Quit harassing me and focus on your wife. I'm fine. SPEAK WHEN I'M HOME. A.

He pressed send and jumped out of the car.

There was a rare hum to the hotel as he strode through it – he was used to it being so quiet. The noise seemed to be coming from the restaurant. A quick glance through the open doors at the end of the corridor and he could see Faith's parents talking to Joe, the husband of the pregnant lady. Chloe and Stuart were there too, but on a different table, their faces poring over what looked to be Chloe's iPad. Giles was sitting with Margaret, a mince pie in his hand and a smile on his face. Some people he didn't know were standing chatting to each other, one of the women holding a baby. Was that Faith's nephew? The little mite he'd looked after for a while?

Suddenly Faith came in to view and Adam froze. He couldn't face her just now. Not since he'd made an absolute prick of himself not once but twice today. First lashing out at her over the call from Emma, then insisting on forcing an old lady out in the snow.

He turned to head off to his room but as he did, their eyes met and awareness slammed through him. She probably hated his guts now. What a shame his body didn't realise it.

He stood transfixed as she said something to her parents before heading out of the restaurant. Towards him.

Every muscle in his body tensed and for a split second he considered running to his room, shutting the door and turning the lock. But he hadn't phoned Emma back yet, and one cowardly action a day was about all he could stomach.

'Dr Ferguson got back okay?'

'Of course,' he replied tightly, resenting the question even though he knew it was asked out of concern rather than to make a point.

Hurt flashed in her gorgeous eyes and Adam knew he was failing left, right and centre with this woman. 'I wanted to warn you of our new guests.'

He frowned, looking over her shoulder into the restaurant. 'The ones with the baby?'

'No. That's Jack and my sister, Charity. She and Hope have come today in case the roads are too bad to travel tomorrow.'

His eyes swept further round the room. 'Giles and Margaret?'

Her breath came out in a gentle exhale. 'They're going to stay until their electricity is sorted.'

He found it too hard to look into her eyes. 'Thank you.'

'No, thank you for warning me about them.' When he

plucked up the courage to glance at her face, the compassion he saw there sent alarm bells ringing through him.

'Emma and her parents checked in half an hour ago,' she said in a rush.

For a moment the words didn't penetrate. All he could see was Faith's beautiful eyes, wrapping him up in warmth and kindness, neither of which he deserved. But then what she'd said began to work its way through his paralysed brain, and fear trickled through him, freezing his organs in its wake. 'They're here.' He almost choked on the words.

Eyes swimming in sympathy, she nodded. 'Apparently Emma was visiting her parents when she called.'

'They were buying a holiday home in Keswick.' Slowly the memory came back to him. *But why the hell were they up here?* he thought wildly. They always spent Christmas down south, hundreds of bloody miles away.

'Yes. So when she found out you were here ...' Faith paused, guilt flooding across her face. 'When I opened my big mouth and told her where you were, they made a snap decision to come.'

'But the snow ...' His brain felt like mush as it struggled to comprehend what was happening.

'Emma's husband – Frank – drives a Discovery. They made it here just before it got really bad.' His expression must have looked as dazed as he felt because she gave his arm a brief, reassuring squeeze. 'I didn't give them your room number, so you don't have to see them, but Emma asked me to give you hers. She and her husband are in number seven.'

Numbly he thanked her, then took a step away before he gave in to temptation and reached out for her. He'd given up the chance to feel those arms wrapped around him. Her heart beating against his.

'You should talk to her, Adam,' Faith said softly. 'No good ever came of pushing people away, or burying your thoughts.'

Pride made him bristle. 'You don't know what you're talking about.'

'You've not told me what happened, so perhaps you're right.' He took the jab on the chin, knowing he deserved it, though it stung like a bugger. 'I do know I'm the first woman you've slept with since your wife left you, though. That suggests you've got some unresolved issues. As does the way you're avoiding your wife's family.'

'Ex-wife,' he countered bluntly, eyes glancing over her shoulder and back into the restaurant. The more he stared at the people congregated there, the more he began to see a pattern. A rush of harsh laughter escaped him. 'Look at that group in there; your sisters, Chloe, Giles, the people from the car crash. All people you're helping in some way.' He almost laughed again when he caught sight of Nip and Tuck, chasing each other round the room like a pair of mop heads on speed. 'Damn it, even your dogs were from a rescue centre, weren't they? And that's what you're doing to me too, isn't it? I'm another one of your rescue projects.'

Two red spots appeared on her cheeks. At first he thought it was embarrassment, but one look at her flashing eyes and he knew differently. 'Since when is it a crime to want to help others?' She shook her head in a dismissive gesture. 'Stop being a coward. Go and talk to the woman who's bothered to travel through the snow to see you.'

Faith turned away sharply and Adam knew however angry she'd been with him before, he'd just made the situation a million times worse.

As he watched her stride back into the restaurant, his heart plummeted, dragging painfully at his shoulders, tearing at his chest. He had serious doubts whether anything Emma could throw at him – and he knew she hadn't tracked him down just to say hello – could make him feel any worse than he did right now.

Chapter Nineteen

Tears stung Faith's eyes as she walked back to the restaurant. Damn Adam Hunter and his sad, lost expression. His harsh, accusing words.

Trying to swallow down her misery, she headed for the kitchen. The brothers were still there, preparing the final dishes for the day. When she'd only had a few guests booked, all planning to eat elsewhere on Christmas Day, closing the restaurant to keep the brothers happy had seemed like a good idea. Now she was beginning to doubt her sanity. Maybe Adam was right. She was too much of a soft touch to run her own business.

Stop thinking about him.

'You have a crowd now, *si*?' Mario said as she stepped inside. 'They all stay here?'

Ripples of panic slithered through her. 'The way the weather is looking, I think so, yes.'

He dipped his head, looking at her with his dark Italian eyes. 'When we agree to have tomorrow off, we thought only a few guests. Now the hotel is full.'

The irony wasn't lost on her. 'Half of them are my family. We'll muddle through.'

'Are you sure? We can come and cook the turkey for you.' Antonio this time. He was the younger of the two. Quieter.

'And trudge through all this snow when you could be having a lie-in, and a meal made for you?'

Antonio looked towards his brother and a silent conversation went on before Mario nodded and turned to her. 'We won't see our family tomorrow now. Too much snow. So it's just us. We could come in. Cook for everyone. We live only two kilometres away. The walk here will not be too much of a ... what did you say ... trudge?'

A bubble of hope floated up inside her. 'You don't mind?' she almost squealed.

Mario gave her a wide smile. 'You were kind to agree to close the restaurant. We will cook a turkey for you.'

She bit into her lip. 'Umm, we're going to need more than one. Mum's got one big enough for our lot, plus a spare. The neighbours Giles and Margaret have brought theirs—'

'Relax.' Mario put a hand on her shoulder and started to push her out of the kitchen. 'You do your job, we do ours. We'll leave croissants and cereal out for tomorrow morning for anyone up early. We be here at ten. Now what do you English say ... shoo.'

'Grazie, grazie,' she shouted over her shoulder, and knew without looking that they were rolling their eyes. It was the only Italian she'd picked up in the four months they'd been working together.

Relief made her steps considerably lighter as Faith went to find her sisters, who were now talking to her parents. Nip and Tuck, who she'd not had the heart to keep locked up now it was too snowy to run outside, were lying docilely at her father's feet. Clearly playing chase was exhausting when you only had little legs. As she walked towards them, her eyes skimmed over the other tables, resting finally on her niece, who was still talking to Stuart. *Interesting.*

Hope caught sight of Faith and frowned. 'Everything okay?'

'Of course.' Faith forced a smile. 'Especially now Mario and Antonio have agreed to make Christmas dinner for us tomorrow.'

'My stomach says thank you,' her father murmured.

'You looked upset earlier, though,' Hope persisted. 'After you'd talked to the guest in the corridor.'

'Oh, he's more than a guest,' her mother supplied unhelpfully.

And now both Hope and Charity were staring at her. Before Faith could question what was happening, her sisters had whispered to their husbands, and the men were leading her father out of the restaurant. It left only Faith, three pairs of inquisitive female eyes. And a sleeping baby.

'Let me get this straight,' Hope said finally, when Faith had given them all the highs, and subsequent lows, of her doomed affair. 'You think you've fallen in love with a man who lives down south, who has a hang-up about his ex-wife and who hates Christmas.'

'But is a star when it comes to looking after dogs and wee babies.' Her mother glanced at her sympathetically. 'Let's not forget his good points.'

Charity dropped a kiss on her son's soft downy hair. 'Anyone who managed to get this one to stop crying that day was a hero in my eyes.'

Hope's gaze travelled to where her daughter sat. 'And if the change in Chloe is anything to go by, it seems he has a way with teenage girls, too.' She patted Faith's hand. 'Though I know most of that is down to you. She told me how you've helped her. Listened to her when I was too busy to.'

Faith smiled sadly. 'I was only able to listen because it's been quiet here, so don't put yourself down. And Adam's helped a lot. Sticking up for her, talking to her, showing her exercise routines.'

'Yes, what is it with him and exercise?' Hope let out a little giggle. 'Chloe seems to think he's an exercise God.'

'Something went on with his wife, now ex-wife,' Faith added quickly as she watched the horror creep across their faces. 'Whatever number the woman did on him made him hate himself for a while.' It also made him secretive, reclusive, emotionally unavailable, prickly and unwilling to trust, she thought miserably.

But God, when he looked at her with those tortured eyes, she was putty in his hands. She wondered where he was now. Whether he was actually talking to Emma or whether he'd locked himself in his room, allowing whatever demons were haunting him to have a free rein.

The door opened and Adam found himself staring straight into the cautious blue eyes of his sister-in-law. Ex sister-in-law, he reminded himself. He tried to hold her gaze, to keep his shoulders square and his back straight.

Tried not to remember the last time he'd seen her.

Her eyes widened as they took him in, moving from his face, down his body and back up again. 'You look different.'

Self-consciously he rubbed a hand over his jaw. 'It's the beard.'

'Maybe. You're also ...' She waved a hand up and down. 'Bigger.'

There was a tremor in her voice, a hesitancy in her expression. *She's nervous*, he realised, and the thought almost blindsided him. He was the one in the wrong. He was the one so far on the back foot he was tipping over.

She pulled the door further open. 'Come on in.'

Frank, her husband, immediately stood up from the sofa. After giving Adam a quick, firm handshake he gave his wife a long, meaningful look. 'I'll be in the foyer if you need me.'

The door closed with a thud behind him and immediately the room filled with a tense, uncomfortable silence.

'I'm surprised to see you here,' he blurted finally. 'I thought your parents always came to you for Christmas.'

She gave him a knowing look. 'Which is why you thought you'd be safe up here, huh?'

'No, that's not ...' He trailed off, horribly aware she was right.

'As luck would have it, when you once again didn't reply to my invitation, we all decided to come up to Mum and Dad's cottage for a change.'

Following her pointed response, the room once again lapsed into a strained silence. Adam shifted on his feet, scratching at the prickles he could feel at the back of his neck. What did you say to the woman you'd been avoiding for three years? The woman who'd been like a sister to you, but whose own sister you'd almost destroyed.

The woman whose nephew you'd killed.

But then she stunned him by reaching for his hand and clutching it between hers. 'It's so good to finally see you again. I've missed you,' she whispered, her eyes glistening with tears.

Shocked, confused, he gaped at her, his hand feeling all wrong inside hers, yet he didn't want to grab it back. Didn't want to escape the precious contact. 'You … what?'

Her eyes glanced up at the ceiling and she shook her head, letting out a small, sad sounding laugh. 'Is that so hard to understand? You're my brother, Adam, in everything but name. We grew up together. Of course I've missed you since you disappeared out of my life three years ago.'

'You must hate me.' He almost choked over the words. 'How can you miss me?'

'Hate you?' Her hands squeezed round his even more tightly. 'Why would I hate you? You're family.'

The tightness he'd been feeling round his chest since he'd knocked on the door became unbearable. He yanked his hand away, stalking to the other side of the room. 'Ruth does,' he said flatly.

Emma swore, which was so unlike her. 'My sister has said a lot of things she didn't mean. A lot of things she shouldn't have done.'

'Ruth said what she was feeling.' And as long as he lived he'd never forget her words, or the expression on her face as she'd spat them at him. It had gone beyond anger. Beyond desolation. He'd not just broken their marriage, he'd damn near broken her.

'Ruth was a wreck,' Emma countered, her eyes brimming with compassion. 'She'd just lost the baby. Her emotions were too raw for her to think rationally.'

Adam deliberately turned away from Emma, the pressure on his chest making it hard for him to breathe. 'When defences are down, people speak the truth,' he choked out.

'Oh Adam.'

He heard the sadness, the pity in her voice and he wanted to flee from the room. To get in his car and drive far, far away from her, from the hotel. From the people he'd managed to hurt. And if the expression on Faith's face – when he'd accused her of making him another rescue project – was anything to go by, the people he was *still* hurting.

He froze as a pair of arms slid round his waist. Emma peered up at him, her eyes suspiciously bright. 'Don't tell me you've spent the last three years believing what Ruth said?'

A shudder ran through him as those words echoed once more inside his head. 'I was there,' he told Emma stiffly. 'I know the part I played.'

'It was an accident.'

'One I could have prevented.' Adam felt a searing pain in his chest as his heart began to crumple. 'Ruth didn't want to leave. I made her. When we had the accident, I was driving. I caused our son's death.' He felt the shameful sting of tears on his cheeks. 'I don't blame her for leaving me. For hating me. It's what I deserved.'

Suddenly Emma tugged at his hand, pulling him until he sat down on the bed. He was so shocked he didn't stop her. 'What you deserved,' she said fiercely, her eyes blazing as she stared down at him, 'was to have your family supporting you through your grief.' She gave a shake of her head, her voice growing quieter. 'Your own parents were useless, as always.'

Adam couldn't disagree with that one. He'd never been close to them, always aware he was a nuisance. A complication they hadn't planned and didn't especially want to have to deal with. They'd become so estranged it had been a shock to see them at his son's funeral, though they'd dashed back to France the moment their duty had been done. His whole childhood had been the same. A series of duties they'd ticked off over the years. Make sure he's fed and clothed, tick. Enrol him in a good school, tick. Attend parents' evening, tick. See him safely off to university, a final tick. Parental duties ended.

The bed dipped as Emma sat down next to him, her hand clasping his. 'Everyone was so concerned about Ruth,' she whispered. 'We didn't pay enough attention to you. Didn't appreciate enough that you lost a child, too.' Her eyes brimmed with tears. 'I should have realised that. Should have been there for you. The last time I saw you ...' She bit down on her lip, shaking her head.

'You asked me to leave,' he said roughly, the rejection feeling as sharp now as it had three years ago.

Her hand tightened on his. 'And I bitterly regret it. Ruth was in the living room and I panicked. I thought if I was friendly to you, she would see it as a betrayal.' Tears began to slide down Emma's face. 'Instead, I betrayed you, which was unforgivable.'

'No.' The word was wrenched from him. 'It was totally understandable. It's just I didn't know that. I thought you felt like Ruth did. Thought you hated me, too.'

'Oh Adam.' Emma wiped at her tears with the back of her hand. 'You have no idea how much I regret how I handled things in those early days. By the time I woke up to how badly I'd ignored you, and your needs, it was too late. You'd disappeared. All I had was your work number and your mobile number. Which you kept refusing to answer.'

Adam's mind was struggling to make sense of the last few minutes. He'd spent so long running away from Emma it was hard to fathom he was now in the same room as her. And she didn't hate him.

'I didn't phone back because I couldn't bear to hear the disappointment in your voice,' he said finally. 'I knew by hurting your sister, by letting her down in the most terrible way, I'd let you down, too.'

'I can't believe you thought that.' She stared back at him, looking both confused and exasperated. 'Why do you think I kept asking you to spend Christmas with us? Why do you think I wanted to speak to you so much I kept phoning you?'

He let out a short, bitter laugh. 'I know you, Emma. You haven't got a nasty bone in your body. Despite what I'd done, you felt some sort of misguided duty towards me because of our shared past.' And he'd had enough of people putting up with him because they felt they had to. Not because they wanted to.

Emma gave him a shove. 'Jeez, for a smart guy, you can be exceptionally stupid. You're my big brother, Adam. I phoned because I worried about you, especially at this time of year. And because I wanted to see you. And because I love you.'

Emotion reared inside him, a tight band around his chest, a hard lump in his throat. As tears stung his eyes he rubbed them, not wanting to embarrass himself again. 'I wish I'd answered,' he whispered.

Her arms came around him once more. They were slender, too short to fully wrap round him, but he welcomed their weight just the same. 'So do I.'

They remained like that for several minutes, him absorbing her comfort like a sponge, until he jolted, suddenly remembering what Faith had told him. 'Your parents?'

'Miss you too,' she replied quickly, her head resting against his shoulder. 'They're in the room next door.'

His body shuddered as he drew in a breath. 'I'm not sure I can—'

'When you're ready.' She smiled up at him, eyes full of understanding. 'Remember, just because they were there for their daughter, didn't mean they agreed with what she said.' Her eyes dropped to where their hands were still clasped. 'In those first few months after the accident Ruth was hanging by a thread. We worried she was going to take her own life. We had to get counsellors in, keep a watch on her.'

Numbly he nodded. The day of the accident Adam had lost the two most important people in his life. His wife, and his unborn child. Ruth had told him she never wanted to see him again – and she'd kept to that. Any overture he'd made – and there had been plenty in those first few months – she'd thrown back in his face. Wracked with guilt, torn up with grief, after a while he'd stopped trying.

Taking a deep breath, he asked the question. 'How is she now?'

Emma smiled. 'She's good, thank you. She'd like to talk to you.'

Adam leapt up from the bed. 'No.' His heart rattled his ribs. 'I couldn't.' He felt himself starting to shake. No way could he face her again after what he'd done to them. No way on this earth. 'Please tell me she's not here, too.'

Emma must have sensed he was near to breaking point because she rose and put a gentle hand on his arm. 'Relax. Ruth isn't here, no. That's why we thought it was a good opportunity to go to the cottage. She's spending today and tomorrow with … a friend. We're hoping to see her tomorrow night.'

'Right.' He could barely squeeze the word out.

'Nobody's going to make you do anything you don't want to do.'

He backed away a few steps, fighting to get his breathing under control, his heart rate back to something that wasn't supercharged.

Finally Emma broke the silence. 'So, what's with you and the very attractive hotel manager, huh?'

He blinked at the sudden change in conversation. 'Why do you ask?'

'Because she's the one who answered your mobile when I phoned.' Emma cocked her head to one side, seeming to study him. 'And she seemed awfully protective of you earlier. Wouldn't give me your room number.'

'It must be hotel policy.'

Emma gave him another smile, this time more … sly. More knowing. 'If you say so.' She reached up to kiss his cheek. 'Frank and I are staying here with Mum and Dad tonight and eating Christmas lunch here tomorrow.'

'You can't,' he blurted, still reeling from everything he'd heard. 'The restaurant's closed.'

'Faith did warn us of that. She also said she and her family were cooking and had enough turkey if we wanted to stay.' Emma gave him a sly smile. 'She seems a very capable woman.'

Adam kept his lips firmly shut. No way was he falling into that trap.

'Will you join us for Christmas lunch?' Emma's eyes begged him. 'Please?'

Almost of its own volition, his head tipped forward in a single nod of acceptance. It was the third invitation he'd had for Christmas lunch over the last few days – first Faith, then her mother, now Emma. It seemed he was destined not to spend this Christmas day alone.

Emma beamed, kissing his cheek and thanking him, her obvious pleasure almost too much for him. The moment her chatter dried up he made his excuses and almost fled down the corridor. He was so desperate for the sanctuary of his own room. Once there he flopped onto the bed, his head a mess, his heart not feeling any better.

Emma doesn't blame me. That was what he kept telling himself. And it nearly drowned out what Ruth had yelled at him three years ago.

Until he closed his eyes.

That was when the image that haunted him burst vividly into life. Ruth at the funeral, hunched against the cold, her expression lost, sobs wracking her slim frame. She'd not been simply upset, or heart-broken. She'd been destroyed.

He knew, however kind Emma's words had been, they'd never drive away those the woman he'd once loved had hurled at him across their son's grave.

Chapter Twenty

In the last hour Faith had shown another three unexpected guests to their rooms, courtesy of the weather. She let out a gentle sigh as she strode back to the restaurant area. The snow had prevented many families getting together tonight. Thank goodness hers was already here.

A small smile tugged at her as she passed by the Christmas tree, remembering how the little boy and girl had almost vibrated with excitement as they'd left a snack on the hearth for Father Christmas and Rudolph. She hoped their parents would remember to eat the mince pie and nibble on the carrots when the kids had gone to sleep.

The restaurant was noticeably quieter now than it had been an hour ago when the guests had been tucking in to dinner, and the room had buzzed with the sound of conversation and laughter.

The only guest who hadn't been there, she remembered on a wave of misery, was Adam. Had he been too upset to leave his room? Still too angry to risk bumping into her? Not long ago she'd harboured hopes that their Christmas affair would blossom into something more. Something that distance and careers wouldn't prevent.

Now it looked like it was dying prematurely, killed off through anger and ill feeling.

She found her sisters and their husbands gathered round one of the large tables, chatting with her parents. On the next table sat Chloe and Stuart, their shoulders touching as they gazed at whatever they were watching on the iPad. The way they kept glancing at each other and grinning lifted Faith's heart a little. At least someone was having luck on the romance front tonight.

'You're kidding me.' Hope's face brimmed with delight

as Faith told them about the new arrivals. 'You really just checked in three guys on their way to a pub quiz?'

'Err, yes.' Faith eyed her sister suspiciously. 'Why are you so pleased they got caught in the snow?'

'Isn't it obvious?' Faith's face must have looked clueless because Hope rolled her eyes. 'Duh. It's Christmas Eve, and you've got the whole flipping nativity scene going on right here in your hotel.'

'I have?' Faith glanced at the rest of her family for help but they just shrugged, seemingly as baffled as she was.

'Yes,' Hope hissed. 'Those guests whose car slipped into a ditch.' She nodded over to where Chloe was sitting. 'Romeo over there's family.'

'You mean Joe and his pregnant wife, Mary.' Slowly the penny began to drop.

'Exactly. And you have a shepherd, Giles.'

'Sheep farmer,' Faith corrected. 'And there's only one of him.'

Hope batted her objection away. 'Don't spoil the fun. Now you have the final piece.'

'Three men going to a pub quiz?'

Hope grinned. 'Three wise men.'

The rest of the table collapsed in groans, interspersed with fits of laughter. 'You can count me out if your Mary gets into full character tonight,' her father interrupted. 'I've witnessed enough births for one lifetime.'

Even as she laughed with the rest of them, Faith had a flashback to Adam, and how panicked he'd looked earlier when helping Mary. How he'd insisted on dragging Dr Ferguson out in the blizzard. The man had so many secrets. So many demons he seemed to be battling.

When the laughter died down, Hope's husband Tom gave Faith a pleading look. 'Are you going to invite us back to your digs? It's Christmas Eve and I don't have a drink in my hand.'

Faith rose to her feet. 'I think I can manage some whisky. Or some eggnog,' she added, glancing at her father. Trying not to think of the last man she'd mentioned eggnog to.

Her father's eyes lit up and he stood up smartly. 'Why the bloody hell didn't you say earlier?'

As they trailed off back to hers, Faith noticed Stuart give Chloe a quick peck on her cheek before walking off towards his room.

When Chloe caught her eye, her cheeks flushed. 'He's welcome to come, too.'

Chloe gave an awkward shake of her head. 'Nah. It's okay. I'll see him tomorrow.'

Faith gave her side a gentle nudge. 'Do you like him?'

'He's okay.'

'Just okay?'

Chloe was clearly fighting not to smile. 'Maybe a bit more than okay.' Chloe nudged her back. 'How about Adam? Do you like him?'

Chloe's voice was teasing. She didn't know how badly her affair with Adam had faltered over the last twelve hours. 'He's okay.' Before Chloe could ask anything further, Faith changed the subject.

It was half past ten. Charity and her husband had left a short while ago, baby Jack having had enough. Her parents were yawning. Hope and Tom were curled up on the sofa by the fire, looking content. Chloe had just disappeared back to her room.

The knock on her door startled them all.

The sight of the man standing outside shocked her further.

'Adam.' Her heart did a crazy leap as her eyes travelled across his strapping chest and up to his face. 'Are you okay?'

His small, tight smile didn't reach his bloodshot grey eyes. 'Honestly? I'm not sure.'

She hesitated, torn between inviting him in and slamming the door in his face. Part of her was still angry with him. She'd answered his phone and then tried to help him. She wasn't sure either action merited the way he'd spoken to her. Then again, he clearly had his reasons for not wanting Emma to know where he was, and Faith had totally blown his cover.

Plus he looked so vulnerable. So achingly sad.

The sound of laughter echoed from her sitting room and Faith gave Adam an apologetic smile. 'My parents and sister are still here.'

Disappointment flooded his face. 'Then I won't disturb you. I just …' He tugged a hand through his hair. 'I wanted to apologise. I've been a git to you today.'

'You've had a tough day.'

His laugh was short and humourless. 'You could say that.' His hand fell to his face and he rubbed at it, making her aware of how drawn he looked. How tired. 'It doesn't excuse my behaviour.'

Behind her, Faith heard footsteps.

'We're just off to bed, dear.' Her mother gave her a wink. 'Happy Christmas. See you tomorrow morning.'

As her parents disappeared down the corridor, Hope and Tom came up to her, yawning theatrically. A moment later they were bidding her goodnight.

She didn't know whether to be cross or pleased at their rather obvious exits. 'It seems my visitors have fled.'

Adam stared back at her, a myriad of emotions swirling in his eyes. He was hurting, she could see that, but there was more. He looked lost. 'I still don't want to intrude,' he said softly, his gaze darting away from her. 'Maybe it's best if I go.'

'Do you want to go?'

A short exhalation of breath. 'No.'

Faith pulled the door open wider. 'Then come in.'

Silently they walked into her sitting room. She wondered what he thought as his eyes skimmed over the twinkling fairy lights, the empty glasses, two remaining mince pies and multitude of chocolate orange wrappers that littered the coffee table. The stocking her mother had already filled for her and hung above the fireplace. Did he want to flee from the reminder of the time of year that clearly held such awful memories for him?

Her eyes shot up to his face but she couldn't read his expression.

'Do you mind?'

He indicated to the sofa and her heart ached. Last night he'd made love to her on that sofa. Tonight he was asking permission to sit on it. 'Of course not. Would you like a drink?'

As he lowered his big body he shook his head. 'Better not. I've already raided the minibar in my room.'

Unlike previous evenings, she chose to sit in the armchair opposite him. He gave her a wry smile but didn't comment. Instead he shifted forwards, resting his arms on his knees. 'I owe you an explanation.'

'No, you don't.' She didn't want him talking to her because he felt he should. She wanted him to tell her because he trusted her. Because he thought they had something worth pursuing when he went home, no matter how difficult it might be.

His head lifted and the bleakness of his expression left her fighting to breathe. 'I've ruined things, haven't I?'

How was she meant to answer? Was he asking because he wanted two more nights in her bed, or because he wanted more? Two more nights she could give him, but more seemed impossible. Not when he was still so clearly hung up on his ex-wife.

When she didn't reply, he rose stiffly to his feet. 'I'd better go.'

Faith felt a rush of longing, of wanting. Though alarms were going off in her head, warning her another night with him would make his leaving even more painful, she ignored them. 'You don't have to go,' she found herself saying. 'And you don't have to explain.'

He angled his head, clearly confused.

'We only have two more nights. We can forget everything and just enjoy them.' She stopped before she added *Enjoy Christmas*.

Adam felt as if his head was going to explode. He didn't know why he'd come here. Oh, he knew he wanted her. In his arms, beneath him, on top of him. On the floor, her sofa, her bed. Anywhere she'd let him take her. But if that's all it had been, he'd have found the strength to stay away. What was the point in prolonging something that had no future? Something else had drawn him here though; a yearning, a longing he had no control over. For hours he'd sat in his room, nursing drink after drink, trying to come to terms with what Emma had told him. For so long he'd assumed everyone had blamed him for what had happened. It was a shock to find that Emma and her parents hadn't.

While the news had come as a huge relief, had lifted some of the oppressive weight he'd been carrying with him the last few years, he knew two other people still held him accountable. His ex-wife. And himself.

The thought had left him restless, aching, miserable as hell. Would he ever be free of the guilt? Ever be himself again? A few minutes later he'd found himself knocking on Faith's door. With her, he'd had glimpses of the man he wanted to be.

'Are you staying or going?'

Faith's terse words jolted him out of his introspection. One look at her face and he knew she'd taken his silence the wrong way. In a heartbeat he was lifting her into his arms.

'Staying.' His voice sounded desperate but he didn't care. He needed this woman, the safe haven of her arms, the thrill of her body, more than he'd ever needed anyone. 'Please, let me stay.'

Her body melted against him, her lips finding the side of his neck. 'Then take me to bed.'

He needed no further instructions. Within moments he had her exactly where he wanted her. This time though, beneath the joy, the heat, the heavy throb of desire, sadness poked and prodded. Even as he kissed her soft skin, caressed her. Even as he slid blissfully into her heat, Adam found her words going round in his head.

Two more nights.

Her message couldn't have been clearer. There would be no attempt at a long distance relationship for them. When he checked out on Boxing Day, it would be goodbye.

'Adam?'

He blinked, gazing down at the woman beneath him, her cheeks flushed, her eyes heavy-lidded. Shaking away his thoughts he angled his hips, thrusting harder, causing them both to gasp.

If they only had two more nights, he was going to make absolutely sure they were nights she'd remember.

The bedside clock flicked over to midnight and Faith stirred in his arms, easing herself up on her elbow to kiss him lightly on the mouth.

'Happy Christmas,' she murmured. Before he could say anything, she placed a finger over his mouth. 'Humour me. *I'm* feeling particularly happy.'

Adam smiled. 'I have you in my arms. Trust me, I'm very happy right now.'

Something flickered in her eyes, and her smile slipped a little. 'I wish you could stay happy.'

His heart shifted and he hugged her closer, silently wishing the same thing. Funny thing was, if he could stay right here in her bed, never let the real world intrude, he could easily see it happening.

It was so long before she spoke again, he thought she'd dropped off to sleep. 'Did your talk with Emma help?'

As she'd made it clear she didn't want an explanation, Adam stuck to the simple truth. 'Yes, a little.'

He felt the curve of her mouth against his skin. 'Does that mean I'm off the hook?'

Laughter rumbled through his chest and he kissed the top of her head. 'You're more than off the hook. I should be thanking you for interfering.'

Her body shuddered gently against his side. 'I don't like how that sounds.'

He reared up, pushing her off him and onto her back, taking her by surprise. Then he took hold of her hands and pinned her to the bed so she couldn't turn away from him. 'Faith Watkins, I want to formally thank you for answering my phone and telling Emma where I was. Thanks to your ... intervention,' he settled on, 'I've been reunited with someone I thought I'd lost forever.'

Her smile reached right inside him, warming places that had been closed off for so long. 'Then I'm glad it worked out. Emma seems really nice.'

Adam dipped his head and kissed her nose. 'She is. Far more like a sister than a sister-in-law.' As he wanted to share at least something of his past with her, he shifted to his side and started to talk. 'Ruth, my ex-wife, was my best friend all the way through secondary school. Her family was like my second family. Her sister, Emma, the sibling I didn't have. Her mum and dad, the parents I would have chosen.'

Understanding shone through her eyes. 'Because they took notice of you when your own didn't.'

'Yes.' The need to touch her was so strong he reached out to smooth his hand down her neck.

'So when you and Ruth split up, you thought they'd take her side?'

'They were right to take her side,' he corrected. And just like that, the heavy weight he'd temporarily shrugged off threatened to crush him again. Determined not to let it, determined to restrict Faith's bedroom to just him and her, Adam bent his head and started to kiss her.

Within moments he was lost to a world where nothing mattered but the press of her flesh against his.

Chapter Twenty-One

Christmas Day

Faith eased onto her side, taking a moment to study the man lying next to her. The first man she'd ever woken up next to on Christmas morning, she noted with a jolt of surprise. No matter who she'd been dating, she'd always gone home on Christmas Eve, waking on Christmas morning in her childhood bed.

This year it was all change. Her family had come to her place. And she had a man in her bed.

His face looked younger when he was asleep, she noted as her eyes skimmed it. It was as if the burdens he carried were no longer pulling at him, relaxing the creases around his eyes. What would he look like without the beard? Younger again, perhaps. She had to admit she loved it, though. It gave his face a rugged, edgy look that was incredibly sexy. Add that to his powerful physique and, whether asleep or awake, Adam Hunter was a deeply attractive man. The fact that he had no clue how attractive he was just added to his appeal.

She recalled his admission last night – that he and Ruth had been childhood sweethearts – and knew it confirmed what he'd already hinted. She, Faith Watkins, was only the second woman he'd slept with. The thought pulled once again at her heart. It might have been only a fling, but he'd surely remember her as the years rolled by. She wouldn't be a notch on a crowded bedpost. She'd be the woman who'd awakened his sexuality again.

Leaving him free to fall for the next woman he became close to.

Or perhaps to go back to the ex-wife he clearly wasn't over. Her heart twisted and Faith jumped out of the bed. She needed to let the dogs out. Tidy up the glasses left from last night. Make some coffee. Anything to stop thinking beyond today.

When she opened the back door Nip and Tuck scampered outside, coming to a skidding stop as their paws hit the snow. Moments later, having done what they needed to do, they darted back in again. Looking at their silly faces, their noses covered with snowflakes, her mood lifted.

Focus on now. Focus on now. She uttered the words to herself as she made two coffees and carried them to her bedroom.

It was empty.

'Adam?'

She peeked around the corner into the en suite. No, he wasn't having a shower.

She called his name again, feeling stupid. Had he woken up regretting last night? Regretting being in her bed this morning? Staring down at the two coffees in her hand she started to feel sick.

The sound of her doorbell ringing made her jump. Thrusting the drinks down she walked through to the hallway and peered through the peephole.

Relief had her throwing the door open.

'I wondered where you were.'

His hair was rumpled, his clothes – last night's jeans and shirt – creased. His smile a touch sheepish, yet the combination made her hormones stand to attention.

'Sorry. I just popped back to my room.' She glanced down to the large brown envelope he was holding, decorated with a red ribbon – and her heart thumped. He must have seen her reaction because his smile slipped. 'Don't get excited. I haven't got you a present. Well, not as such. And I pinched the ribbon from one of your decorations.'

God, he was so adorable. A great hulk of a man standing awkwardly in her doorway, shifting from one foot to the other. Reaching for his hand, she drew him inside and led him into the sitting room. 'Number one, I wasn't expecting a present,' she told him as they sat facing each other on the sofa. 'Number two, what on earth does *not as such* mean?'

'It means no money was exchanged.'

She eyed him curiously. 'Did you pinch it?'

His laugh was a mixture of humour and offence. 'No. And no more questions, or you'll start to build it up into something bigger than it is.'

'Do you want yours?'

Grey eyes widened, his expression more than surprised. 'You got *me* something?'

She'd debated whether to or not, knowing it said boyfriend rather than fling. But then she'd gone to see the owner of the gym to talk about mutual promotion ideas and the present had leapt out at her. Yesterday she'd wondered if she'd wasted her money. 'I haven't wrapped it yet,' she warned.

Sadness crept into his expression. 'You didn't plan on giving it to me.'

'I wasn't sure if you'd want a present from me,' she corrected. 'I know you don't like Christmas. And then, well, we spent most of yesterday at loggerheads. I wasn't sure we'd see each other again, other than when you checked out.'

'I can't imagine a time when I wouldn't want to see you.' His voice was quiet but had a hoarse edge to it. 'Faith, I ...' he trailed off, glancing away before seeming to gather himself. 'I'm sorry for yesterday. This last week with you has been the best I've had in such a long time.' His eyes stared straight into hers. 'You have no idea how much it meant to me. How much you mean to me.'

Her heart began to beat wildly and Faith struggled with how to reply. Was he hinting at something more, a future beyond tomorrow? Yet how could there be with the presence of his ex-wife looming between them? Whatever had happened, he hadn't really moved on from it. He'd admitted at the start that he wasn't in the right place for a relationship, and now she'd seen the truth of it with her own eyes.

'This time has meant a lot to me, too,' she said softly. *Keep it simple. Keep to the boundaries already set.*

Needing to dial down the heavy blanket of emotion, Faith stood and went to fetch the coffees and his present from the bedroom.

When she came back he was hunched over, scrubbing at his face, the sound making a scratching noise against his beard. Her heart gave another painful tug. Would there ever be a time when he didn't look sad? Didn't look so lost?

She forced herself to smile. 'Here you go.'

Adam snapped his head up. Faith, a strained smile on her face, was handing him a plastic carrier bag. He couldn't believe she'd got him an actual present. As touched as he felt, it also left him cursing, and praying that what she'd bought him was something trivial and inexpensive. When he'd woken to an empty bed this morning he'd had time to think; usually when he woke next to Faith his thinking was done with the part of his anatomy that lay below his waist. Realising it was Christmas morning, and knowing how much Faith loved Christmas, he'd had the genius idea of giving her what he'd been working on over the last few afternoons, as a Christmas present.

Now, knowing she'd planned his present, actually *bought* him something, he felt like an unthinking prick.

She was waving the bag under his nose, her smile becoming more genuine as she rolled her eyes at him. 'Santa calling Adam. Time to open your present.'

Cautiously he took the bag from her. It felt soft. Not an impersonal box of chocolates then, or a bottle of something alcoholic. Pulse racing, he peered into the bag and drew out a large black cotton T-shirt. When he unfolded it, his smile was instant and real. On the front was the picture of a weight lifting bar, and beneath it the words: *Eat, Sleep, Lift, Repeat.*

'Thank you.' His throat felt tight, his voice rough.

She must have sensed he was genuinely pleased because her smile was brighter than ever as she sat down next to him. 'You're welcome. Are you going to try it on?'

Hastily he shrugged off yesterday's crumpled shirt, feeling a ripple of pride as he noticed the way her eyes were drawn to his naked chest. Deliberately he twitched his muscles.

She laughed. 'You caught me. I can't get enough of your body.'

He slipped the T-shirt on – it fitted perfectly – before leaning in to kiss her on the lips. 'In case you hadn't noticed, I'm rather partial to yours, too.'

She blushed a little, surprising him because he always thought of her as confident. Then her eyes wandered to the envelope he'd set on the coffee table. 'Do I get mine now?'

Unease flooded through him. He was so damn out of practice at all this; relationships, Christmas, present buying. Or in his case, not buying. 'Sorry I didn't get you a proper gift.'

Her eyes softened and she leaned into him. 'Stop apologising. You told me you hate Christmas. I was hardly expecting you to come bursting through my door with a stocking full of beautifully wrapped presents.'

'But you should.' Shame pricked at him. 'That's what you deserved. Not a brown envelope decorated with a stolen ribbon.'

'Hey.' She cupped his face and he was surprised to find anger in her eyes. 'If you'd done that, I'd have run for the hills. It would have been too much considering we've only known each other a short while.' Her eyes darted over to the envelope. 'Whatever is in there isn't for show. It's real and because of that, I'll love it.'

He had his doubts about that, but he kept them to himself and handed her the envelope. 'Here's your non-Christmas present.'

Unceremoniously she shoved the ribbon off and ripped at the envelope. 'Careful,' he winced. 'I hadn't figured on you attacking it, or I'd have warned you to go easy.'

She halted, giving him a sheepish smile. 'Sorry. In case you hadn't realised, I love surprises.'

He watched with increasing tension as she carefully drew out the sheets of paper. Her eyes scanned the drawings, then glanced up at him. Before he could work out her expression she was poring over the drawings again.

'You don't have to use them.' God, his heart was racing more than it did during a serious work-out. 'I just thought I'd make myself useful while I was here.'

'It's the extension I talked about,' she whispered, raising one hand and pressing it to her chest. 'I can't believe you were even listening to me rabbit on about it, never mind ...' She trailed off, shaking her head. When she finally looked at him again, he was astonished to see tears in her eyes. 'The pool room, the side extension. You've added hints of the old building, but not tried to make it look the same, which never works.'

He cleared his throat. 'Is it okay? You can take the bits you like and discuss it with another architect—'

Her mouth covered his, stopping all speech, which was fine by him because he'd never been good with words. He guessed, by the way her body was climbing over his, her hands running under his shirt, that she was pleased with the plans he'd drawn.

'I love them,' she whispered, her breath hot against his neck. 'They're perfect.'

So are you, he wanted to say, because it was true. He'd never met a woman so giving, so smart, so damn sexy. But her body was pressing against his and the desire to talk was easily eclipsed by the desire to take her in his arms again.

Chapter Twenty-Two

Faith looked around the crowded restaurant and felt a burst of pride. It was true nearly half of those tucking into the amazing turkey dinner, courtesy of Antonio and Mario, were her family. Also true that of the others, most were here not through choice but because last night's heavy snowfall had made many roads treacherous to drive on. Still, listening to the busy hum of conversation, scanning her eyes across animated faces wearing party hats, tables crowded with cracker remains, the warm glow of the fire in the wood burning stove, Faith had a sense of what was possible.

'Lord of all she surveys.' Her father smiled over at her. 'Admiring your new kingdom?'

'More like feeling grateful it's not just me and the dogs.'

He chuckled. 'My daughter's hotel was always destined to be busy over Christmas. Had to be some reason you dragged that ruddy great tree in here.'

Feeling stupidly emotional, Faith had to take a drink before she could speak. Maybe that was what was making her so sappy. Too much wine. 'A few people's misfortune turned into my good fortune. If it hadn't been for the weather and Giles's faulty electrics, today would have been a different story.'

His hand reached out to grasp hers. Rough, the fingers slightly bent now, the joints swollen with arthritis, it still held surprising strength. 'All businesses need a drop of luck. Those who succeed follow up on that luck with hard work and discipline. I know you'll provide the latter two.' He nodded towards the tables of guests: the family with their two little kids, who'd decided to stay for lunch and visit their family later, when the roads were expected to be clearer as the snow was beginning to melt; alongside them, the guys from the pub quiz who were sharing a table with Giles and his wife; then there was Joe, Mary and, sitting next to Stuart, a happy looking Chloe. In the corner sat Emma and her family, with Adam. Their table wasn't wearing party hats. It was a table of quiet conversation, rather than raucous laughter but Adam was smiling and looking surprisingly relaxed for a man eating with his ex-wife's family. 'And in that lot,' her father continued, including all of the diners with a wave of his arm, 'you have a bunch of avid supporters who'll help spread the word. This time next year, there'll be no room at the inn.'

'Maybe this time next year the inn will be looking to expand.' Faith knew she was running ahead of herself. Still, if you were going to dream, you might as well dream big. And that was so easy to do now she'd seen what her hotel *could* look like.

Her father chuckled. 'That's my girl.'

A few moments later she became aware of her father studying her. 'What? Have I got bits of sprout stuck between my teeth?'

'No. But for the last minute your eyes haven't left that Hunter bloke.'

Guiltily she tore her gaze away from Adam's dark head. 'Sorry. I was just remembering what he gave me this morning.'

Her father made an odd, strangled noise and then began a coughing fit. On the other side of her, Faith's mother laughed. 'Darling, I just came in on the end of that conversation. And unlike your father, I'm dying to hear what Adam gave you this morning.'

Her father made that noise again, and Faith began to giggle. 'Jeez, Dad, get your mind out of the gutter. I was talking about the designs Adam drew up for me.'

'The man has designs on you,' her father muttered, which made Faith laugh even harder.

'And why wouldn't he have?' her mother countered. 'Our daughter is a smart, beautiful woman with her own business. Of course men are going to want to pursue her.'

Faith's smile slipped a little. Pursuing her when she was in the same building was very different to pursuing her when she was at the other end of the country.

'Now, about these designs.' Her mother turned her sharp gaze towards Faith. 'What were they for?'

She could feel herself starting to blush, which was ridiculous. She wasn't that thirteen-year-old girl being quizzed on the love letter the boy next door had sent her. The designs felt that important to her, though. Felt as if, with every clever stroke of his pencil, Adam had tried to convey feelings he hadn't verbalised. 'Some ideas for the extensions I bored him about one evening.'

'Adam's an architect?' Tom, Hope's husband asked.

'Yes.'

'And the plans are detailed?'

Faith didn't know much about architects' drawings. 'Well yes. It's not a sketch, if that's what you mean. He's put measurements in there.' He'd listened when she'd told him about making a quadrangle, she thought with a flutter. Listened and remembered every detail.

Tom blew out a breath. 'Then congratulations. If you like them, you've just saved yourself a small fortune in architect fees. I should know. We just paid three grand for drawings of our house extension.'

Automatically her gaze flew to Adam, and the black T-shirt he was still wearing. It really did fit him perfectly, hinting at the beautiful body beneath. But it had only cost her fifteen pounds.

Her mother touched her arm. 'He would have done it out of a desire to help. Not to have you fretting over the cost.'

As if aware they were talking about him, Adam looked up and caught her eye. He gave her a small smile, though his eyes said more. They said he wished he was sitting next to her. Wished they were alone.

Warmth surged through her veins, pooling between her thighs.

'I remember a time your father looked at me like that,' her mother murmured, causing her father to cough yet again. 'So, is the delectable Mr Hunter still planning on going home tomorrow?'

Reluctantly Faith dragged her eyes away from Adam and onto her mother. 'Yes.' And just like that, her chest felt tight, the turkey that had been merrily digesting now sitting heavy in her stomach.

'You're going to miss him.' Her mother didn't form it as a question. 'Any plans to see him again?'

The air rushed out of Faith's lungs. 'Not so far.' Would he ask tonight? Tomorrow morning just before he left? Even if he did, would it be wise, considering the chance of them actually being able to see each other on a regular enough basis to continue a relationship was pretty much zero? And that's before she factored in the feelings he obviously still had for his ex-wife.

Faith's gaze slipped away from his and immediately Adam felt its loss. There was something about Faith, about the way he connected with her, that didn't just flame his desire. It soothed him. Made him feel hopeful for a future that held more than the emptiness of the last three years. But tomorrow he would be saying goodbye to that connection. He couldn't help but feel he'd be saying goodbye to that hope, too.

He tried to focus back on his lunch, and the people he was sharing it with. For the most part he'd enjoyed it. Emma's mother, Cathy, had opened her arms to him the moment she'd seen him. Her simple gesture had made a hundred stilted words redundant. Then her father, Peter, had shaken his hand, looked him squarely in the eye and said, 'It's great to see you again, son.'

Adam had been too choked to reply. For three years, he'd believed he'd lost this substitute family. He'd understood – of course they had to side with their daughter. Yet incredibly here they were, sharing Christmas lunch with him. Three people who understood why he was still haunted by the day. Understood why he couldn't laugh and joke and wear party hats. Not yet, not while it still felt raw.

He could however sit at a table with them and eat turkey. Share conversation about everything he'd missed over the last three years.

'And Ruth?' he asked, resting back against his chair. So far they'd all been careful to avoid her name but he'd had enough of dancing round the topic. 'What's she up to these days?'

Cathy glanced at her husband, clearly not sure how to answer. In the end it was Emma who answered on a huff of frustration. 'We should tell him.' She turned to Adam. 'The friend I told you Ruth's spending Christmas with? It's a guy she's been seeing for the last six months. She seems really taken with him. I think he, more than anything, has helped her become her old self again.'

As the words registered, Adam braced himself for his response, but none came. There was no sting of jealousy, or pang of regret. No flash of anger that she'd got on with her life while he'd still been wallowing. Actually, maybe there *was* some anger, but it was directed at himself, not her. Why had he let what she'd said to him rule his life for so long?

Because you believed it.

And the gut-wrenching part of the whole sorry mess? He still did.

Reaching for his wine glass, he took a big gulp and forced his focus back on the conversation. 'I'm glad she's doing well.'

Cathy studied him, her eyes shining with understanding. With compassion. 'She'd like to—'

'I already mentioned that to Adam,' Emma cut in. 'I don't know about you guys, but even though I'm stuffed I'm going to help myself to some of that Christmas pudding. And drown it with brandy sauce.' Beneath the table, Adam gave her hand a grateful squeeze. 'Any other takers?'

'Months old dried fruit and suet?' Adam shuddered. 'I'll pass.'

Faith was back at the buffet. The brothers had outdone themselves today, piling up the heated trays with everything anyone could possibly want from a Christmas lunch. There had been turkeys, crisp roast potatoes, a selection of stuffing, sausages wrapped in bacon, parsnips, perfectly cooked Brussels, their flavour helpfully hidden by the pancetta they'd been sautéed in. Very little remained.

Now her eyes devoured the choice of trifle, mince pies, fruit salad. Or Christmas pudding. Okay, there was no choice.

'That looks like heaven.'

Having landed a generous portion of the pudding into her bowl, Faith turned to see Emma watching her. 'I'd be willing to wager it tastes like heaven, too. And a million calories.'

Emma screwed up her face. 'Calories don't count at Christmas.'

'Let's hope it's true.'

She was about to leave when Emma spoke again. 'You and Adam. You seem to have something going on between you.' She peered over at her. 'Sorry if I sound nosey. It's just Adam's important to me. And I get a sense he's important to you, too.'

Unsure what to say, Faith went with a noncommittal, 'oh?'

Emma laughed, her blue eyes glinting. 'You're as bad as

Adam. I told him about the way you wouldn't tell us his room number and how it made me think there was something going on between the pair of you, but he wouldn't admit to anything. Said it was hotel policy.' The laughter eased, her face turning curious. 'It's more than that, though, isn't it? You sounded protective of him.'

'He's our first guest.' Faith gave her a professional smile. 'I guess that gives him a special status here.'

'He is special.' Emma briefly touched her hand. 'I hope I'm not the only one who can see that.'

Faith didn't know what to say, what to think. 'Don't you want Adam and Ruth to get back together?' she blurted. They were clearly all so close; she couldn't see how, now he was back in the fold of his ex-wife's family, he wouldn't soon be going back to his ex-wife, too. His first and only love.

Emma looked momentarily taken aback. Then, slowly, understanding dawned in her eyes. 'He hasn't told you what happened, has he? Why my sister divorced him?' Faith shook her head. 'Maybe you should ask him. He needs to talk about it and it might help you understand him more.'

Faith's hand clutched at the bowl of Christmas pudding as she watched Emma walk back to her table. When Adam had offered to talk about that part of his life she'd turned him down, afraid he was doing it because he felt he had to. But if Emma was right, talking might help him as much as it would her.

Chapter Twenty-Three

Adam gave Emma one last hug before she ducked into the passenger seat of the Discovery. Her parents were already in the back, her husband in the driving seat and looking keen to set off before it got too dark.

'Stop worrying,' she told Adam for the umpteenth time. 'The snow has been melting fast since this morning. Plus the travel websites say the Lakes were the worst hit. As soon as we get onto the motorway, we should be okay.'

He didn't like the thought of them driving in the snow, though. Not one bit. They bloody knew how dangerous icy conditions could be. But he also knew they needed to get back. Emma's in-laws were coming round for lunch on Boxing Day. And Ruth would be expecting to see them tonight.

'Please take care,' he managed, gripping at the door handle.

'I'll text you as soon as we're home.'

His stomach twisted anxiously as he watched their car ease out of the car park.

He didn't relax until he got Emma's text several hours later.

You can stop worrying now, we're home. Enjoy your evening. Say thank you to the pretty hotel manager from us. E x

She'd added a damn winky face emoji.

He stabbed out a reply, his fingers far too big for the silly touch-screen keyboard.

Pretty? I hadn't noticed. Glad you're home safely. Thank you for coming. A x

With a sigh he put down the phone and flicked over to another channel, bored of the film he'd been watching.

He'd seen *The Great Escape* too many times. Then again, now he realised the choice was that, *Finding Nemo* or *It's a Wonderful Life*, maybe he'd finish the ruddy film. See if Steve McQueen managed to escape this time.

It flickered on in the background but his mind wasn't on it. It was on the hotel manager he hadn't noticed was pretty. Probably because to him she was more than that. Stunning. Gorgeous enough to make his heart stop. They were more fitting descriptions.

The restless feeling returned. He wanted to see her, spend as many of his last remaining hours as possible with her, but her family were here. He couldn't impose.

Heaving out another sigh, he settled back to watch the film.

An hour later, just as Steve McQueen was captured yet again, there was a knock on his door. He shifted off the bed, telling himself not to get his hopes up.

But when he opened the door, those hopes rocketed skywards. 'Hey.'

Faith gave him a big, warm smile. The one that reached into her eyes and bathed him in it. 'I wondered if you're up for a glass of whisky and a turkey sandwich?'

'Do you come as part of the deal?'

She reached up to give him a soft kiss on his lips. 'Yes.'

He cupped her face and kissed her back. 'Count me in.'

'The rest of my family is playing Monopoly downstairs,' she told him as she opened the door to her place.

Halfway inside, he halted. He knew how important her family were to her. 'Do you want to join them?'

'Are you kidding?' She slipped off her shoes, bringing the top of her head down to his shoulder level. 'I swear my father cheats. He always ends up with hotels on Mayfair and Park Lane.'

'So I'm here because you hate losing Monopoly?'

Pulling at his hand, she led him into her sitting room and

pushed him down onto the sofa. Then she crawled onto his lap. 'You're here because I missed you this afternoon. Because I want to make the most of you before you go.' Her mouth trailed kisses along his jaw. 'And because I hate losing at Monopoly.'

Laughter shot out of him and he shook his head as he gazed down at her. 'What is it about you?' he murmured.

Her head, currently resting under his chin, shot up. 'What do you mean?'

He hadn't meant to say it out loud. 'I just realised I haven't laughed since I left you this morning.'

'I make you laugh?' When he nodded, her lips curved into a smug smile. 'I'm going to take that as a huge compliment. Want to know a secret?' Before he could answer she was talking again. 'When you first arrived here I thought you'd never smile, let alone laugh.'

It hadn't been too long ago that he'd felt the same way. 'I hadn't done much of either until I came here.'

The body wrapped snugly in his arms tensed and Adam drew her head back so he could look at her. 'What is it?'

She kept her head down, her fingers fiddling with a button on his shirt. 'Yesterday you offered to tell me what had happened to you. Why you hate Christmas.'

Now he was the one whose muscles were tensing. 'I did.'

Finally she looked up. 'Will you tell me now?'

His heart began to race. A fact she was bound to notice as she was pressed against him. 'Why the change of mind?'

She bit into her lip. 'Just something Emma said to me.'

'Emma? What on earth does she have to do with this?'

'She thought it would do you good to talk to someone about what happened.' There was a hesitancy to Faith's voice, a tremor he didn't associate with her. It made him realise she was as nervous about what he might say as he was about saying it. 'Emma also said I might understand you more if I heard it.'

That damn hope started to rear up inside him again. 'Is it important to you to understand me more?' *Because I thought this was just a fling to you*, he wanted to add, but kept his mouth shut. Too scared to hear her confirm it.

'Yes. Is that okay with you?'

Was it okay that she wanted to know him more? A big resounding yes. Was it okay that he talked to her about what had happened? A bloody definite no. He didn't want to see it change the way she thought of him.

This wasn't about what he wanted, though. 'I thought I was coming here for turkey sandwiches and whisky.'

Her hand flew to her mouth. 'Sorry, I totally forgot.' She began to wriggle off him, but he held onto her.

'You deserve to know why I acted like such a prick for a lot of the time I've been here.' He took in a deep breath, trying to find his balance. 'And I've lost my appetite for the turkey.'

A frown appeared between her eyes. 'You don't have to do this.'

'I know.' Knot after knot began to form in his stomach. 'Before I do, I wouldn't say no to the whisky.'

Faith could see Adam retreating into his quiet, reserved shell as he sat on her sofa and drank his whisky. She had half a mind to tell him to forget it. She didn't want to know any of it after all. But she remembered Emma's words. It would do Adam good to talk about it.

'So.' She curled up next to him and gave him an encouraging smile.

'So.' His large chest rose and fell, and the hand holding the whisky tensed around the glass. 'I think you already know Ruth and I met at school. She was my first crush, first and only girlfriend.' He lifted his gaze to hers. 'Until you.'

Instantly a tide of emotion swept through her. This wasn't a man who played fast and loose. He loved seriously, deeply. The look in his eyes suggested his feelings for her ran seriously and deeply, too. 'When did you get married?' she asked, more in an effort to divert her attention from her own feelings than a desire to know the answer.

'Nearly four years ago. We were heading that way anyway, but Ruth fell pregnant.'

Faith's heart jumped. 'You have a child?'

And that's when the mask he'd put on, the feelings he'd been so clearly determined to control, disintegrated before her eyes. She knew, without him telling her, that they'd lost the baby.

Adam gulped back the rest of his whisky, then leant forward to place the glass on the coffee table. As he did so, his hands shook and her heart ached for what he'd been through. What he'd lost.

'Ruth lost the baby when she was eight months pregnant. We were ...' He inhaled sharply, shoving a hand through his hair. 'We were on our way home from visiting her parents on Christmas Eve. The car spun off the road and landed in a ditch. By the time the ambulance came, by the time she got to hospital, the damage had been done.' He was talking in a rush now, clearly desperate to get the explanation over. 'She gave birth prematurely, and the baby survived for a short while, but the placenta had ruptured and ...' Another ragged breath. 'Our son died on Christmas morning.'

Tears welled in her eyes as she saw the agony in Adam's. 'I'm so sorry.' Silly, useless words, but she didn't know what else to say. Grabbing his hand, she kissed his palm, her mind flashing back to yesterday. 'That's why you were so worried for Mary.'

'Yeah.' He scrubbed the hand she wasn't clutching across his face. 'I acted like a total nut job, dragging that poor retired doctor out in a blizzard.'

'She didn't mind. And if she'd known what you'd been through, she'd probably have camped on the floor next to

Mary all night to keep an eye on her.' Each time he revealed something more about himself, she fell for him a little more, she thought hopelessly. 'Now I can see exactly why you hate Christmas. It holds too many terrible memories.'

'Yes.'

The way he said it, heavily, as if he was trying to wrestle with some of those huge weights he lifted, made her realise there was more to the story. 'Your marriage didn't recover from the loss?' she hazarded.

'You could say that.'

She could see how hard this was for him. How rigidly he held himself, how tight his expression was. Whatever else he had to say, she decided, she didn't need to hear. She'd put him through enough.

But before she could tell him that, he was talking again.

'Ruth blamed me for the accident.' Though his voice was flat, his eyes looked tortured. 'She blamed me for the death of our son.'

Faith's hand automatically tightened over his. 'Why?'

'The roads were icy that night. Snow had started to fall. She didn't want to risk driving home. Said we should stay at her parents' for the night. I ... I persuaded her we'd be fine.' He hung his head, tugging his hand away from hers. 'It was our first Christmas as husband and wife. I wanted us to wake up in our own bed.'

Her heart aching, she smoothed a hand down his rigid back, the action as much for her benefit as for his. 'Of course you did. You weren't to know you were going to have an accident. That's impossible to predict.'

'No.' He wouldn't look at her. 'Ruth was right to blame me. Driving on icy roads *is* risky, yet I insisted on driving anyway. We didn't have a four-wheel drive. We were going to buy one for when the baby ...' He paused, his Adam's apple working overtime as he swallowed, clearly fighting for control. 'We were in my rear-wheel drive. Everyone knows they're poor in the snow. I took a risk with our son's life. With all our lives. All because I selfishly wanted her to myself.'

Faith felt as if her heart was being ripped in two. How much guilt, how much grief had this man stored inside him all these years? 'Ruth wasn't right to blame you,' she told him bluntly. 'People in love support each other. They don't screw with their minds, heaping on guilt for something that was clearly nobody's fault.' She was angry, she realised. Coldly, furiously angry. 'When you made the decision to drive, did you think, even for one moment, you were going to end up in a ditch?'

His big body stilled. 'Of course not.'

'Why not?'

He looked at her as if the answer was obvious. 'It was snowy but the roads weren't treacherous. At least I didn't think they were.' He choked over the words. 'We only had six miles to drive. I thought we'd be okay.'

She wrapped her arms around him then, squeezing his body, feeling a tremor run through him. 'Then it was a horrible, horrible accident. And you have to stop blaming yourself for it.' She had a sudden image of Adam lying on his bed, her nephew curled on his chest, and guilt dragged at her insides. 'Oh God, I made you look after Jack. No wonder you were so cross with me. I thought you were freaking out because, you know ... men and babies.'

For the first time since he'd started talking, his face carried a hint of a smile. 'There was a bit of that, too.'

And yet he'd looked so perfect with Jack; the baby and the gentle giant. She felt another rush of sadness for the man who'd lost the chance to comfort his own son.

'Ruth accused me of ...' He trailed off, hanging his head again. 'She said I was responsible for his death.'

At the strangled words, Faith's head snapped up and she stared at Adam incredulously. 'She's a bitch.' Even as she said it, Faith knew the description was unfair. Ruth's words would have been said out of crazed grief, not spite. Still, Faith's instinct, her whole being, was centred on protecting Adam.

He smiled, though it didn't reach his eyes. 'Not a bitch, no. Just a woman, mourning the loss of her baby.' He slumped back against the sofa and shut his eyes. 'I understood why she said it. But …' He shook his head, his breath coming out in a judder. 'By God, it hurt.'

It was then, as she held his shuddering body in her arms, Faith realised she'd done more than fall for this man. She'd hurtled headlong into love with him.

'*Impossible situation*,' she muttered to herself.

Slowly his large frame started to relax, and he shifted so that he was holding her now, her head against his chest. 'Thank you.'

She glanced up at him. 'What on earth for?'

'Listening. Not judging. Defending me.'

'Always, always.' And he didn't know how true those words were. 'Ruth's family don't blame you, do they?'

He gave her that small, tight smile. 'Apparently not.'

'But you thought they would,' she murmured, speaking her thoughts out loud. 'That's why you kept avoiding Emma's calls.'

'That, and the fact that she was a reminder of Ruth, and everything that had happened. Everything I'd lost.'

She felt a pang of unwanted jealousy. Did he mean what he'd lost in terms of his son, or his marriage? The only woman he'd ever loved? *Don't go there*, she told herself. He'd had enough heaped on his plate this evening. It was time to change the mood. 'How do you feel about that turkey now?' she said after a while. 'Do you want some sandwiches?'

He sighed, his hands moving to her face, smoothing across her cheeks with such incredible gentleness. 'I want you,' he whispered, touching his mouth to hers. 'Just you.'

Always. The word was there again, only this time she kept it to herself.

Chapter Twenty-Four

Boxing Day

Adam took a final look around the room that had been home for the last ten days. He wouldn't miss it, he decided. As nice as it was, he'd had enough of living within the confines of four small walls. Enough of eating food cooked by someone else, too. Again, as nice as that had been. As for trudging off to a gym each day to work out instead of walking down to his basement ... Yeah, when he thought about it, there was a lot to look forward to in going home.

As long as his thoughts didn't include picturing himself eating alone, sitting in front of the television, alone. Lying in his bed. Alone.

Misery clung to him as he zipped up his holdall and walked out of the door. Faith would be on the reception desk to check him out, as she'd promised earlier this morning. After he'd made love to her one final time.

Made love to her. Not had sex with her. He knew the distinction. Knew when they'd come together they were no longer two people having a fling. Hadn't been for a few days, at least not on his side. His heart had become so tangled up with her now he couldn't think straight any longer. He'd dumped a lot on her last night, yet she'd absorbed it, considered it, and come to his defence. For as long as he lived, he would never forget how angry she'd been on his behalf.

Her head turned towards him as he walked up to the desk and dropped his bag on the floor. So many things he wanted to say, needed to say, but he wondered if now was the right time.

'So.' It had become their standard conversation opener,

only this time her accompanying smile looked like he felt. Wobbly. 'I hear the snow's nearly all gone. You should have a good trip back.'

Pain lanced through his chest and when he spoke his voice sounded thick and foreign to him. 'There's nothing good about driving away from you.'

Her eyes glistened with unshed tears and she drew in a sharp breath, letting it out slowly before she spoke again. 'Well, thank you for being our first guest, Mr Hunter.' Her voice shook. 'I hope you enjoyed your stay.'

His mouth felt like it was full of sand. 'I did,' was all he could manage.

She handed him the invoice, and he didn't miss how it trembled in her hands. Heart in his mouth, he covered her hand with his. 'Faith.'

He didn't know what he was going to say, but before he could say anything she was shaking her head. 'No. Don't say anything or I'll break down in tears and I really, really don't want my guests to see the hotel owner blubbering like a fool.'

'This isn't goodbye,' he said firmly. He didn't know what the hell it was, but he couldn't walk out of the place thinking he wasn't going to see her any more. It would kill him.

'I hope not.'

'I'll phone—'

'Please don't,' she cut in and he jerked as if she'd shot him, snatching his hand back.

Her eyes tracked his movements and she let out a half laugh, half sob. 'Sorry, I didn't mean don't phone. I meant please don't make any promises. This last week has been intense. Surreal.' Tears crept slowly down her cheek and he reached to wipe them away, his thumb trailing over her soft skin. At once her hand clasped his, a sad smile crossing her face. 'We both need to take a step back, get on with the mundane for a while. Take time to process.'

He knew she was right. What man falls in love over ten days? It was daft to think it had happened to him. And yet ...

'You don't mind if I call you?'

She rolled her eyes. 'Of course not. I just don't want to be the sad woman waiting for the call that never comes. I'd rather no promises, no mention of anything more than what we've just had. Which was awesome, by the way,' she added on a rush, kissing his hand before releasing it.

Emotion lodged high in his throat and for the second time in as many days Adam felt he was going to cry. Yesterday it had been about the past. Today it was for a future he could see, but wasn't sure was attainable. 'It was, as you say, amazingly awesome.'

He handed over his credit card and silently she completed the transaction. Then there was nothing left for him to do but pick up his bag and walk out. Except he didn't think his legs would let him do that.

She must have realised, because she touched his shoulder and gave him a light shove. 'Go,' she whispered, tears now streaming down her face. 'Prolonging it just makes it worse.'

Stiffly he nodded. Without saying anything further, he forced his legs to walk away from her.

The moment the door shut behind Adam, Faith felt her heart crumple. She bent over, the pain in her chest a physical one, as if her heart really was breaking.

Blindly she stumbled into her office. Once she'd closed the door behind her she put her head in her hands and let all the tears she'd tried to hold back fall freely. Silently she cursed herself for stopping him when he'd started talking about making plans. This wouldn't feel so final, so devastating, if she knew she'd hear from him again.

She hadn't wanted him calling her because he'd promised to though – and a man as rock-steady as Adam would always follow up on his promises. He'd never play games with a woman, forget to call, treat her lightly. No, if Adam said he would call, he would make sure he did just that. Still, she wanted him contacting her because he couldn't *not* do it. Because he couldn't function without hearing her voice. Because he'd come to realise he no longer loved his ex-wife. He loved her.

There was a light tap on the glass and she glanced up to see Chloe. Quickly Faith grabbed at a tissue and wiped her eyes. Then she plastered a smile on her face and opened the door.

It clearly wasn't much of a smile because Chloe, at times sullen, at times awkward, reached forward and gave her a hug.

'Adam's gone, hasn't he?' she asked as she drew back, giving Faith's face a quiet study.

Faith tried to smile. 'What gave it away?'

Chloe shrugged, though there was amusement in her eyes. 'Just a good guess.'

Faith put her hands on Chloe's shoulders, returning the scrutiny. 'Enough about me, how about you and Stuart? I guess he'll be off today, too.'

'Yeah, but it turns out he doesn't live that far away.' She blushed, the first time Faith had ever seen her niece properly blush. 'We've made plans to see each other on New Year's Eve.'

And though her heart was breaking for herself, and the plans she didn't have, it lifted for Chloe.

Thankfully the rest of Boxing Day was so busy Faith didn't have much time to dwell. She had guests checking out, followed by two sets of guests checking in. They were a surprise last-minute booking, courtesy of a recommendation from Joe and Mary. Her dad had been right, Faith thought as she stripped one of the vacated beds ready for the new arrivals. The hotel had gained a set of fans over the last few days.

Once the new rooms were ready, Faith was about to head back to the office when something stopped her, drawing her towards Adam's room instead. No longer his room, she reminded herself, feeling the awful drag on her heart. She should leave it for the housekeeper who was back in tomorrow. She didn't need to see the empty room.

Before she knew what she was doing, she was opening the door.

Tears flooded her eyes the moment she saw the neatly made bed. Typical of the man that he'd left the place tidy.

It shouldn't hurt this much, she thought as she walked towards it. He was supposed to have been a bit of Christmas excitement. Not a man she'd fall in love with. Not a man who'd break her heart when he left.

Gingerly she touched the pillow. Imagined his head on it. Stupidly she bent down and inhaled. Longing tore through her as the scent of his familiar aftershave wafted up her nose.

On a sob she climbed onto the bed, hugging the pillow to her. And wept. It was while she was trying to pull herself together that she heard her phone ping. Glancing down she noticed a text from a number not in her phone.

Got your number from Chloe. Hope you don't mind. This isn't me calling you, it's me texting you. I'm back home now. And missing you. A x

Fresh tears fell down her cheeks but her heart felt lighter as she typed out a reply.

I love that you texted me. I miss you too. Faith x

Chapter Twenty-Five

Two days after Christmas

Adam stood on the doorstep, hands fisted at his side. *You can do this*, he told himself for the umpteenth time since he'd arranged to meet her. After all, he'd done the hardest part already. Making that first contact, that first call, had taken every ounce of strength he'd possessed. Why was he so damn scared of seeing her? It didn't matter any more what she thought, did it?

Drawing in a deep breath he pressed the buzzer.

One second, two, three … his heart sped up as he waited for the door to open.

Suddenly there she was. A hesitant smile on the face he knew so well.

'Adam.' She looked as awkward as he felt.

'Ruth.' He took a moment to study the woman he'd once known so intimately. Her hair was shorter now, with blonde highlights he didn't remember. Her eyes were the same blue as her sister's. Her face looked calmer, softer than the last time he'd seen it. When she'd been yelling at him.

The image flashed back to him and he slammed his eyes shut, bracing his hand on the door frame.

Dimly he heard her voice beckoning him into the house. On legs that felt wooden and unstable he followed her through into her sleek modern sitting room. No wood-burning stove or exposed bricks for her, he noted, his mind unconsciously making comparisons with Faith's cosy front room.

'Can I get you a drink?'

It was polite to accept one, but Adam didn't want to linger, to draw this conversation out. He wanted them to say what they needed to say to each other, and then he'd get the hell out of here. 'No thanks.'

Her lips curved in a sad smile. 'I suspect I'm the last person you want to share a drink with.' Because she was right, he kept quiet. 'Thank you for coming here anyway.'

'Emma said you wanted to see me.'

'Yes.' She indicated for him to sit down, then carefully sat on the opposite end of the sofa. Her eyes were downcast and he knew, because he knew her, that she was trying to remember the words she'd been practising since his phone call. Finally she looked up at him. 'I wanted to apologise for what I said the last time we saw each other.'

It was a sad fact that they hadn't spoken since the funeral. After she'd refused to answer his calls he'd retreated into his own shell, giving up on them just as surely as she had. On his first wedding anniversary, he'd found himself served with divorce papers. Bitterly he'd signed everything asked of him. Friends for ten years, lovers for eight, yet they'd managed only five months as man and wife. 'You were upset.'

'Yes.' She wrung her hands together. 'That didn't excuse what I said.'

He felt his throat begin to tighten. 'You spoke the truth as you saw it.'

'No.' Her reply was so sharp it startled him. 'I was lashing out, desperate for someone to blame,' she continued, more measured now, but still as firm. Words she'd rehearsed? 'It didn't seem right that I should lose a child … we should lose a child,' she corrected, her eyes seeking out his. 'That we should lose something so precious, to an accident. A bit of ice on the road and suddenly our whole world turned upside down.' Her blue eyes clouded, the hands resting in her lap becoming agitated. 'I needed it to be more than that.'

She drew in a deep breath and rose to her feet. Because he couldn't think of anything to say, Adam kept quiet.

Suddenly she was walking towards him. Sitting right

next to him and taking his hand. 'It wasn't anything more though,' she said quietly, eyes looking directly into his. 'Two years of therapy has told me that. There was nothing either of us could have done.'

His hand felt stiff inside hers. 'Except not get in the car.'

She held his tighter. 'Perhaps. But that was a joint decision. I might have suggested staying at my parents', you might have said you wanted to go home, but we both took the decision to get in the car. And who's to say if we'd driven over the next morning instead, things would have been any different? It was still cold. That ice would still have been there.'

'Maybe.' It would take a long time to fully convince himself of that.

She withdrew her hand from his and lightly touched his beard. 'This is new.'

'Not really. I've had it for nearly three years.'

Her eyes closed and she bit into her lip. 'I used to know everything about you. When you had a haircut. When you went a day without shaving.' She dropped her hand to her lap and let out a deep sigh. 'You grew it after what I'd said, didn't you? Tried to become someone different because I made you hate the person you were.'

'Not consciously, no.' At least he hadn't at first.

Tears welled in her eyes. 'I made you think it was your fault. All this time, that's what you believed, isn't it? Emma told me as much, but I didn't want to accept it. Now I'm looking at you, I know she was right.'

'I was driving.'

She let out a strangled sounding laugh. 'And thank God you were. If it had been me driving we might all have been killed.'

Incredibly his lips twitched. 'Driving wasn't one of your strong points.'

'I was crap. Still am.' Her hands reached for his again. 'I've missed you, Adam. I'm so sorry I pushed you away.'

'You were hurting.'

'Yes, but I should have turned to you for comfort. We should have been able to comfort each other. Instead I drove a wedge between us.'

Faith had said something similar. The fact that Ruth hadn't turned to him in her hour of need, and that he'd given up on her, made him wonder if their marriage would have survived even without the accident.

Her big blue eyes lifted to his. 'Do you think you can ever forgive me?'

'There's nothing to forgive,' he told her gruffly. 'I never blamed you for what you said. How you felt towards me.'

She looked stricken. 'No, you blamed yourself, which is worse. If you can forgive me, you have to forgive yourself. Please.'

'I'm working on it.' He'd said the same words to Damon, not long after meeting Faith, only then he'd meant he was working on being happy.

Forgiving himself would be a huge step in that direction.

He stayed with Ruth for another hour, finally accepting that drink. They filled each other in on the last three years and it felt, if not like old times, then at least like two friends. She told him of the new man in her life and he listened, happy for her.

At the same time wondering if he, too, would have that second chance at happiness.

On his way home, he swung by Damon's house.

His friend greeted him in paint-spattered jeans. Adam tried, and failed, not to smirk.

'Wife's got you working, I see.'

'I'm my own man. If I'm painting the bedroom it's because I want to.'

Adam laughed. 'Sure it is. I mean, what man wants to be watching sport instead of painting his bedroom two

199

days after Christmas?' He peered at the brush Damon was holding. 'Good shade of pink, too. Matches your cheeks.'

Damon let out an expletive before standing aside to let him in. 'If you're coming in, I'll give you a brush. You can say goodbye to those fancy jeans.'

'I'll pick up a brush if you promise to listen to what I have to say.'

Damon held out his paint-spattered hand. 'Deal.'

Five days after Christmas

It had been four days since Adam had walked out of the hotel. Four days in which, aside from his first text, Faith hadn't heard from him.

Damn the man, she wasn't going to think about him. She'd meant what she'd told him right at the beginning. She was far too busy for a relationship right now.

Speaking of busy. Faith slipped behind the reception desk and clicked open the bookings. Her eyes skimmed the calendar, noting with satisfaction they'd had another booking since she'd last looked. On seeing the name, her heart jumped.

'Chloe. This booking for tomorrow.' Her niece was sitting on the stool, staring down at the phone that was a permanent fixture in her hand. Thankfully now what she read on there made her smile. Faith knew Hope had offered to speak to the parents of the so-called friends leaving snide comments, but in the end it hadn't been necessary. Now Chloe had a boyfriend of her own, a boy a year older and at a different school, which was apparently *legit cool*, the nasty comments had dried up.

'Earth calling Chloe. I'm sure Stuart won't mind if you leave it, say, a minute, before replying?'

Finally her niece glanced up, rolling her eyes. 'Okay, okay. What?'

'When did you take this booking for an A. Hunter?'

'Oh, yeah. Five minutes ago. This woman called, wanting a double room for two nights.'

'A woman? Are you sure?'

Chloe looked at her in a way that only a teenager could. 'Duh, I do know the difference.'

Still, Faith couldn't stop the butterflies buzzing in her belly. 'Was she booking for herself? Did she give a first name?'

Chloe gave a frustrated huff. 'I don't know, right. She just asked for a double room for an A. Hunter for two nights. I said great and entered it in the computer like you told me to. She gave a number.'

Faith studied the number. It wasn't one she recognised. And why would it be? There must be thousands, no millions of A. Hunters. It had to be a coincidence, that's all. It didn't stop her mind from imagining it was Adam though.

Perhaps Adam and a woman.

Dread rose inside her, sending cold shivers down her back. Adam wouldn't be so cruel as to book into her hotel with another woman. He'd known how she felt about him. It had to be an Alice, or an Amanda Hunter looking to spend New Year in the Lakes. With a huff of annoyance at herself, Faith stepped away from the screen.

'You're wondering if it might be Adam, aren't you?' Chloe asked quietly.

'You said it was a woman who called.'

Chloe lifted her shoulders. 'She could be booking it for him.'

Or for both of them. Faith pushed the unhelpful thought away. 'The idea had crossed my mind.'

'I can always phone her back. Ask her.' Before Faith had a chance to say anything, Chloe grabbed at the phone and began dialing the number on the screen. Faith's pulse began to rocket. Oh God, she was going to be sick, she was going to …

'It's gone to voicemail. Woman's voice says we've reached Anita. We can leave a message if we want.'

'No.' Faith pressed a hand to her churning stomach. 'No, let's just forget it. It's clearly not Adam.'

Chloe gave her a sympathetic smile. 'You miss him, huh?'

Briefly Faith shut her eyes. The moment she did, an image of Adam came into view. It always did. Sometimes he'd have that small smile on his face. Sometimes his gaze was heated. Often, she saw just his eyes; beautiful, yet at times so horribly sad. 'Yes,' she whispered, answering Chloe's question. 'I miss him.'

Chapter Twenty-Six

New Year's Eve

Though she'd told herself a hundred times it wasn't Adam – it was Anita Hunter who'd be checking in – Faith still found herself watching the hotel door like a hawk. It was five o'clock on New Year's Eve and here she was, sitting by herself on the reception desk, pining after a man who wasn't going to turn up.

Next year she needed to get a life. Maybe keep her vague promise to phone Patrick.

The thought made her shudder, and once again she cursed Adam Hunter. She couldn't even imagine being with another man now.

Just then the door creaked open. Faith's head snapped up and over towards the entrance.

Immediately her heart leapt, bouncing off her ribs. Tall like Adam, muscular like Adam. Dark-haired, too. The same clear, smoky grey eyes. But this man was clean-shaven. No heavy stubble hiding the strong line of his jaw. Where Adam had been sexy, rugged, this man was stunning.

His eyes swept across the reception desk, halting when they found her.

'It *is* you.' She could barely manage the words.

His mouth lifted in the small smile that made her heart ache and every cell in her body sigh. 'How many other Adam Hunters do you know?'

She knew she was gaping at him like some half-wit but she couldn't seem to do anything else. Her body was frozen to the stool. 'The booking said A. Hunter. Chloe took it. Said it was a woman's voice on the other end.'

'Yes, I've been a bit busy. I asked Anita to book it.'

She swallowed the lump now sticking in her throat.

'Anita?' Automatically she angled her head, trying to look past him.

A frown formed on his face and he ducked, meeting her eyes. 'What are you looking at?'

'Not a what, a who. You said Anita ...'

'Our office manager.' The bag he'd been holding slumped to the floor. 'Good God, you didn't think I'd be bringing another woman with me?'

Anger edged his usually quiet voice. It seemed to bump her out of her trance. 'No. I ... no. I didn't think the booking was for you. But then I saw you, and you mentioned Anita, and for a horrid moment I didn't know what to think.' Her words were tumbling over each other. 'What happened to the beard?' It was just one of the hundreds of questions running through her mind. Was this for real? Had he come to see her, or was he just passing through?

He walked towards her. Three of those long, long strides and he was standing right up against the reception desk. 'Faith.' His voice was back to soft, back to the voice that spoke to her in her dreams. 'I know we have a lot to talk about but can we just. Can I just ...' He exhaled in frustration, moving round the counter so he was standing next to her. Towering over her. Then, with a tenderness that totally belied his appearance, he placed one arm under her legs and another round her shoulders, lifting her up.

Before she knew what was happening, he was kissing her. And kissing her. His mouth hungry, as if whatever he was taking he couldn't get enough of. It seemed kissing her like that wasn't enough though, because soon she was eased onto the reception desk and he was standing between her legs, his hands on her face. Kissing her again, his whole body pressing into her.

She closed her eyes and gave in to the pleasure, inhaling him, running her hands up and down those big muscular arms.

'Hi there Adam.'

Faith froze at the sound of Chloe's highly amused voice. Hell, she'd forgotten her niece was changing in the office, ready for her New Year's Eve date with Stuart.

Adam drew back and laughed, looking slightly embarrassed. 'Hey there Chloe.'

'I'm, err, about to go.' Chloe's eyes danced with barely suppressed glee as she looked back at Faith. 'I just wanted to let you know Stuart's step-mum has just given birth. He's got a baby sister.'

'That's …' Faith coughed and tried again. 'That's wonderful.' All the questions she'd usually ask – the weight, how Mary was – just weren't there. Not with the force of Adam's smouldering gaze on her.

'Well then.' Chloe smirked, giving them both a little wave. 'Happy New Year.'

As the front door clunked shut behind Chloe, Adam pressed his forehead to hers. 'That,' he murmured huskily. 'I just needed to do that.'

Laughter caught in her throat. 'I'm a big fan of that. Though I'd rather not have had an audience.' Her fingers shook as she ran them over his face, along his clean-shaven jaw. 'I loved the beard, but I have to admit. I'm also a big fan of this.'

'I was hoping you would be.'

'Why?'

He smirked. 'Because I want the woman I plan on taking to bed to fancy me?'

'No, no.' She smoothed her hand across his chin. 'I mean why did you shave it off?'

'Ah.' He caught her hand, wrapping his fingers round it. 'I don't feel the need to hide who I am any more. Adam Hunter was always clean-shaven. I guess I figured it was time he made an appearance again.'

Faith studied him. The lines of his face, the depths of his eyes. 'You look more at peace. Happier.'

He smiled then, properly, bringing her hand to his mouth and kissing it. 'I'm working on it.'

For a few magical, humming seconds they gazed into each other's eyes.

A cough from the other side of the reception desk interrupted the moment, making her jump. Not again. With a rush of horror Faith realised where she was sitting. And who was between her legs.

Adam saw her expression and grinned, lifting her up and onto the floor. When she turned to greet the visitor, her stomach dropped. 'Mrs Bannister. Sorry. I ... err—'

Sally Bannister put up her hand. 'No need to explain.' Her eyes ran appraisingly up and down Adam. 'I can understand the distraction. I just wanted to check everything is ready for tonight? My party are on their way.'

Faith grappled for her professionalism. 'The room is all ready, the tables set up.' She was aware of Adam easing back, out of the way. 'Mario and Antonio are in the kitchen prepping as we speak.'

Sally finally cracked a smile. 'Good. I'll go and get ready. If you could make sure my guests—'

'Are checked in, shown to their rooms, told where the dinner will be? Of course. We thought champagne and canapés by the tree at 7.30?'

Sally's smile actually widened. 'Excellent. Thank you.'

As she walked away Faith let out a long breath.

'You got the booking after all?' There was surprise and a hint of something that sounded like awe in Adam's voice.

'Of course.'

'But how?'

Faith grinned. 'I wish I could say it was my powerful negotiating skills. Turns out everywhere else was fully booked. In the end she came back, not quite cap in hand, but certainly a lot meeker than before.'

His face seemed to fall a little. 'I guess this means you're busy tonight?'

'I have to be on call if needed, yes.' She moved closer, putting her arms around him, just because she could. 'But Mario and Antonio have the food covered and Becky, our restaurant waitress, has agreed to work tonight. I believe that leaves me free to entertain my new guest.'

His eyes darkened and he trailed his finger down her face. 'Do I need to check-in?'

She pouted, letting out a mock sigh. 'There goes my two-night booking.'

Bending his head, he dropped an exquisitely tender kiss on her lips. 'I'll make it up to you.'

Draping her arms around his neck, she beamed up at him. 'Promises, promises.'

Several hours later and Adam still hadn't managed to deliver on his promises. Oh, he was definitely ready to, but it was hard to deliver anything when the person you were delivering it to wasn't there. First Faith had been busy settling in the new guests, then last minute nerves had her deciding she needed to be downstairs to make sure everything went smoothly for the party, after all. Adam was left to sit and wait for her in her sitting room. Watching *The Big Fat Quiz of the Year* on TV. Two fluffy mutts for company.

'Not quite how I imagined it,' he muttered. Tuck, or was it Nip?, cocked his head, as if he understood. 'Not that I'm complaining,' he added, scratching him behind the ears. 'I know she has to work. I know running this hotel takes up most of her time. Of the spare time she has left she has her family to see, then her own personal needs. I recognise there isn't much left over for me.' He also knew he'd take whatever crumbs she was prepared to offer.

The other dog nuzzled in closer, putting a paw on his thigh. Adam grunted. 'That could be the most action I get tonight.'

The longer he waited for Faith, the more anxious he became about what he was about to say. He hadn't missed the way she'd remained behind the reception desk when he'd walked in. There had been no rush to greet him, no flinging her arms around him, no beaming smile on her face. Instead she'd looked shocked. What he didn't know was whether it had been shocked in a *wow, this is amazing* sort of way, or shocked in a wary, *I hope this guy isn't about to turn heavy on me, because while I like him, I don't want him hanging round too often* sort of way.

Two pairs of ears twitched, and then suddenly the dogs were scrambling off the sofa and darting towards the door. 'Charming.' He stared after them as they bounced up and down in the hallway, waiting for the door to open. 'I'm the one who's been giving you tummy rubs all evening.'

But as Faith walked in, laughing down at them, kicking off the gorgeous heels she'd teamed with her sexy little black dress, Adam felt like bounding up to her, too. He had to consciously make sure his tongue wasn't hanging out.

When she'd made sufficient fuss of the dogs, she smiled over at him. 'Sorry it took so long. I didn't want to give either of the Bannisters a chance to complain.'

'It's not a problem. I've had great company.'

For a split second she looked confused. Then her eyes followed his and she giggled. 'The pair of them are good listeners, though they do tend to hog the best seat on the sofa, next to the fire.'

'They're also up for a good tummy rub, though they're a bit stingy on reciprocating.'

Her gaze remained on his. 'I'm always up for a tummy rub, too. And I reciprocate.'

Lust shot through him and all the words he'd been rehearsing flew out of his mind. 'Are you free for a while?' His voice sounded so hoarse it was barely recognisable.

The corner of her mouth curved. 'Define a while.'

He jumped to his feet. 'The way I'm feeling right now, it won't take very long.' She was laughing as he bundled her up in his arms and strode towards the bedroom. Still laughing when he kicked the door shut, much to the disgust of the dogs.

She only stopped when he placed her on the bed and started peeling off her stockings. A sight more than worth the wait.

Passion spent, Adam drew Faith firmly against his side. Immediately he felt his pulse start to quicken. Nerves, this time. He had things to say, and he could only hope she wanted to hear them.

'The last time I was here you told me you didn't want me to make any promises,' he began. Immediately he felt her stiffen in his arms.

'I said what we'd had was like a whirlwind. We needed to take a breath. Not make promises we might not want to keep when we got back to real life.'

His heart began to thump. 'Why do I get the feeling that while you're saying *we*, you actually mean *I*?'

Her head lifted, possibly because she couldn't hear him over the pounding of his damn heart. 'You're wrong. I actually mean *you*.'

'Me? You think I'm the one who doesn't know how I feel?'

He felt her withdrawing from him. Not just physically, though she sat bolt upright by his side, hardly touching him, but emotionally.

'You're the one with the ex-wife you clearly have unresolved feelings for.'

The heart that had been pounding away now stuttered. 'You think I'm still in love with Ruth?'

'Aren't you?'

Her head remained down so he couldn't see her expression,

but he read the uncertainty in her voice. The sadness, too. 'Faith, Faith, Faith.' Shaking his head, he cupped her face, bringing her eyes up to meet his. 'I love you.' His gaze swept over her, letting her see everything he was feeling. 'Whatever I felt for Ruth changed irreversibly three years ago.'

Her eyelids lowered, leaving him once again unable to see what she was thinking. 'How do you know?'

'How do I know I love you?' He smiled, kissing the end of her nose, making her look at him again. 'I think about you all of the time, and I mean all of it. I can't even buy a damn can of deodorant without wondering if you'll like the smell, can't watch a TV programme without reminding myself to ask if you've seen it. Can't look at my phone without wanting to talk to you. These last few days without you have been hell. I've not been able to sleep. Mornings are grey and cold, even when the sun's out. But mostly I ache everywhere when I'm not with you. And I can't picture a future without you in it.'

She blinked, then blinked again, her hazel eyes glistening. 'Seriously?'

He wished to God he knew if that was a *wow, fantastic*, seriously, or an *oh shit*, seriously. Turns out spilling his guts had been the easy part. Waiting for her reaction was a million times harder. 'Yes, seriously.' *Now please put me out of my misery*.

Faith's heart felt as if it was about to explode. *He loved her*. She so wanted to believe it. So wanted to tell him everything he'd just described was exactly how she felt, too. There was just one major stumbling block.

'Before, when I asked how do you know, I actually meant, how do you know you no longer have feelings for Ruth?'

Disappointment flooded his face and Faith felt terrible. He'd told her he loved her and here she was, withholding from him. Still banging on about his ex-wife. Yet she'd seen how he'd reacted just at seeing Ruth's family. And she knew Ruth was the only woman he'd slept with, the only woman he'd ever loved. She had to be sure she wasn't setting herself up for heartbreak. To ease the sting of her question, she touched his cheek. 'Please. Before I tell you how I feel, I need to know.'

He nodded, his expression grave. 'I understand. I meant what I said earlier though. When a woman you thought loved you accuses you of murdering her son, it crushes something inside.'

Faith's hand flew to her mouth. 'Oh my God, she didn't say that.' But she knew, from the anguished look in his eyes, that she had.

'In case you're worried how I might feel about her now,' he added, 'I saw Ruth a few days ago. I went because she'd asked to see me, but also because I finally realised I needed closure.'

Faith's voice was having trouble making itself heard. 'What did she want?'

'She wanted to apologise for what she'd said.' He sighed, taking Faith's hand and placing it over his heart. 'I was glad I went. Relieved to hear her tell me she no longer blamed me. Even as she was telling me that though, I couldn't stop thinking of you, of how fiercely you'd defended me. It made me realise I actually no longer cared what Ruth thought. It mattered more what you thought. And if you didn't hate me for what I'd done, if you didn't think it was my fault, then maybe in time I could stop thinking that, too.'

That was it. Her heart opened, enveloping him, absorbing every big, delicious part of him until it felt heavy and swollen. And gloriously full. 'Of course it wasn't your fault.' Tears ran freely down her cheeks as she held his face in her hands. 'And of course I love you, too. I knew before you left, but I was too scared what you felt for me wasn't the real deal. I was terrified that now you were reunited with Ruth's family, it wouldn't be long before you were reunited with her, too.'

She almost melted at the ferocity of the love blazing from his eyes. 'What I felt for Ruth doesn't come close to what I feel for you.' He kissed her then, a deep kiss full of need and longing. 'And you need to know that I'd never let you go, like I did her. I'll fight for you until the end of my days.'

Love mixed with joy, mixed with hope, and bounced around her chest. 'But how are we going to make us work? Between the hotel and you living in the south …?' She trailed off when she saw him smile.

'My business is expanding. After a bit of prodding on my part, Damon agreed we need an office in Manchester. That's what I've been busy doing the last few days. Looking for office premises. Looking for a small flat so I can live there Monday to Thursday.' He grinned down at her. 'I'm rather hoping Friday to Sunday I can get myself some cheap digs in the Lakes.'

'Oh God, I can't believe it.' She was overwhelmed. She'd gone from convincing herself she'd never see him again, to the promise of three days a week.

'Is that a good I can't believe it? Because trying to second guess what you've been thinking over the last ten minutes has been killing me.'

'It's not just good.' She took his face between her hands and kissed him. 'It's amazingly, spectacularly brilliant.'

He kissed her back, feather-light kisses that teased and aroused. 'Does that mean I get the cheap digs?'

She smiled against his lips. 'The digs you can pay for. The hotel manager you get to keep for as long as you want.'

He gave her a loaded look. 'I have a feeling that's going to be forever.'

Faith melted against him, her sigh one of pure happiness. 'Forever works for me.'

Epilogue

Faith stood back and admired the giant Normandy fir standing proudly, no, make that magnificently, in the middle of the hall.

'Don't tell me. They didn't have a smaller one.'

She laughed, twirling round to find her father standing behind her. 'They did, but I had to put all these decorations somewhere. Besides, it's a thing of beauty.'

'Aye, it is that.' Her father wasn't looking at the tree though. He was looking at her.

With a rush of love, she went to hug him. 'You're looking pretty dapper yourself.'

He put a finger down the back of his collar, stretching it. 'Damn thing's shrunk since I last wore it.'

Faith giggled. 'There is another explanation.'

He scoffed. 'With the tiny portions your mother gives me? Don't be daft.'

She could have told him it was more than likely Antonio and Mario's calorie-laden puddings that he seemed to sample most weeks, but she kept quiet.

'Someone has to take care of your waistline for you.' Her mother glided down the stairs in that elegant way she had that Faith could only admire and had never been able to emulate.

More love filled her heart. 'Mum, you look stunning.' She'd chosen a deep emerald-green dress which brought out the colour of her eyes.

'Thank you my dear. Not half as beautiful as my daughter, though.'

A babble of voices sounded from the foyer and Faith

glanced round to find her sisters and their families walking in. Little Jack – now a lively toddler – immediately raced over to the reception desk and tugged at the garland draping from it.

'Jack, no,' Charity squealed, rushing over to him.

'Perhaps a good thing you closed the hotel for the next two days,' her father murmured. 'Place might need re-building by the time he's finished with it.'

'Don't. We have enough building going on as it is.' The extensions Adam had so beautifully drawn out were now underway. She'd refused when he'd offered to help financially. It was only in the summer, when he'd told her he wasn't loaning her money, he was investing in their future, that she relaxed enough to give in. Now she couldn't wait to see how his ideas would translate from paper into real life.

Faith looked beyond her sisters and felt tears rush into her eyes. 'Oh, Chloe. You look amazing.'

And she did. Her awkward, slightly overweight niece with the clumsy boots and madly coloured hair was now a stunning young woman. Amazing what a year, exercise and a besotted boyfriend could do. Her hair, back to its natural brunette, fell like a sleek curtain down her back. Her deep blue velvet dress clung to her toned body.

Chloe smiled, glancing over to Stuart who grinned back at her.

'Well, Antonio and Mario have laid out some champagne in the restaurant area.' Faith grasped her parents' hands. 'Shall we?'

Her father's eyes lit up. 'What the bloody hell are we doing here then? Lead the way.'

Adam fiddled with his tie. Red, Faith had insisted, so red he'd bought. It went with the rose in his lapel, he guessed. Probably went with his eyes, too.

'Stop playing with that damn tie. It's fine.' Damon – the

same man who'd insisted on taking him out and getting him drunk last night, hence the red eyes – scowled over at him.

Adam heaved out a sigh and stepped back from the mirror. 'Feels funny being in this room again.'

'You're not supposed to see the bride the night before the wedding. Bad luck and all that.'

'I don't need luck.' He smirked back at Damon. 'Faith and I deal in love, not luck.'

Damon made a gagging sound. 'Jeez, big man. Don't go all soppy on me. My breakfast will come up.' Then he sighed and went to clasp his shoulder. 'But I guess, if we're going to do this soppy shit, I might as well say this. It's bloody good to see you looking so happy, mate. Especially considering the time of year.'

Adam swallowed, then swallowed again just in case. If he was going to have an emotional meltdown today, it was going to be in front of Faith. Not this man staring at him with something that looked suspiciously like the emotion Adam was trying to keep at bay. 'Faith wanted to get married on Christmas Eve. Said the time of year should hold some happy memories, too. I'll still remember …' *Shit*. His voice sounded choked.

Damon came to his rescue. 'I know. At least this way you won't forget your wedding anniversary though, hey?'

Grateful for his friend's humour for once, Adam laughed. 'No chance of me forgetting today. No chance at all.'

'So, as your best man, I guess it just remains for me to ask if you're sure you want to do this?'

Adam took in a deep breath and straightened his shoulders. 'Try and stop me.'

He almost ran towards the hallway, hearing the babble of people before he saw them. Faith's family, who he considered to be his family now, were huddled round the giant Christmas tree, drinking champagne. The tree was still too big for the space, but try getting her to see that.

Two mad dogs raced around, chasing each other, the gold bells hanging from their red collars jingling every time they moved.

Jingle bells, he thought with a grin.

Talking to Faith's parents was the kind lady who'd agreed to marry them, despite it being Christmas Eve.

And there, amongst them all, was Faith. Radiant in a deep red dress, laughing at something her brother was saying to her. Suddenly, as if she sensed him, her eyes caught his. He was almost blinded by the love he saw there.

A year ago he'd come to The Old Mill hotel to forget Christmas.

Now he couldn't wait to celebrate it. With Mrs Faith Hunter.

Thank You

Thank you so much for taking the time to read *A Little Christmas Faith*. I get so much pleasure out of writing a book – spending months in a fantasy world with my perfect hero, what's not to love?! The greatest pleasure though comes from hearing that others have enjoyed the fantasy I've created. I'm not alone in that. Authors love feedback – it can inspire, motivate, help us improve. It can also help spread the word. So if you feel inclined to leave a review, I would be really grateful. And if you'd like to contact me (details are under my author profile) I'd be delighted to hear from you.

Love Kathryn

x

About the Author

Kathryn was born in Wallingford, England but has spent most of her life living in a village near Windsor. After studying pharmacy in Brighton she began her working life as a retail pharmacist. She quickly realised that trying to decipher doctors' handwriting wasn't for her and left to join the pharmaceutical industry where she spent twenty happy years working in medical communications. In 2011, backed by her family, she left the world of pharmaceutical science to begin life as a self-employed writer, juggling the two disciplines of medical writing and romance. Some days a racing heart is a medical condition, others it's the reaction to a hunky hero...

With two teenage boys and a husband who asks every Valentine's Day whether he has to bother buying a card again this year (yes, he does) the romance in her life is all in her head. Then again, her husband's unstinting support of her career change goes to prove that love isn't always about hearts and flowers – and heroes can come in many disguises.

For more information on Kathryn:
www.twitter.com/KathrynFreeman1
www.kathrynfreeman.co.uk

More Choc Lit

From Kathryn Freeman

A Second Christmas Wish

**Do you believe in
Father Christmas?**

For Melissa, Christmas has
always been overrated. From
her cold, distant parents to
her manipulative ex-husband,
Lawrence, she's never
experienced the warmth and
contentment of the festive
season with a big, happy family
sitting around the table.

And Melissa has learned to live with it, but it breaks her
heart that her seven-year-old son, William, has had to live
with it too. Whilst most little boys wait with excitement for
the big day, William finds it difficult to believe that Father
Christmas even exists.

But then Daniel McCormick comes into their lives. And with
his help, Melissa and William might just be able to find their
festive spirit, and finally have a Christmas where all of their
wishes come true …

Read a preview at the end of this book.

Available in paperback from all good
bookshops and online stores. Visit
www.choc-lit.com for details.

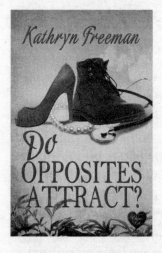

Do Opposites Attract?

There's no such thing as a class divide – until you're on separate sides

Brianna Worthington has beauty, privilege and a very healthy trust fund. The only hardship she's ever witnessed has been on the television. Yet when she's invited to see how her mother's charity, Medic SOS, is dealing with the aftermath of a tornado in South America, even Brianna is surprised when she accepts.

Mitch McBride, Chief Medical Officer, doesn't need the patron's daughter disrupting his work. He's from the wrong side of the tracks and has led life on the edge, but he's not about to risk losing his job for a pretty face.

Poles apart, dynamite together, but can Brianna and Mitch ever bridge the gap separating them?

Find out more and purchase in the kindle store (Kindle UK, Kindle US, Kindle Australia, Kindle Canada)

Purchase from your eBook provider or visit www.choc-lit. com for more details.

Available in paperback from all good bookshops and online stores. Visit www.choc-lit.com for details.

Too Charming

Does a girl ever really learn from her mistakes?

Detective Sergeant Megan Taylor thinks so. She once lost her heart to a man who was too charming and she isn't about to make the same mistake again – especially not with sexy defence lawyer, Scott Armstrong. Aside from being far too sure of himself for his own good, Scott's major flaw is that he defends the very people that she works so hard to imprison.

But when Scott wants something he goes for it. And he wants Megan. One day she'll see him not as a lawyer, but as a man … and that's when she'll fall for him.

Yet just as Scott seems to be making inroads, a case presents itself that's far too close to home, throwing his life into chaos.

As Megan helps him pick up the pieces, can he persuade her that he isn't the careless charmer she thinks he is? Isn't a man innocent until proven guilty?

Search for the Truth

Sometimes the truth hurts …

When journalist Tess Johnson takes a job at Helix pharmaceuticals, she has a very specific motive. Tess has reason to believe the company are knowingly producing a potentially harmful drug and, if her suspicions are confirmed, she will stop at nothing to make sure the truth comes out.

Jim Knight is the president of research and development at Helix and is a force to be reckoned with. After a disastrous office affair he's determined that nothing else will distract him from his vision for the company. Failure is simply not an option.

As Tess and Jim start working together, both have their reasons for wanting to ignore the sexual chemistry that fires between them. But chemistry, like most things in the world of science, isn't always easy to control.

Available in paperback from all good bookshops and online stores. Visit www.choc-lit.com for details.

Before You

When life in the fast lane threatens to implode …

Melanie Taylor's job working for the Delta racing team means she is constantly rubbing shoulders with Formula One superstars in glamorous locations like Monte Carlo. But she has already learned that keeping a professional distance is crucial if she doesn't want to get hurt.

New Delta team driver Aiden Foster lives his life like he drives his cars – fast and hard. But, no matter how successful he is, it seems he always falls short of his championship-winning father's legacy. If he could just stay focused, he could finally make that win.

Resolve begins to slip as Melanie and Aiden find themselves drawn to each other – with nowhere to hide as racing season begins. But certain risks are worth taking and, sometimes, there are more important things than winning …

Nice boys don't kiss like that!

Too Damn Nice

Do nice guys stand a chance?

Nick Templeton has been in love with Lizzie Donavue for what seems like forever. Just as he summons the courage to make his move, she's offered a modelling contract which takes her across the Atlantic to the glamorous locations of New York and Los Angeles. And far away from him.

Nick is forced to watch from the sidelines as the gawky teenager he knew is transformed into Elizabeth Donavue: top model and the ultimate elegant English rose pin-up, seemingly forever caught in a whirlwind of celebrity parties with the next up-and-coming Hollywood bad boy by her side.

But then Lizzie's star-studded life comes crashing down around her, and a nice guy like Nick seems just what she needs. Will she take a chance on him? Or is he too damn nice?

Available in paperback from all good bookshops and online stores. Visit www.choc-lit.com for details.

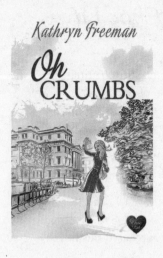

Kathryn Freeman

Oh Crumbs
Kathryn Freeman

**Sometimes life just
takes the biscuit …**

Abby Spencer knows she can
come across as an airhead –
she talks too much and is a bit
of a klutz – but there's more
to her than that. Though she
sacrificed her career to help
raise her sisters, a job interview
at biscuit company Crumbs
could finally be her chance to
shine. That's until she hurries in late wearing a shirt covered
in rusk crumbs, courtesy of her baby nephew, and trips over
her handbag.

Managing director Douglas Faulkner isn't sure what to
make of Abby Spencer with her Bambi eyes, tousled hair
and ability to say more in the half-hour interview than he
manages in a day. All he knows is she's a breath of fresh air
and could bring a new lease of life to the stale corporate
world of Crumbs. To his life too, if he'd let her.

But Doug's harbouring a secret. He's not the man she thinks
he is.

Available as an eBook on all platforms.
Visit www.choc-lit.com for details.

Introducing Choc Lit

We're an independent publisher creating
a delicious selection of fiction.
Where heroes are like chocolate – irresistible!
Quality stories with a romance at the heart.

See our selection here:
www.choc-lit.com

We'd love to hear how you enjoyed *A Little Christmas Faith*. Please visit **www.choc-lit.com** and give your feedback or leave a review where you purchased this novel.

Choc Lit novels are selected by genuine readers like yourself. We only publish stories our Choc Lit Tasting Panel want to see in print. Our reviews and awards speak for themselves.

Could you be a Star Selector and join our Tasting Panel? Would you like to play a role in choosing which novels we decide to publish? Do you enjoy reading women's fiction? Then you could be perfect for our Choc Lit Tasting Panel.

Visit here for more details…
www.choc-lit.com/join-the-choc-lit-tasting-panel

Keep in touch:
Sign up for our monthly newsletter Spread for all the latest news and offers: www.spread.choc-lit.com. Follow us on Twitter: @ChocLituk and Facebook: Choc Lit.

Where heroes are like chocolate – irresistible!

Preview
A Second Christmas Wish

by Kathryn Freeman

PROLOGUE
Christmas Day, almost three years ago

The dining room was so silent Melissa could hear her knife scraping the plate as she cut through the turkey. Why didn't Lawrence talk to his parents, for goodness' sake? Why did he just sit there, his face like thunder?

Her eyes scanned to her in-laws. Attractive yet cold, aloof. Perhaps it was no wonder Lawrence couldn't talk to them. His parents belonged to an era when the Lord and Lady of the manor ruled their household with a rod of iron. When guests who stepped out of line were silenced with a sharp tongue and a stern look. When children were seen and not heard.

Lawrence was fast turning into them.

Next to her, William started to become restless, kicking his legs under the table, shifting about in his seat.

'Finish your meal, darling,' she whispered.

He shook his head. 'Not hungry.'

Lawrence's black eyes darted across the table at them and William immediately froze. Melissa touched his small hand reassuringly. 'Okay, if you're sure you've had enough you need to sit patiently while everyone else finishes.'

'He's got the appetite of a sparrow,' Lawrence's mother stated witheringly. 'He should be made to eat his meal.'

Melissa bit the inside of her cheek and fought for control.

'It's Christmas day. William should be allowed to do whatever he wants on such a special day, don't you think?'

'If you give children an inch, they'll take a mile,' she retorted, then glanced over towards her son. 'You're very quiet, Lawrence. The turkey not to your satisfaction?'

Lawrence clattered his knife and fork onto his plate and drained the contents of his third glass of wine. 'I have no appetite for dry turkey,' he announced, shooting Melissa a cutting glance.

'I'm sorry,' she whispered, then bit her lip, angry with herself for being so timid. 'Perhaps if you put some more gravy on it?'

'Drown overcooked turkey with lumpy gravy?'

She felt tears prick. Did he have to be so rude to her in front of his parents? In front of their son?

'Manners,' his father scolded. 'What's got into you today?'

Lawrence reached for the wine bottle and refilled his glass. 'I'll tell you what's got into me. My darling wife announced a few days ago that she's leaving me.'

Melissa's heart bounced inside her rib cage. Oh no. She'd begged him not to raise the subject today. She'd wanted to give William a Christmas to remember – for the right reasons. 'I don't think today is the time to discuss this,' she said, unable to stop her voice from shaking.

'Why not?'

She turned to William, who was hanging his head, staring at his lap. 'Because Christmas is a time for smiling. For having fun. Especially when you're nearly five.'

'And are you having fun, William?' Lawrence asked his son coldly.

William's head shot up. 'Yes.'

Lawrence continued to glare. 'Is that how you've been taught to address your elders?'

'Yes, Sir.'

'And what constitutes fun in your book?'

Confusion flickered over William's face and Melissa reached for his hand again, this time holding onto it. 'Your father just wants to know which part you've enjoyed most today.'

For a brief moment his eyes filled with joy. 'Opening my presents from Father Christmas.'

Lawrence snorted. 'Father Christmas, eh?'

'Yes, Sir.'

'You seriously believe one man goes round to all the children in the world delivering presents in one day?'

Melissa inhaled sharply. 'Don't,' she hissed. 'Please, I beg you, don't ruin this day for him.'

'Ruin it?' Lawrence thrust his glass onto the table with such force some of the wine spilt, forming a blood-red stain on the white tablecloth. 'I rather think you're the one who's ruining things.' His eyes flicked over to William who looked impossibly small on the large antique chair. 'Let me save you a lot of heartache later in life, son. Love, rather like Father Christmas, doesn't exist.'

'He does,' William shouted, shifting agitatedly in his chair. Melissa had never heard him answer his father back, ever.

'If you believe that, then you're as big a fool as I am.'

William started to cry and, as he scrambled desperately off his chair, he sent his plate clattering to the floor.

'You bloody idiot,' Lawrence bellowed.

Melissa slid off her chair and scooped her sobbing son into her arms. 'You're the idiot, Lawrence,' she replied as evenly as she could. 'Mr and Mrs Raven,' she said, nodding over to her in-laws, 'I'll leave your son to entertain you. I'm going to take William upstairs.'

* * *

She spent the rest of the day playing games with William in his playroom. Because it was a far better way to spend Christmas afternoon than sitting with his stuffy parents, Melissa almost felt like thanking Lawrence for his petulant outburst at the dinner table. Almost. But she would never forgive him for taking the magic out of the day for William. Though she'd tried to reassure him Father Christmas did exist – that his father thought he was being funny saying he didn't – she wasn't sure William believed her.

When he was finally asleep in bed, Melissa walked hesitantly back downstairs. She found Lawrence sitting by himself in the lounge, staring into the fire. With the crackle of the logs, the cosy glow of the flames and the fresh smell of the pine tree she and William had carefully decorated, the scene should have brought her a warm, fuzzy Christmas feeling. It didn't.

The man on the sofa was too cold, the atmosphere far too tense.

'Decided to come back down, have we?' Lawrence stood and walked towards her, his dark eyes glittering menacingly.

'You upset your son today,' she accused, fighting for calm though her heart was hammering. 'How could you do that?'

Irritation flickered across his face. 'You mollycoddle him too much. He's turning into a real mummy's boy, frightened of his own shadow. He needs toughening up.'

'He's a few days away from being five.' She dared to look up at him. 'I asked you not to discuss the separation today. It wasn't the right time.'

'I beg to differ. My parents had a right to know.' He bent his head and she caught the smell of stale wine on his breath, mingling with his exotic aftershave. 'I still find you incredibly attractive, Melissa.'

The words – ones she'd heard often over the years – were

almost a purr. Once she'd believed them. Now she knew it was his way of keeping control. One minute charming, the next cruel, it made sure he kept her unbalanced. 'And you're still trying to manipulate me,' she retorted, twisting her body away from the confines of his. 'I won't be pushed or pressured by you anymore.' Back ramrod straight, she raised her chin. 'You got away with it when I was young and naive. Now I'm old enough to fight back.'

Lawrence took a step away, his long hair falling away from his sharp features. 'How is telling my wife she's attractive, trying to manipulate her?'

'You blow hot and cold, and I'm tired of second guessing your mood. Tired of feeling on edge all the time, wondering how you're going to react to me. How you're going to treat your son.'

His lip curled. 'You make me sound like an ogre. Have I ever hit you, hurt you?'

'Physically, no.' Damn, her voice had started to tremble. She took in a deep breath before speaking again. 'You had an affair, Lawrence. Did you really think that wouldn't hurt me?'

He laughed harshly. 'That was ages ago and there were reasons for that. Reasons I've explained and you accepted.'

'It doesn't mean I forgot, or forgave. I can't trust you any more. I can't trust your mood, your fidelity, your treatment of William. I want out.'

'So you've already told me.' Reaching out a hand, he ran his finger down her cheek. 'Do you remember the day we first met? You were modelling my new range and I'd never seen a more exquisite creature, yet when I went to introduce myself you were so unsure, so shy. I knew right then you were not only going to be a superstar, you were going to be my wife.'

'And you made sure of both.' Her life had changed almost overnight. He'd thrust her into the limelight, turning her from a painfully shy, unheard of young model into Melissa Raven, supermodel and wife to the hottest designer in the country. 'I'm grateful for what you gave me,' she added, moving away from his touch. 'But now I want to live my own life, not one made for me.'

He sighed, dropping his hand and swivelling dramatically on his heel before settling elegantly onto the sofa. 'It's a mistake,' he barked coldly. 'Without me backing you, your career will tumble.'

'You think I care that much about wearing clothes and smiling for the camera?'

He glared back. 'You will, when the glamorous lifestyle you've enjoyed comes to an abrupt end. Still, it's your loss. I'm not going to beg you to stay.'

Chewing on her bottom lip, she fought for the courage to ask the most important question. 'Will you want joint custody of William?'

His dark eyes widened in surprise, and then he started to laugh. 'Of course not. We both know I never wanted the boy.' Then his features turned sharp. 'But for appearance's sake I'll want to see him now and again.'

'Fine.'

Joy flared at the knowledge he wasn't going to fight her for William and for a brief moment she wanted to put her arms around Lawrence. Thank him for letting her have her son. But one look into his eerie dark eyes and the impulse died. 'I'm going up to my room.'

Those eyes watched her carefully. 'It's Christmas day. Surely you aren't going to leave your husband alone on such a … what did you call it? Ah yes, such a *special* day.'

Though she wanted to escape upstairs, she didn't. Out

of habit, and a desire to keep the peace, Melissa did what her husband asked of her. She spent the rest of Christmas evening with him.

Later that night though, as she opened the door to her bedroom – the one she'd moved into last week, next door to William and at the other end of the corridor to Lawrence – she promised herself next year it would be different. She and William would spend Christmas in their own house.

And with a bit of luck, away from Lawrence's oppressive, controlling presence, they might both learn to loosen up and live a little.

CHAPTER ONE

At the knock on the door, Melissa sighed and grabbed at the bag of sweets she'd left on the side. Halloween seemed to be the only time they ever received visitors. Tentatively she opened the door.

When she saw who was there, all she wanted to do was slam it shut again.

'Lawrence.'

He gave her a twisted smile. 'Melissa.'

She should ask him in, she thought, then dismissed the idea. She was done being subservient to Lawrence. It was nearly three years since she'd left him. Now she did what she wanted, not what was wanted of her. 'What brings you here?'

'Aren't you going to invite me in, first?'

'No. I repeat, what are you doing here?'

He sighed dramatically. 'Fine, if we must discuss private matters on your doorstep. The reason I'm here, my darling Melissa, is to ask to see my son over the Christmas holiday.'

Every cell in her body seemed to freeze. Right now she bitterly regretted her decision to let Lawrence know where she'd moved to. At the time she'd harboured a crazy hope that he might change once she'd left him. Might wake up to realise how lucky he was to have such a beautiful son and want to build a proper relationship with him, one borne of love and patience, not disinterest and domination.

The last few years had only proved how delusional she'd been.

'Christmas?' she finally managed. 'How do you expect me to plan that far ahead? I haven't even thought about it yet.'

'Which is why I'm telling you now. I'll be spending a lot of my time in the States over the next month, but I'm back in England for Christmas. Evangeline wants to meet him.'

'Evangeline?' Her mind instantly recalled the dark-haired woman she'd shared both a catwalk and a husband with. Evangeline hadn't smiled because it caused wrinkles, and hadn't talked to the other models because she thought she was above them all. 'Why her?'

'What do you mean, why her?'

'Why would she want to see William?'

'Because he's my son.'

Melissa registered the implication, that Lawrence was now dating the super bitch, and felt nothing. No anger, no bitterness, no jealousy. Just a calm *nothing*. She almost smiled. Almost. 'Why do *you* want to see William?'

Lawrence gave her one of his arrogant smirks. 'Don't most fathers want to see their sons? Especially over Christmas?'

'You're not most fathers. In fact, you've barely been one at all.'

'Come now, you're being cruel.' He gave a dismissive

shake of his head. 'It's not my fault I've had to spend most of the last few years out of the country. Let's just say I want to make up for lost time.'

'You want to update your image more like.' She knew her ex-husband, and the world of fashion he was driven by. As one of the country's leading designers he was constantly setting new trends, many of which continued into his personal life. When she'd first met him he'd been the sophisticated bachelor. A party-animal, enjoying his freedom following a strict upbringing. When he'd married her, he'd morphed into the glamorous, attentive husband. At least as far as the media were concerned. Since their divorce, his star had started to wane. 'Is William the latest attempt to prop up your dwindling image? Are you trying for super dad?'

'Sarcasm doesn't suit you.' Scorn filled his features, making him appear cruel.

'Well, whatever your reason, you can't take him away for a few days. He hardly knows you. It would terrify him.'

'Still frightened of his own shadow?'

Her hand clutched tighter onto the door handle. 'William is a shy, sensitive seven-year-old who needs love and support. Not a fickle father who bullies him.'

Lawrence's mouth hardened. 'You're exaggerating. I simply instilled some much-needed discipline into him. And besides, it's my right to see him.'

'Just as it's my duty as a mother to do what's best for him. God, Lawrence, you've only bothered to see him once since I left you.' And that stilted afternoon would remain with her for a lifetime. 'If you want to build a relationship with him, I can't stop you. But you'll do it my way, or not at all.' Melissa marvelled at how calm she sounded. He'd never know by the tone of her voice how much she shook inside. How terrified she was that Lawrence would simply push her aside and take William away.

'And what is your way?' Lawrence asked, leaning his shoulder against the wall, his hands loosely shoved into his pocket.

'We all go out together, at a time and place of my choosing.'

Lawrence snorted. 'Oh my dear Melissa, I hardly think you're in a position to dictate terms. The custody agreement clearly stated I would have access to him when I wanted.' His dark eyes skimmed over her face, scrutinising, assessing. 'You're harder than the shy girl I married. It doesn't suit you.' Straightening, he carefully secured his flamboyant wine-coloured fedora onto his head. 'I'll be in touch.'

Melissa waited until he'd driven off before slamming the door and collapsing on the bottom stair. God, how she wished he were right, and she had become a tougher version of the girl he'd married. If she had, she wouldn't feel this absolute terror whenever she saw him. At twenty-eight she might have learnt to act confidently, but inside she was still intimidated by him, and she hated herself for it.

'Mum, are you okay?' William stood at the top of the stairs, his dark hair spiked up at awkward angles and his round grey eyes looking worried.

Forcing a wide smile onto her face, Melissa stood and beckoned him down. 'Of course I am. Come on young man, I've got something I want to talk to you about while I make the tea.'

Wariness added to the worried look in his eyes. 'Is it about Dad?'

Her heart squeezed painfully. 'Why do ask?'

'That was him just now.'

She wondered how much he'd heard – clearly enough

to make him worry. Taking hold of his hand, she gave it a quick squeeze. 'Your dad just needed a quick word with me, that's all. Now come into the kitchen because I want to tell you about these tennis lessons I'm trying to set up for you.'

'Simon plays tennis.'

Relieved that the tension had disappeared from his face, Melissa laughed. 'I know. How would you like to play, too?'

He wrinkled his nose. 'But it's winter. People don't play tennis in the winter.'

'Ah, that's where you're wrong. If you play indoor tennis, you can play all year round. I used to love playing when I was younger.'

William shrugged. 'I dunno.'

She stifled a sigh. William was always so reticent about trying anything new. 'Well, the tennis player I used to love watching, who happens to be Simon's uncle, runs a tennis centre with courts inside, so you can play even when it's snowing.' And while her experience with Lawrence had left her distrustful of men, especially rich, successful, overly confident men, she wasn't averse to the idea of drooling over Daniel McCormick from afar.

'Is it going to snow?' Latching onto the last part of her sentence, William's eyes shone with something close to delight. 'I want it to snow for Christmas.'

'That's a while away yet.' Smiling, she dipped down to kiss the top of his head. 'But who knows, by then you might have to walk through the snow to play tennis. Maybe strap the rackets onto the bottom of your feet to help you.'

He started to giggle and the sound warmed her heart. She only wished she heard it more often.

Sitting in the café in his tennis academy, Daniel eyed his sister over his coffee cup. 'Let me get this straight. You're asking me to find a space in my coaching programme for the shy seven-year-old son of your friend. I'm expected to be warm and friendly to them both, but under no circumstances come onto her?'

Alice smiled sweetly back at him. 'I always knew you were good at assimilating information. Come on, you can find little William a space, can't you? She'll pay, you know. She isn't poor. And Simon will love having his friend in the same group.'

Daniel sighed and reached his hands behind his back to stretch out his shoulders. Injury had forced him to give up his professional tennis career several years ago and every now and again he felt a twinge in his right shoulder where they'd had to operate. It became worse when he tensed up, like he was now. *Sisters*. 'I'm pretty sure I can find William a place, yes. But assuming the mother is as lovely as you're saying, why am I not allowed to chat her up? She's single, isn't she?'

Alice shifted back against her chair. They shared looks – dark hair and brown eyes – but not temperament. Where he was calm and patient, Alice was impetuous. Where he was laid-back and easy going, unless he was on a tennis court, Alice was gregarious and at times temperamental. Daniel was thirty-three and still single. Alice, older by three years, was onto her third husband.

'We're talking about Melissa Raven, Daniel. Haven't you heard of her?'

Daniel searched his mind, but came up blank. 'Should I have?'

Alice let out an exasperated sigh. 'She was the face of the Raven fashion label for years. Surely you've heard of Raven? You've probably got a suit made by them somewhere in your wardrobe and you're just too ignorant to know it.'

'Hey, if we're going to start trading fashion insults I can think of a few horrors you've worn over the years. I still remember that fluorescent-green dress.'

She gave him the traditional sister put down – sticking her tongue out at him. 'I was just trying to tell you that Melissa was a famous model and that Lawrence Raven, the world-renowned designer, was her husband.'

'I take it they're divorced?'

'Yes, and she goes by her maiden name of Stanford now. I've only known her for two years, since William and Simon became friends at school, but long enough to know she doesn't like talking about her marriage. I think she went through a pretty bad time and still carries a lot of pain and mistrust. She tells me she's sworn off men.'

Pushing his empty cup away, Daniel raised a dark eyebrow. 'If that's the case, neither of you have anything to fear from me.'

'Oh no, I know you too well. You won't be able to stop from trying to charm the socks off her. She's just your type.'

'First, I don't try and charm. I charm. Second, what do you mean, my type? I wasn't aware I had a type.'

Alice smirked. 'Not in the traditional sense of blonde versus brunette, no. But you do always hanker after women who are both gorgeous and smart. Then you get let down because that combination are usually also arrogant and pushy, which you hate. Melissa is stunning, clever, but actually quite shy.'

Feeling slightly irritated now, Daniel glanced at his watch. 'Much as I'd love to carry on discussing your version of what I might find attractive, I'm afraid I've got to dash.' He rose from the table, unfurling long, muscular legs encased in navy track suit bottoms. At six and a half feet tall, he dwarfed most people he met, including his sister. Bending down, he placed a kiss on her cheek. 'Tell this friend of yours that she and William can come by next week. And I promise to keep my hands off her.' He walked away a few steps before looking over his shoulder and giving Alice a wink. 'At least for now.'

CHAPTER TWO

The moment Daniel caught sight of the two women and two boys walking through the reception area towards him, he swore softly. He hated it when his sister was right. Even from a distance, and having not yet spoken to her, Daniel knew the tall, slender blonde walking alongside Alice was most definitely his type. She walked with the easy grace he'd expect from an ex-catwalk model. Her head held high, her elegant frame fluid in its movement. As they came closer he could make out the striking angularity of her face. It shouldn't work, he thought as his sister waved at him. Melissa's mouth was too full, her grey eyes too large, her cheekbones too sharp. Yet as she came to a halt in front of him, Daniel could only stare. Of course it worked. The combination was stunning.

'Daniel, meet Melissa and her son, William.' He was only dimly aware of Alice making the introductions. His eyes, his mind, his focus, were all on Melissa.

'Uncle Daniel, I'm going to beat you today.'

The sight of his nephew, Simon, leaping up and down in front of him, knocked Daniel out of his trance and he grabbed the boy by his legs, dangling him upside down. 'What did you say?' he remarked gruffly, swinging him slowly from side to side.

'I said I'm going to beat you,' Simon giggled from his upside down position.

In a routine he'd begun when Simon was just a toddler, Daniel slowly raised his nephew up and down. 'Who's the best tennis player in the family?' he growled, allowing Simon's face to come perilously close to the floor.

'You are,' Simon squealed, clearly ready to come back to earth.

As he carefully put his nephew back on his feet, Daniel glanced at the quiet boy standing next to Melissa. 'Do you think you're going to beat me, William?' he asked, grinning down at him.

William shrank back, clutching tighter to his mother's hand. 'No, Sir,' he replied quietly, his eyes watchful and unsure.

'Is that because you don't want to be dangled by your feet?' Daniel prompted, his voice more gentle this time. William was one nervous little boy.

'Yes,' William whispered.

Daniel searched for the beginnings of a smile on the boy's serious young face, but wasn't sure he could find one. 'Very wise. Perhaps Simon here will learn some sense from you.' He ruffled his nephew's hair before turning back to William's mother. 'Now is probably a good time to mention that I don't hang all the children here by their feet. Only family members.'

'I'm glad to hear it.'

For a moment Daniel stared into her clear grey eyes but then her lids lowered and she dropped her gaze to the floor.

Damn, he'd embarrassed her.

'Have you bought me a new racket yet?' His nephew piped up, breaking the slightly awkward silence.

'Simon,' Alice admonished. 'I know it's only Daniel, but that was still rude.'

'Thank you, I think.' He smiled wryly at his sister before

turning back to Simon. 'Why would I want to buy you a new racket?'

'Because it's nearly Christmas.'

'Okay, I'll bite. Even though we're only just in November, why would I want to buy you a racket because it's *nearly* Christmas?'

'Because you buy me a tennis racket *every* Christmas.'

As Simon's face lit up with laughter at his own joke, Daniel bit back a smile. 'Maybe this year I'm going to be less predictable.'

'Nah. I like you being pre … whatever. I get an awesome racket.'

More laughter, this time with Simon and Alice joining in. When his eyes shifted over to Melissa though, she was looking everywhere but at them, as if she felt out of place.

As the laughter died down, she cleared her throat. 'Thank you for finding a space for William. I know you're fully booked, so I really appreciate you letting him join.'

'No problem.' He couldn't seem to stop staring at her. If Alice was right, and the lady had sworn off men, it was a crying shame.

'Shall I go with the boys and get them changed while you talk to Melissa about the set-up?' Alice's glare said it all. *No flirting, no asking her out.*

'Yes, ma'am,' he replied, both to her verbal command and the unspoken one. Turning to Melissa, he gave her an encouraging smile. 'If you'd like to follow me?'

Her eyes flickered to him and then to her son. Wary about being alone with him, or wary of letting her son out of her sight? 'We'll catch up with William and Simon on the court in a minute,' he reassured, though if it was being alone with him that had her all het up, that was unlikely to help. Still, she followed him as he led her down the corridor, which had to be a start.

Melissa followed behind the giant of a man who was her friend's brother. He seemed friendly and easy-going enough, but she couldn't help feeling slightly uneasy. She wanted to be flattered by the admiring looks Daniel had just been giving her – after all, she'd had a crush on this man for years – but instead all she felt was uncomfortable. She simply wasn't interested in becoming the focus of any male attention. Even from one who looked every inch as attractive in the flesh as he had done on the television.

Daniel opened the door to a large office dominated by a black desk with an in-tray in danger of buckling under the weight of its contents. To the side of the desk was a glass-fronted display cabinet and inside it row upon row of gleaming silver trophies.

'Are all those yours?' She nodded over to the trophy cabinet.

He gave her a grin she'd have described as sheepish, had it not been on the face of a strapping six and a half foot athlete. 'Yeah. I know it's a bit corny to have trophies on display, but I figured they looked better here than on my mantelpiece at home.' He laughed at himself. 'Besides, I worked blood, sweat and tears to win the damn things. I reckon I owe it to myself to show them off once in a while.'

'Yes, you do.' She'd watched him win a fair few of them.

While Daniel moved round to sit at his desk, Melissa slipped cautiously into the black leather chair facing him. In his tennis playing days the man sitting across from her had been known as a handsome charmer and it wasn't hard to see why. The combination of rippling athleticism, dark good looks, compelling brown eyes and a dazzling smile was hard to ignore.

'Is it something I said?'

She blinked. 'Sorry?'

'You're staring at me. Don't get me wrong, I'm not averse to having a woman stare at me, but in this case I get the feeling it's not because you like what you see.'

'Oh no, it's not that at all.' His lips twitched and she realised how that sounded. 'What I mean is … well, to be honest I was thinking how relaxed and easy-going you were. Then I remembered how you used that charm on court to sucker the competition.'

He let out a startled laugh. 'I did?'

'You know you did. One minute you were entertaining the crowds with a wise-crack. The next you'd turn deadly and rip your opponent to shreds. I believe they nicknamed you the Laughing Assassin.'

He laughed, coughed and laughed again. 'Oh boy. I hadn't realised you were a tennis fan.'

She felt herself starting to blush, which hadn't happened to her in years. 'I wasn't just a tennis fan,' she admitted. 'I was a Daniel McCormick fan.'

His gaze crashed into hers and for a moment she was transfixed by his deep brown eyes. An almost forgotten feeling of attraction tugged at her, warming her skin, tickling her senses.

'Has William ever played tennis?'

Grateful for the safer topic, she smiled. 'No, not really. I've been out on the local courts a few times and tried to help him hit the ball, but he hasn't received any proper coaching.'

'Did he enjoy it?'

She watched him pick up a pencil and twirl it through his long, tanned fingers.

'Melissa?'

Shaking herself, she focused back on the conversation. 'Sorry, yes, William does enjoy tennis. That's why, when I mentioned it to Alice, she offered to speak to you.' She decided to leave it at that, even though it wasn't just an improvement in William's tennis skills she was hoping for from the academy.

'He's quite shy, isn't he?'

'Yes.' She sounded abrupt and defensive but couldn't help it. The question put her on edge.

Daniel's dark eyebrows rose up a fraction. 'It was just an observation. I didn't mean to imply it was a bad thing.'

'I know.' She sighed and took a moment to remind herself this stranger was also her friend's brother.

'I understand you and his father are divorced?'

'We are, yes.' She wondered how much more Alice had told him, and felt her posture slowly stiffening.

Daniel narrowed his eyes, his expression hard to read. 'Does he still see William?'

Abruptly her chin shot up. How much more did he really need to know? He was only going to give her son tennis lessons, after all. 'Sorry, but I'm not sure that's any of your business.'

Daniel took the barbed retort on the chin. 'Fair enough. Is there anything else you do want to tell me? I'm afraid you're going to have to fill out some forms. Just the usual stuff, name and address, any allergies or illnesses we should be aware of. Emergency contact.' He smiled at her look of alarm. 'I can assure you we've only had to use that once, when one of the mums forgot to pick up her daughter because she thought the session finished an hour later.'

'William's pretty healthy. No illnesses, no allergies.' Just a fear of his arrogant, overbearing father, she added to herself.

But that would go in time, now it was just the two of them. Already she'd seen an improvement. It was an extra reason not to let another man into her life again. It simply wasn't worth the risk.

'Excellent. If you could fill these in for me while you're waiting for us.' He pushed a couple of forms at her. 'Then the only thing left to do is see him play tennis.'

He stood and once again Melissa was struck by his size. Quickly she got to her feet, though even with her model height she felt dwarfed by him. It wasn't just his physique that intimidated though. It was his air of confidence, of sureness. His *presence*.

More aware of him than she wanted to be, she followed him out of his office.

Enjoying a drink in the café opposite the courts, Melissa found her eyes constantly straying towards the young tennis players William had joined. She was acutely aware of how he hung back, even though his best friend, Simon, was there. The group, a mixture of boys and girls, all seemed determined to prove to Daniel that they were the best. All except for William. His shyness, in direct contrast to the confident children around him, was almost painful to watch.

'He'll soon settle in when he gets to know Daniel and the other children better,' Alice remarked gently.

'Yes, I know.' It didn't stop her worrying, though. Happy wasn't a word that sprung to mind when she watched him. Oh he laughed when he was with her, but his quietness around others was wrong. She worried it was more a reflection of his state of mind, than his true character.

Daniel changed the exercise, getting the children to throw a ball at each other and catch it on the bounce. He demonstrated with one of the girls, pulling comic faces when she dropped it, much to the amusement of his young audience. Clearly his brand of easy charm worked equally well with children as it did with adults.

'Does he miss the tennis?' she asked Alice, intrigued that a top ranking professional could find contentment teaching basic tennis skills to children.

'You wouldn't think it to watch him, or to talk to him.' She paused, eyes on her brother. 'There were a few weeks, right after he knew his career was over, when he was very down. It was heart-breaking to see.' Briefly her face filled with sadness. 'But then he pulled himself together and focused all his energies on taking his career in another direction. I don't know if he still yearns for what might have been. I only know that he's put his heart and soul into these academies and is rightfully proud of what he's achieved.' Alice turned to her. 'He's a good man, Melissa. He would suit you very well.'

Melissa almost dropped her cup. 'Oh no you don't. I've already told you, I'm not interested in another relationship. The scars from the last one are far too raw, for both me and William.'

Alice merely shrugged and took a sip of her drink. 'Don't worry, I heard you and I won't be doing any stirring. It doesn't stop me thinking you're wrong, though. And we are coming into the season of goodwill to all men.'

Melissa groaned. 'Don't remind me. I've never really enjoyed Christmas, but after Lawrence's sudden appearance on my doorstep last week, I've started to dread it. I expect I'll spend most of December terrified he'll try to see William again. I ran out of goodwill towards that particular man a long time ago.'

Alice looked at her sharply. 'Did he make any threats?'

'No, not in the sense you mean. He just made it clear that he wanted to see his son over Christmas, which is odd because the last time he saw either of us was nearly two years ago, on William's sixth birthday.'

'He's not what you'd call a doting father then,' Alice remarked dryly.

'Not at all. William's birthday was … awful.' No words could adequately convey how distressing and difficult the few hours had been. Seeing her son change from happy in the morning, to tense and miserable in front of his father.

'Are you going to let him see William?'

'I told him he could only see him if I was there, too.'

'And was he happy with that?'

'No.' She sighed. 'Truth is, neither am I. I don't want Lawrence seeing William at all. He'll only intimidate him. And me.'

Alice squeezed her hand. 'It'll sort itself out. As Lawrence didn't bother to see William last Christmas, I can't imagine he'll try very hard this time. Don't worry.'

But asking a worrier not to worry, was easier said than done.